THE SILVER SHADOW

BOOK 2

IN LORE TRILOGY

JESSICA HARDEN

Ordering Information:

For details, contact jessgowrite226@gmail.com

Print ISBN: 979-8-218-12328-4

eBook ISBN: 979-8-218-12329-1

Printed in the United States of America on SFI Certified paper.

First Edition

To Robin,

Whose insight and honesty is what brought this story to life.

Thank you.

PROLOGUE

No one knew where the disease started. It would appear out of nowhere and spread like wildfire from town to town, affecting everyone. This disease wouldn't have been a bad thing if we had known how to stop it.

It would start with a fever, but it was nothing like a normal fever. It overtook you, leaving your body burning one minute and ice cold the next. Then the final stages began. Your eyes turn completely black, with no color or white left. Then black-spidery veins appear at your temple and slowly spread throughout your entire body. The whole thing happens within hours. By the time it starts, it's already too late.

No one knew how the disease spread, so as soon as you showed signs, society would shun you. You would be cursed to live out the rest of your short, miserable hours alone and in pain.

The baby had silver eyes. Not only was it an unusual eye color for someone to have, but her twin brother had dark eyes like his hair. When he came out first, the midwives assumed his twin would also share this quality. They were shocked to see her silver eyes catch in the light of the lanterns. Some thought dark magic was afoot and refused to be anywhere near her.

The twins were born on the eve of the Arak, short for Arachnid, outbreak. This is what the townsfolk had started nicknaming it, believing it had come from spider bites that left the inky black web-like trails down the infected body. Everyone was afraid and looking for something to blame for the disease outbreak. Most of the people in the town decided to blame the twins.

Their mother already had a few names picked out, depending on the gender of the babies. The boy's name was Peter, a normal strong sounding name for the man he would someday surely become. The girl's name was meant to be Piper since they were twins and twins typically had similar-sounding names. However, when her mother saw those silver eyes, she knew that the name she had picked out no longer worked for the daughter she held in her arms.

"Hello, my little Silver," she whispered and pressed her lips to her tiny head.

Names had power, which the twins' mother was aware of. At the last moment, her mother made an impossibly important choice and changed something she had been planning for the nine months she had carried them. This was the most important gift her mother ever gave her, and her mother was very much aware of it.

The twins grew up as normally as they could. There were still people in their town that blamed them for the disease that had spread throughout the lands. The very disease that took their father from them right after they were born. Their mother was now a widow, which she wore with grace.

She insisted on having a funeral, even though most victims of Arak were burned in large piles with no ceremony. Everyone who attended the funeral agreed that the grace in which she held herself, made it painful just to look at her. While most of the widows who've been a victim of the disease had wept and raved at the injustice of it all, the twins' mother stood stoic. A child in each arm, she never wept or wailed. The only sign that she was in any distress was the tears that silently streamed down her face. It was apparent to anyone that the twins parents had loved each other in a way that was somehow visible, a love that would stretch far beyond any disease or even the reaches of death. The twins were too young to have understood this, of course, but they would later hear the stories the townsfolk gossiped about while doing the weekly shopping.

The town the twins were born in was one right off the sea. From their cottage, they could see the white breaks of the waves from a room on the north side of the house. This just so happened to be the room that they were born in, which might have something to do with the twins' love of the sea. It became apparent to their mother as soon as they were able to crawl, the twins somehow knew where the water was no matter where they were.

One day, when they were barely old enough to walk, their mother got quite a fright when after taking her eyes off of them for two seconds, they were no longer standing next to her. After an hour of searching, she found them, perfectly safe but playing in the shallows of the waves. She knew then that they must have saltwater in their blood and no amount of her trying to stop them would do any good. So after a great deal of supervision and safety training on how to swim and the dangers of riptides, the twins were free to go to the beach as often as they liked.

This was a situation that worked just fine for the twins. They spent most of their days playing on the beach and exploring the joys of what the ocean can bring. It was on one of these adventures when the twins were around six that they discovered something that would change the rest of their lives forever.

There was a starfish that had lost its way in one of the waves that had washed up onshore. Silver, having no fear of anything on the beach, walked up to it reaching out her hand to grab it and place it back in the water. Right before her hand reached it, she paused and cocked her head to the side as if listening to something. "What's wrong, Sil?" Peter asked, with the special nickname he had just for her.

"The starfish is talking to me," she said, leaning in closer to hear it better.

"What is it telling you?"

"Be quiet and I'll tell you!" After a few moments of intense listening, Silver nodded and straightened up. "The starfish told me a secret. He made me promise not to tell anyone!"

Peter looked at her, annoyance clear on his face. "But I'm not just anyone! I'm your brother. Your older brother, so that means you have to tell me."

Silver puffed out her cheeks. "Oh fine! The starfish said–" she broke off abruptly. A seagull had started circling above their heads. "Oh no! We have to save the starfish!" She yelled running back to it. Peter ran right behind her, trying to think of a way to keep the seagull away from the starfish and his sister.

They weren't that far from the shore, but running through sand, even for the most experienced runners, is difficult. The seagull above them squawked and started making a beeline towards Silver, trying to get to the starfish in her hands.

Unsure of what he was planning to do but knowing he had to do something to protect his sister, Peter planted his feet and turned to face the seagull head-on. In his mind's eye, he saw exactly what the seagull was going to do. It was almost like watching a dream but everything happened in slow motion. He saw the seagull dodging his first swing with a stick and flying over his head to his sister knocking her to the ground. The image faded, and they were back in real-time. Peter knew what he had to do.

Noticing a stick at his feet, he picked it up to brandish it as a weapon. Knowing which direction the seagull was planning on flying, he lifted his stick and swung with all of his might. The seagull squawked at the impact and hit the sandy ground with a thump. Rolling to right itself, it gave one final squawk of anger and flew off into the distance.

Silver, having successfully put the starfish back in the ocean, came to stand by her brother. "That was amazing! How did you do that?"

"I don't know," Peter said, looking down at the stick in his hands. "I saw what would happen before it happened. Then I just knew what to do."

Silver looked at the distance, where the seagull was now a speck in the sky. "Well, let's go home."

Peter nodded and dropped his stick. They both walked hand and in hand back to their cottage.

A few years passed, and the twins grew up without telling anyone about their gifts. It was a secret they had decided to keep between themselves. A few years before, they had seen a woman who had been accused of witchcraft, tied to a stake in the middle of town. Their mother had dragged them away but not before the screams started. Since then, the twins had made a pact never to speak of their powers to anyone. The screams of the woman haunted both of their dreams after that day, and they held the fear of being discovered in their hearts like a weight.

Even still, their powers grew with them. Silver could now call animals to her, and Peter could see the future but only when something bad was about to happen. They had no idea why they were given these gifts, but they were grateful for them.

Apart from spending time on the beach, the twins had one other favorite activity: racing. Every day as soon as they were done collecting things for their mother, they would race up the hill to see who was the fastest. They were keeping an ongoing tally of who had the most wins. So far they were tied, but Silver was planning on changing that today.

As they raced up the hill, Silver, who was in the lead, saw something strange. There was a small crowd of people gathered around their house. She slowed, giving Peter just enough time to catch up to her. He was about to pass her when he noticed why she had stopped.

Looking at each other anxiously, they ran up the rest of the hill together. They shoved their way through the crowd who were all talking quietly among themselves.

"Children! Someone stop them!" they heard a voice behind them shout. All those adults who had gathered turned towards them and reached out their hands trying to stop them. But the twins were fast, and easily dodged all of them before bursting into the house.

Their mother was slumped over the kitchen table, a blanket draped around her shoulders. She was shaking and covered in sweat. She lifted her head at the sound of the door banging open.

"Oh children," she said, with tears gathering in her eyes. "Don't come any closer! And listen to me very carefully."

The twins looked at each other in panic and edged slightly closer, but without touching her. Her breath was coming out in shallow gasps, and she was struggling to say what she knew she had to. "I'm not going to be around much longer, so listen to my words. Take care of each other. You two are the only family you have left."

"No Mama! You'll get better! We'll heal you!" they shouted at the same time, trying desperately to hold onto the hope that was beginning to leave them.

The tears spilled over and made trails going down their mother's face. "Be brave for me, alright? And take care of each other. I love you both so much."

"There you are!" a voice came from behind them. They whirled around to see one of the merchants who they had seen just last week at the marketplace. "Get the children away from here!"

"No Mama!" Silver lunged away, but the old merchant was too quick for her and in no time had both of them. They kicked and screamed, biting and fighting the whole time trying to get back to their mother.

The merchant was strong and he dragged them away from their childhood home with arms like iron. No matter how they cried and begged, he didn't turn around. He continued to drag them away from everything they had ever known.

CHAPTER ONE

Silver

"Sil?"

Silver jumped, the sound of her brother's voice pulling her out of her thoughts. She shook her head trying to clear it of the last of the memories that clung to her. It had been a long time since she had last thought of that day. She could still hear her and Peter's cries in her head as they were being dragged away.

"What is it?" she asked, still not taking her eyes from the horizon.

"Just checking on you," he said, leaning lazily on the railing next to her. "You seemed like you could use some company."

Silver nodded, taking a deep breath of clean salty air, feeling the gentle rock of the ship under her. "I don't know if it's a twin thing or a future telling thing, but you always seem to know when I go to dark places."

"Oh, definitely a twin thing," said Peter, with a completely straight face. "Future thing is nice and all, but it's nothing in comparison to the twin sense. We could call it the Twense."

Silver made a face at him. "Ugh, that's awful, Peter."

"Well, what do you think about Swin?"

They were both quiet for a minute.

"No," said Silver.

"Definitely not," Peter replied, scratching his chin. "Twense it is!"

Silver rolled her eyes at him. "And who is going to use this new made-up word?"

"All the twins in the world obviously," he replied, hardly bothered by her lack of belief in his greatness.

"How are they going to hear about this newfound made-up word to describe something that probably isn't going to come up in conversation on a regular basis?"

"Well, we're at sea," he said, gesturing to the whole expanse of water surrounding them. "All we have to do is spread the news in a little town here, a little town there, and then before you know it, Twense becomes a household word!"

"Peter, Twense will never become a household word."

"You don't know that. After all you, my dear sister, have said the word Twense a total of three times."

"I've only said it once, Peter."

"Well, I've said it twice, and you've said it once so I'm combining our efforts. You know, because it's a Twense thing."

Silver rolled her eyes again, beginning to worry she would get a headache. She loved her brother but goodness his quick tongue was sometimes too much for her. Not that she couldn't keep up with him but she wasn't really in the mood today. She was still a little shaken from her memory which is probably what led her to ask, "Do you think Mom would be proud of us?"

It was a moment of vulnerability that she was only comfortable showing to her brother. The grin slid off his face, slowly turning into a look of contemplation. She knew he would take his time in answering because he liked to think through his thoughts before speaking them in serious matters, which was the complete opposite of how he acted normally. Even knowing this, she found herself getting anxious at how long it was taking him to answer.

"I think she would," he said, after an agonizing moment.

"Why? We haven't done anything worthy. She was a great woman and we're... well..." she trailed off not knowing how to finish the sentence.

"Pirating," Peter offered, helpfully.

"We're merchants," she said, stiffly. "How could this make her proud?"

"Well, she told us two things before we left. They were: take care of each other. I think we've done a pretty good job of that."

"It's debatable. I think your horrible puns will be the death of me."

"You know you love them!"

"I don't."

"Anyway," he said, turning the conversation back to where they started. "The other thing she said was, never forget that she loved us. Now I think that love may surpass even piracy. I mean, it's not like we've killed anyone!"

"Peter, we have killed people."

"Just a couple," he said, brushing off her comment. "Besides, it was self-defense."

"We boarded their ship."

"Are you going to shoot down everything I say?"

Silver took another breath of salty air. "No, I'm sorry."

"Apology accepted. Now in all seriousness, I think Mom would've been proud. We fulfilled the two things she asked of us." He gave her a gentle bump with his shoulder. "Where is all this coming from?"

Silver shrugged and looked back out at the horizon.

"It's crazy to think it's been twelve years," he said, slowly.

Silver didn't answer but her hands gripped the railing a bit harder than needed. She still wasn't over her mother's death. Even though it had been so long, she still felt the sting of pain. It wasn't debilitating as it had been at first, but there wasn't a day that went by where she didn't think about her mother. It still hurt after all this time, and she wasn't sure that the pain would ever fully go away. There was a part of her that died with her mother that she never thought she would get back.

Peter's hand softly slid onto hers. She looked over at him and saw the same pain that mirrored her reflection in his eyes. "Me too, Sil."

She nodded, gripping his hand in her own as they mourned together.

"Captain?" A tentative voice came from behind them.

Silver turned to see their newest crew member, the timid orphan from a seaside village that had also been completely wiped out by Arak. No one else had been willing to take him aboard for fear of spreading the disease. That was how they had picked up most of their motley crew.

"What is it, Tom?" Silver asked, trying to keep the annoyance out of her voice. It wasn't Tom's fault she was in a mood. She knew he was easily frightened like a rabbit, but she had no idea what he could need.

"Sorry to be interrupting you and the first mate and all," he said, twisting his cap around in his hands. "But the Sailing Master wanted to know where to steer the ship, and he asked me to ask you."

"Well done, Tom," said Peter, slapping him on the back, "I will personally deliver the next location to the Sailing Master. Why don't you go below deck and see what kind of work needs to be done there?" Tom nodded and scurried away like one of the many rats that had found their way into the ship.

"Poor boy, I think you may have frightened him," said Peter, giving her a reproachful look.

"I hardly said two words to the boy!"

"Now, now," Peter held up a finger. "There you go again. You're awfully peckish this morning, Captain."

Silver pinched the bridge of her nose, trying to keep her patience. "Peter," she said through gritted teeth. "You're not helping me."

"Then tell me how to."

She looked up at him and saw the concern in his eyes, then all the anger left her. Taking a deep breath, she tried to gain a little control of herself. "Things aren't going the way I thought they would, and now with all of these people relying on me, I just..." she trailed off, her gaze drifting back to the expansive ocean. Somehow, she found great comfort in the magnitude of the ocean. It reminded her of her own insignificance, which lifted some of the weight from her shoulders.

"Why don't we start with the Sailing Master? Where are we off to next?"

"Tell him we're heading northward. There is an island I have heard about that I'd like to go see."

Silver jumped off the rowboat and felt the coolness of the ocean surf as it soaked into her pants. The Island in question was rather small. Much smaller than the stories had made it sound. The voyage to the Island had gone without a hitch. There were no storms, no strange winds, or anything to remark on. The whole trip took about ten days to complete with warm weather and all-around perfect sailing conditions.

Too perfect if you asked Silver, which no one had. The only one who seemed remotely suspicious of their good luck was the Sailing Master, John. He was in his mid-forties, making him one of the older members of the crew, and the voice of reason. Occasionally, he would glare at the sky throughout their journey, almost seeming to dare the weather to try something.

Silver began dragging the small row boat to the shore with the other men who had accompanied her to the Island. There were a total of four of them including herself. Peter came, of course, he was never far from her side. Then there was John, who always came with them on land adventures, saying they would need a navigator unless they liked being lost. And the newly added Tom, who was so eager to join them, he nearly fell off the ship in his excitement. He was like a puppy, Silver reflected as a large wave came and knocked him off his feet. Luckily, John was there to pull him up by the scruff of the neck. Silver shook her head. She was hoping to get in and out of this island quickly, she didn't know how poor Tom would do in an actual fight.

After wrestling with the waves for a bit, especially on Tom's part, they got the tiny row boat to the shore and were able to look around. There was a huge rock face that ran through the center of the Island. Besides that, there wasn't much else. There were a couple of palm trees scattered around, but that was it.

"What're we looking for, Captain?" asked Peter in his normal, cheerful tone.

She didn't look over at him as she answered, "A special kind of stone."

"Well, it looks like there's plenty of stones here."

"It's a different kind of stone, Peter," she said, as she picked her way around some hermit crabs until she came to the giant wall in front of her. It was dark gray rock, which was a bit odd, considering that this kind of stone was not original to this area. As she got closer, she could almost see what looked like a seam that ran across it in a block-like pattern. She placed her hand on the wall, and the stone was worn smooth. She grinned, knowing exactly what had happened. Tracing her hand along the seam, she heard Peter call, "I see you must be doing some very important inspecting of the wall."

"I am," she called back, not pausing as she continued to search.

"I take it you don't want to explain what it is you're doing?"

"No, I do not."

"Then could you at least tell us what you're looking for?"

Her fingers came across a part of the wall that was different from the rest. She gently pressed down with her two index fingers, and then heard a loud hissing sound. The wall slowly began to transform, the seams becoming visible as the whole thing shifted. The stones began to twist in on themselves slowly, making an opening until it was big enough for even John to go through.

"That is what we're looking for," she answered when all the pieces had finally settled down.

They crowded around what was now a visible doorway. It led down what looked like a flight of stairs into complete darkness.

"What does this mean?" asked an incredulous Tom.

"It means we weren't the first ones to discover this Island."

"Didn't we already know that though? I mean you had heard stories about the island, that's why we're here," said Peter.

"That's true," Silver conceded. "But what we didn't know was how well kept this island was going to be."

They all looked down into the doorway, no one willing to take the first step. "Well," said Silver, adjusting her pistol that was always strapped to her side. "Ladies first, as they say."

"If it's alright by you, Captain," came John's deep voice. "I would like to go first."

Silver's foot was hovering above the first step, which she slowly retracted. While she knew John had the best intentions at heart, she wasn't sure she wanted to be protected in that way. She understood the risk going into this; she didn't need to be coddled. "It's not alright. I am going first," she said, in her best captain voice.

"Come now, Sil," Peter reasoned. "Don't be like that. I know what you're thinking, but the truth is, if you had been anything other than the captain, we would let you go first. As it is, we really can't afford anything to happen to you. This is just the basics of a crew that cares deeply about you."

"Very well," she said stiffly, trying to keep the annoyance out of her voice. She knew Peter was right, but that still didn't stop her from being annoyed. "However, loyal as this crew may be, you won't always be able to protect, me."

"Which is why we're doing everything we can in the times we can protect you," said John, kindly.

Silver nodded, touched at John's caring, but that was something she could never show. Being the captain of an all-male crew was difficult at times, especially when the men wanted to think that being a woman meant that she needed their help in things. She had to demonstrate her capabilities daily to prove that she belonged as the captain. However, she should know that at least with this small group, they saw her only as a captain, a role that she had earned and earned with her own blood, sweat, and tears.

After making some torches from the sad palm trees and some supplies they had brought, John took the first step into the doorway. They waited for a trap or something to be set off. After a few tense moments, nothing happened, so they began their slow descent. John took the front with Silver right at his heels. Next came Tom, and there was a silent agreement he should be somewhere in the middle of the group, with Peter bringing up the rear.

The way down was painfully slow for Silver. She knew why they were taking their time but it still irked her a bit. Adventure was calling deep in her marrow, and taking her time was just making it worse.

John suddenly came to a dead stop, almost causing Silver to run into him. She stopped in time but unfortunately for her Tom was not as quick on his feet. He ran straight into her back, sending her headfirst into John. As the sturdiest person she knew, John hardly budged as the two of them ran into him. Under most circumstances, John would have been fine if Peter had also been paying more attention. Even with all of John's strength, Peter running into Tom after both Tom and Silver had run into him, was enough to send him tumbling down the next step.

Several things happened at once over the next few moments. There was a terrible screeching sound that led to John yelling and all of them taking a tumble down the stairs. After that, there was a lot of yelling and feet and elbows in people's faces and sides. In a giant human-sized ball, they all rolled down the remainder of the stairs and landed with a crash.

They all laid still for a few minutes trying to catch their breath. Silver hurt all over. She couldn't remember the last time she had fallen down the stairs, and stone stairs at that. Slowly, she began to untangle herself from the men, with them doing the same.

"Well, there goes our element of surprise," said Peter, groaning as he stood up rubbing his new bruises.

"John? Are you alright?" Silver asked, kneeling next to him. Their torches had completely gone out when they had fallen, luckily they hadn't caught anyone on fire.

There was a groaning off to her right, which meant he was alive at least. As she felt around, her hand felt something hairy. She pulled back startled, her heart pounding in her chest. "John?"

"I'm alright," came John's tired voice. "This little one on the other hand could use some comforting."

Slowly feeling for each other, John placed the hairy thing into Silver's hands. She had no idea what she was holding until she heard a quiet, "Meow."

"How did a cat get down here?" she asked, slowly stroking the little thing. It was indeed shaking like a leaf, and she tried her best to hold it in a comfortable way.

"No idea," came John's voice from the dark. "I almost stepped on her, poor thing, but luckily I was able to shield her with my body when we fell."

Silver continued to stroke the cat, which seemed to help calm it down. Then she heard, "Who are you?" It was from the cat in which she knew only she could understand. "We're explorers," she answered softly. "We aren't here to hurt you."

"Can you understand me?" the cat exclaimed.

"Yes, I can. Why are you down here?"

"I'm lost," said the cat, sadly. "I lost my master and don't know where to go."

"Well, why don't you come with us for the time being," asked Silver. "Besides, you probably know this area better than all of us."

"Oh, thank you! Now I won't be alone!"

"I'm so sorry!" came Tom's frantic voice from over to Silver's left.

"Tom, it's fine, just watch where you're going next time."

"Or maybe watch the people in front of you. Like a normal person," came Peter's reproachful voice from her right.

"You're one to talk!" came Tom's indignant voice.

"Oh, leave the poor lad alone," said John.

"This is the least of our worries anyway," said Silver, feeling the wall behind her. "Right now we need to figure out where to get some light."

"Oh, I can help!" came the cat's voice and before Silver could stop her, she jumped out of her arms and disappeared into the darkness.

"Wait, come back!" Silver called, reaching out for her in vain.

They waited a few moments in uncomfortable silence and darkness. Then suddenly light flooded the hallway. Everyone shielded their eyes at the sudden brightness.

Once their eyes had adjusted, Silver took a look around. The hallway had light fixtures that seemed to have lit up all at once. They were in a narrow hallway with gray stone walls. The floor was made out of a different kind of stone, Silver wasn't sure what kind. And the ceiling was also stone.

"How did all the lights come on at once?" asked Peter.

Just then the cat came back and jumped straight into Silver's arms. "The cat," Silver answered simply as the cat in her arms started purring loudly.

"But how did they all get lit at the same time? Was it magic?" asked Tom looking around in wonder.

"No, I think it's something else," said Silver, going up to the light to better inspect it. There was no wick or burning fluid but there did seem to be something about it that was strangely familiar. Maybe it was the shape. Silver wasn't sure but had bigger things to worry about.

"Thanks," she said, to the cat who was purring as a sign of contentment. "What's your name by the way?"

"I don't have a name," the cat said, in a sad voice. "My master never gave me one, and I was taken from my family when I was very young."

"Sounds like your master was a piece of work," said Silver "Well, would you like a name?"

Before the cat could answer, Tom said, "What is she doing?"

It was addressed to Peter, which made Silver realize how weird this probably seemed.

"I believe she's gathering her thoughts," said Peter looking at her. "And Tom? She's not deaf you know."

Tom blushed, embarrassed, and looked to the floor sheepishly. "We'll figure that out later," she whispered to the cat. "Right now, we need to figure out where the stone is."

"Oh, there is a big stone in the middle of this place! I can lead you there!" said the cat, excitedly and before Silver had a chance to react, the cat jumped out of her arms again, and began walking briskly down the hall. Silver rushed after her with the men right on her heels.

"Is no one else going to comment on the fact that we're following a cat?" huffed Tom as he struggled to keep up. Everyone ignored him as the cat led them down the winding, twisty stone maze they had found themselves in. After what seemed like forever, the cat finally came to a halt outside of a large stone doorway.

"Here we are!" said the cat, puffing out her chest.

They had come to a dead end without very much light. There weren't very many strange light fixtures, which cast strange shadows against the walls creating an eerie feel to the whole place. As Silver got closer, she saw odd markings on the archway of the doors. Something was etched into the stone itself by what looked to be a very skilled stone worker.

"John? Have you ever seen anything like this before in your studies?"

John leaned in to take a closer look. After a few moments of study, he came back up and said, "It can't be." He continued his study for several agonizing moments until Silver couldn't stand it anymore.

"What is it?" she asked.

"It looks like something from an ancient race. This particular tribe were excellent stone workers and could do what some scholars said was magic. I never believed that part of the study, but there was nothing to prove them right or wrong."

"Why's that?" asked Peter as he came in for his inspection.

"This race was completely wiped out."

Everyone froze in what they were doing. Even the cat blinked her huge eyes up at John. "What wiped them out?" Silver asked, the feeling of unease increasing with each minute.

"No one was completely sure. The scholars who studied them couldn't figure out what it was that did it. They were there one day and completely gone the next."

“So, is it possible they were never wiped out to begin with?” Peter asked, poking at the stone in front of him.

John shrugged. “That theory has been thrown around by the scholars, but there was no evidence.”

“So, an entire race vanished, and no one knows exactly what happened to them?”

John nodded mutely, staring at the stonework in front of him.

“Well,” said Silver, straightening her shoulders. “I guess this means we’re in the right place.”

Everyone quietly looked at the huge door in front of them. “I wonder what’s behind it,” Tom said with huge scared eyes.

“There’s only one way to find out,” Silver said, as she leaned forwards and opened the door. The room was dimly lit with only a few candles burning in the center of the room, leaving the rest in shadows. The stone was there alright, but so was someone else.

CHAPTER TWO

Peter

At first, all Peter saw was the stone that Sil was looking for. It was sitting on a pedestal in the middle of the room, larger than he thought it would be, but small enough he could hold it with one hand. It had a strange cut to it, almost like the top of a diamond. It also was covered in strange markings, although these were different from what had been on the door. They completely covered the stone and each face had a marking. It had a metal belt, which looked similar to copper, that ran around it.

"Fascinating," he said, moving farther into the room. "And what did you say this thing does?" He looked back over his shoulder, and that's when he saw her.

The woman was spread out on a stone table with a white shapeless dress that stopped just below her knees and elbows. Her face was delicate, and she looked young, perhaps a couple years younger than Peter. The thing that captured Peter was her long red hair that spread out behind her creating a halo effect around her.

Peter felt his heart stop for a moment before sputtering back to life. He shook his head trying to clear it and took a look around. As he looked a little closer, he could see the orb was sitting on a pedestal next to her.

The girl somehow seemed to be hooked up to the orb with strange wires that were feeding directly into her arms and legs.

He began a more determined walk towards her when he was jerked back by his arm.

"Ouch," he said, looking at Silver.

"Peter, we can't go barging in here. We don't know what this girl is or if she's a weapon."

"Her, a weapon? Really?"

"You don't know," she whispered, angrily. "That's my point. We need to go into this rationally."

"Fine," he said, shaking off her grip.

"What do we do?" Peter heard Silver ask John. Peter wasn't looking at any of them. His eyes were glued to the girl.

"We unhook her from the orb," Peter said, following the wires attached to her with his eyes. He drew closer at a slow pace, so Silver wouldn't drag him back again.

"Any idea what this stone does?" Silver asked John, ignoring Peter.

"Wait a minute," said Peter, turning on his sister. "You mean to tell me you dragged us all the way here for a stone, and you've no idea what it does?"

"I have a buyer for it," she said, anger flashing across her face at being questioned. "They did not specify why they wanted it, or what the item in question did. I thought we were going to reach an abandoned island and it would be an easy job or I never would have taken it. Are you satisfied?"

Peter gave a curt nod and then turned back to the girl, continuing to edge closer.

"I don't remember reading anything about this stone," came John's voice from behind him. "I would need to get closer to try and translate what's written on it."

"Very well, now we move, but slowly," she added, and Peter felt her eyes burning into the back of his head. "And we don't touch anything."

It was Peter's turn to ignore her as he continued edging closer to the girl. As he got closer, he could see her chest rising and falling. If it weren't for the strange placement, it would have seemed like she was asleep. He was close enough now that he could see the wires were fully embedded in her skin. The skin around the wires was bloody and irritated. His gut twisted at the sight. Whatever they were experimenting with her, ended now.

"Can you read what this is?" Silver's voice asked John, coming from Peter's left.

"I can't read it. These are symbols I've never seen before," John said.

"Are they not from the same language?"

"No, they aren't. Give me a bit, and I'll see if I can translate them."

Peter tentatively reached out his hand and gently touched one of the wires to see if he could detach it somehow. His hand brushed the bare skin of her arm and a vision swept through him, clear and vivid. He was in a room that was stark, blinding white. The girl was with him, and her eyes were wide open, an emerald green that bore into his soul. She was even more beautiful awake. He felt like he couldn't take a breath.

"Please," she said in a voice that rang like a bell. "Help me."

The vision ended as quickly as it had begun, and Peter found himself on his hands and knees gasping for breath. Once his vision cleared, he could see Silver kneeling on the floor next to him with her hand on his shoulder.

"Peter! Are you alright? What happened?"

"I had–" he broke off when he remembered Tom and John were in the room and were also leaning over him. "I'm fine," he said, telling with his eyes what he knew he couldn't say out loud.

Silver gave a nod showing she understood and said, "We'll talk later. Right now we need to figure out what to do."

Peter got back to his feet. He had visions before but nothing ever like that. His were usually slightly blurry around the edges, just slightly out of focus, and no one had ever spoken to him before. Maybe this was something different. He looked back at the girl lying on the stone table.

She looked the same as she had a few minutes ago, nothing had changed for her but it felt like everything had changed for him.

"We need to take her with us," he said, interrupting whatever conversation was going on behind him.

"I'm sorry, what?" came Silver's annoyed voice.

He turned and looked at her before replying, "She needs our help. We need to take her with us."

"She wasn't part of the deal."

"Are we just going to leave her then? Someone who clearly needs help? You'd turn your back on her?"

"Peter, we don't know who she is or what her significance is to this orb. What if people come after her?"

"Then it's all the more reason to take her with us. Please, Sil," he said, coming closer and trying to convey the importance of this with his eyes.

She sighed, exasperated. "Fine, but first we need to figure out how to unhook her from the orb."

"I hate to be the bearer of bad news," said John, slowly. "But we don't have a lot of time to figure it out. We've got company."

Peter looked over in the direction John was indicating. There was a figure in the back of the room, mostly hidden in shadows. The figure was covered from head to toe in a long, black cloak, which probably explains why they didn't see them at first. As the cloaked figure came further into the light, Peter saw abnormally long fingers covered by black gloves folded in front of its body and a hood that covered most of its face. But there was something strange about its face, something that seemed to protrude out of the hood that Peter was having a hard time making out.

It was only when it fully came into the light that Peter understood what he was looking at. It was a beak, one similar to that of a raven or crow. There were two small slits for air and from what he could see, two large gaping holes for eyes. He couldn't tell if this was a mask or the actual creature's face.

"Well, it seems we have visitors," came a voice like molten iron, smooth but with a harshness to it. As it began talking, Peter saw, to his horror, that the beak moved. Either this was a very clever trick or they were dealing with something far bigger than they ever had.

Peter felt Tom begin to tremble beside him. He angled his body, so he was slightly in front of Tom and then said, "Sorry to intrude, we didn't think anyone would be here."

The strange gaping holes turned to him as the creature cocked its head to the side like it was trying to figure him out. "Why are you here?" the creature asked, in its strange metallic voice.

"We're explorers," Peter said, beginning to edge away from the rest of the group. "We travel all over the seas looking for whatever we please."

"And what're you looking for that brought you here?" The creature turned its body slightly away from the rest of the crew, so it could keep its eyes on Peter.

Peter shrugged, continuing his slow trek. "We search for adventure, my friend. This is what makes our hearts sing and why we have come together." He saw the creature look back at Silver so he asked, "Why are you here? We thought this place was abandoned."

The creature turned back towards him. "We are here for the ritual."

"We? So, there are more of you?"

"Oh yes," said the creature in a satisfied voice, with expressionless eyes. "There are quite a few of us here that our mistress has asked personally to attend to."

"Mistress?"

"She is wonderful, powerful, and has asked us personally to take care of this matter, and we are honored to do her bidding and to serve her."

"I see. Well congratulations on having her favor. What exactly is it you all are doing here? And how many of you are there?"

The creature chuckled; it sounded like gears turning over each other. "I see what you are doing. But you won't get any more information from me."

"Well, in that case–" Peter ran towards him full force, which the creature hadn't been expecting, and tackled him to the ground. The creature's head hit the ground with a metallic sound that echoed around the room. The creature's body felt solid, but with a slight give that Peter took to mean it was at least partly living, even if most of it was metal.

"Grab them, and let's go!" Peter yelled looking over at the crew who were now surrounding the girl. His plan to distract the creature had worked, which had given everyone else time to get over to the girl and the strange stone.

"You fool!" came the creature's voice from underneath him. "You think that you, a mere human, can hold me?" Its voice had become louder, almost like it was being projected somehow, and it echoed around the room. Its body began to vibrate, and before Peter knew exactly what was happening, the creature began to move so fast he couldn't keep a grip on it. Just when he thought things couldn't get any weirder, the creature evaporated, turning into a dark black smoke and slipping out from under him.

"Bad news! They can turn into smoke!" said Peter, heart in his throat as he jumped to his feet. "Let's go!"

John was holding both the girl and the stone, which they had wrapped in Silver's jacket. The wires were still connected to the girl but awkwardly, with some of them bent at angles. They didn't have time to make it more comfortable for her, so Peter just hoped they would be able to get out of here, then they'd figure out how to disconnect her.

All the candles suddenly went out, leaving the only light in the room coming from the two double doors they had come in from, which had begun to close. The five of them bolted towards the door with Silver in the front and Peter in the rear. He took a deep breath and let it out slowly, clearing his mind from the panic and focusing. Everything began to move in slow motion as he saw the doors closing before Silver reached them. The five of them were plunged into darkness with no escape. Then he was brought abruptly back to the present. He saw the doors closing too quickly and looked around for something to prop them open. Not seeing anything handy, he sighed and pulled out his sword from his belt. Praying that it would hit the mark, he threw it like a spear.

His luck held out. His sword flew through the air straight as an arrow and embedded itself into the door preventing it from closing. They ran through just as the sword began to bend. Once Peter had gone through, the sword snapped, making Peter wince. Then the doors shut with a final boom.

"John, do you remember the way out?" asked Silver, already breathless. He nodded, conserving his strength knowing they had a long way to go, and began leading the way.

"Wait, what happened to the cat?" Tom huffed as they ran down the hallway.

"I don't think that should be high on our priority list," said Silver in between breaths as they made their way around the corner.

There was the cat, but she wasn't alone. A bird person was with her, and it was standing there calmly with its hands folded in front of him. The cat was circling its legs purring.

"Should we move the cat to the list of priorities now?" Peter asked.

"Traitor," Silver said, glaring at the cat who just purred, ignoring her.

"You cannot escape," said the bird person spreading his arms wide. Its voice sounded triumphant but there was no expression on its face, making it seem all the stranger.

A low rumbling began in the back of the cavern which the group felt pounding in their chests. The rumbling became louder, vibrating the floor under their feet and making it hard to feel their legs.

"We will keep you here with us and–" it broke off as Silver pulled out her gun and fired. It hit the creature's chest, and the bullet embedded itself. The creature looked down at the hole in its chest and fell to its knees. A black, almost oil-like substance began pooling on the floor from the hole, which the group avoided as they made their way forward. When the cat saw them trying to escape, she came after them with her claws out. Unfortunately for her, she wasn't as careful around the oil. As soon as her tiny paw stepped into it, her eyes rolled back in her head, and she passed out.

"Glad we didn't touch that," said Peter looking over his shoulder at the cat as they continued to run. Right as they were about to turn the next corner, Peter, still looking over his shoulder, saw the bird person begin to move.

"Bad news, it's not dead!"

"How did that not kill him?" asked Tom, looking behind them.

"We can talk about it later! Right now let's focus on getting out of here! John, how much farther do we have to go?"

John seemed too tired to respond. "Is it much farther?" He shook his head just as they made it to the long staircase they had fallen from when they first arrived.

They were tired from running so far, John more so, carrying the girl. Peter leaned over to him and said, "John, let me carry her." John shook his head and opened his mouth to argue. "John," Peter interrupted. "I was the one who said we needed to take her. You've done the hard bit. Let me carry her the rest of the way. Plus if that thing comes back we need you to fight it. I'm out of weapons."

John shrugged and gently handed her over. As soon as the girl was in his arms, Peter could feel her body warmth through his shirt. She wasn't heavy, but he could see how tired John was. He wasn't sure if he would've been able to run with her that way, and he was grateful to have someone like John. He tucked her head against his chest and felt her soft breath. So far no more weird visions, but he was careful not to touch her skin again.

The group made their way up the long flight of stairs. None of them knew exactly how long this flight was because they had fallen most of it. The longer they climbed, the more exhausted they became. Their adrenaline began slowing down, now that nothing was chasing them. They took a short break, at what they hoped was halfway up the stairs. Peter pressed his back against the wall and slid down slowly, gently putting the girl in his lap. As he moved her, so she would be sitting more comfortably, his finger accidentally brushed her bare arm.

Again, his vision went dark for a moment before being blinded by white light. He was again in the white room facing the girl. It was weird to think she was still in his arms in the physical world but here she stood across from him. As she turned, she fixed him with her piercing green eyes.

"Please, you have to get up," she said, looking worried.

"Wait, who are you?" he asked, taking a step towards her.

"There's no time, they're coming for you."

He reached out his hand to touch her and just before he reached her, he was brought back to the present. He took some deep breaths and saw the girl was still tucked in his arms. Everyone else was still resting, not noticing his momentary journey. He stood keeping the girl comfortable against his chest. "We need to go," he said urgently, trying to get everyone to stand again.

"We'll get up, just give us a minute," said Silver, taking a few more deep breaths and not making any moves to ever stand up again.

A popping sound made them all jump. They looked down the stairs and saw that at the very far end one of the lights had gone out. Slowly the bulb next to it went out, and then the next one did, blanketing that part of the hallway in darkness. They looked at each other and silently began making their way back up the stairs, this time with a bit more urgency.

The lights continued to go out one by one, slowly picking up speed. No matter how fast they ran, the lights seemed to be directly behind them. The doorway was in sight, and they could see the blueness of the sky and ocean in front of them. Peter didn't feel his arms shaking with exhaustion or his breath coming out in gasps. All he knew was that if they didn't make it to the door, there was no hope of them making it out of here alive. The light bulbs finally overtook them and were now going out ahead of them. Peter felt the blackness closing in around him while keeping his eyes on the doorway ahead.

His heart skipped a beat when he saw the door beginning to close. He held the girl closer to his chest and used her strength to push himself a little harder. He practically flew out of the doorway with Silver and John right at his heels. He looked back to see just a small portion of the door remained open.

John reached his hand in and pulled Tom out by the arm. Tom yelped as the back of his shirt got caught in the stone doorway as his momentum was cut short and was pulled back against the wall. John reached over and, taking a small knife from his bag, cut him out of it. Peter turned and made it to the small rowboat, where he gently placed the girl. He hopped out and began pushing the boat out into the waves. Tom was put in the boat by John before he turned to help Peter and Silver push the boat the rest of the way into the ocean. They got in and began taking turns rowing back towards their ship.

They made it and were able to hoist the boat and everyone safely into the ship. Tom flopped down on the deck shaking slightly.

"What the devil?" came the proper voice of Cedric.

"We found someone who needs medical attention," said Peter, still holding the girl and leading the way into the below decks to the captain's chambers where they usually take the wounded. Cedric followed, mumbling the usual about how reckless they were and how they were going to have enough resources to take care of everyone.

Peter shouldered open the door that led into a spacious room. There was a section with a large table and map where Silver and John had their meetings to discuss the best route. Then there was a small table and washroom in the corner. There was a large bed that took up the other half of the room, which is where Peter made a beeline. He laid her down on the bed and began to unwrap the stone.

"What seems to be the matter with her?" came Cedric's voice as he pushed his spectacles up on his nose, a sign of him beginning his examination.

"That's the thing we aren't sure about," said Peter as he continued to unwrap the stone. He was going slowly and carefully to not pull on the wires that were connecting her to the stone. "She does have all of these wires attached to her, which I'm sure we'll need your help detaching."

Cedric was taking her pulse when he looked around her and said, "Where are the wires?"

Peter finished unwrapping the stone and saw that the wires had disappeared from it. He looked over to the girl and saw that there weren't any wires attached to her either. There weren't any marks where the wires had been. Her skin was as smooth, as if it had never been touched.

"That's odd," Peter said, examining the stone closer. He didn't see any wires or any markings on it either. He realized with a start that he was touching it with his bare hands, which he thought was probably not a good idea, even though it wasn't hurting him. He didn't feel anything at all, the stone just felt like a very smooth rock. Regardless, he decided putting it down would be the best option, so he wrapped it back up in the jacket and placed it on the table. He felt the ship give a jolt as winds caught the sails.

There was a knock on the door, and John came in with Tom trailing behind him. "Cedric, could you take a look at Tom? There was an incident with a stone door."

Cedric nodded and looked over at the girl one more time before seeing Tom. There was a long purplish bruise across his back where the door must have pinched him. There were spots of blood where the force of the doors had broken the skin. Peter felt his heart sink in shame. He was so focused on the girl, he didn't even think about Tom or the others who were with him.

John looked over at him, almost seeming to sense his shame, and said, "Silver needs you on the deck."

"Right, on my way," Peter replied, and with one more look at the girl on the bed, he turned and walked back up the stairs to the main deck.

The man deck was bustling with activity, with crew members running to and fro, yelling directions and replies to each other. He spotted Silver who was at the helm and began making his way towards her. As he walked over, he looked over to the starboard side and saw the island had grown much smaller. He could still see it, but just barely, which meant they were making good time.

He walked up the short flight of stairs and sauntered over to Silver. "You needed me?"

She glanced over at him, with anger burning in her eyes. "What?" he asked, already starting to feel his defenses rising.

"Oh, I don't know Peter, maybe it's that you weren't there to help us cast off. Or the fact that you completely ignored Tom's injuries. I bet you didn't even know he was hurt, did you?"

Peter felt the shame wash over him again, making him bristle. "Well, the ship didn't sink, even though I wasn't on deck. Tom seemed fine. He was walking around and walked himself to Cedric. Look there he is now," Peter finished as Tom came walking out of the captain's quarters. He did seem fine, maybe a little shaken up from the whole ordeal, but he had a pep in his step from his latest adventure. He went around the deck showing off his bandages and telling anyone who would listen about how he got it. "Don't blame me for your decision to take him on this trip. He didn't have to go to the island with us."

"You think I don't know that?" she snapped, glaring at him.

"Well, you act like you don't!"

They glared at each other for a moment before they both simultaneously took a breath and let it out. "I'm sorry," Peter said, running a hand through his hair.

"Me too," said Silver, loosening her grip on the wheel. "We're both under a lot of pressure."

"And a near-death experience," Peter added. "All in a day's work."

She laughed at this. "So, it would seem."

"Lots of sacrifices were made," he said leaning against the railing next to her. "My sword, for example, was lost to this latest adventure. I'm not sure what I will do without it. I feel as though I've lost a friend today."

She rolled her eyes at him. "We'll get you another sword. Keep your shirt on."

"It could have been a lot worse," he said, looking out over the ocean.

"You were certainly taking a lot of risks."

"But that's what saved our necks," he reasoned.

She sighed. "Next time, let's try not to tackle the strange creature that we don't know anything about, alright?"

Peter stood up straight, puffing out his chest he gave a salute and said, "Aye, aye Captain."

She laughed at him, completely breaking the remainder of the tension around them.

"Sil? I'm glad we're okay."

"Me too."

They sat in comfortable silence for a few moments, enjoying each other's company and the salty ocean air. They saw John come out of the captain's quarters and begin walking towards them. "Here comes trouble," Peter said, which got a smile out of Silver.

"Captain, Cedric needs you."

"Is there a problem?" Silver asked as she gave him the wheel.

"Not exactly," he said looking at both of them. "But the girl's awake."

CHAPTER THREE

Silver

Silver walked into her quarters with Peter right at her heels. The girl was beautiful and delicate, her bright green eyes were almost mesmerizing. She was looking at Cedric when they came in, but soon turned her eyes to them. Silver almost felt a shock go through her at the intensity of her gaze. She looked briefly over at her before turning her eyes to Peter. Silver felt him stiffen next to her as the girl's eyes rested on him. "It's you," the girl said in a voice that was clear as a bell.

"Peter, how does she know you?" Silver asked, turning to him.

"I may have touched her when we were in the tunnel," he answered in a husky voice, never taking his eyes off the girl.

"So, that's why you were acting weird then?" At Peter's nod, Silver rolled her eyes but continued. "I believe introductions are in order," Silver said, coming forwards. The girl turned her eyes to her as she approached. "My name is Silver, and I'm the captain of this ship. This is Cedric," she said, gesturing to him. "He is our doctor. And I take it you and Peter have already met."

The girl nodded, showing she understood, before looking back at Peter.

"What is your name?" Silver asked, trying to get the girl's attention back on herself.

"I'm Aisling," the girl answered.

"Do you know why you were in the tunnels? Or why were you hooked up to the stone? Where is it, by the way?"

"On the table," Peter answered but made no move to retrieve it.

Silver sighed and walked over. She unwrapped it, careful not to touch it. Now that she had a chance to examine it, she saw it had about twenty sides that were all smooth and shiny. Each side had a different symbol carved on it except for the front which had one large symbol painted gold and the strange metal band that ran around it.

"That is the stone that they were using on me. They took me to the tunnels for… experiments," she said, looking down and shivering slightly.

"What kind of experiments?" Silver asked, taking her eyes off the strange stone to look at her.

Aisling shook her head, drawing her knees up to her chest, and began to shiver in earnest.

"Why don't we give her some time to recover?" said Cedric, looking at Silver with meaning in his eyes. "Perhaps she will feel better after some time to rest."

"Very well," said Silver, re-wrapping the stone, and placing it securely in a chest she kept nearby. She locked the chest and went over to her wardrobe. She pulled out an extra shirt, pair of pants, and boots and brought them over to Aisling.

"Here, why don't you wear these? They'll be more comfortable than what you have now." Aisling nodded and pulled the clothes closer to her.

"Go ahead and rest. One of us will come and check on you in a while."

"Thank you for being so kind to me," said Aisling, in a quiet voice. "And thank you for rescuing me." She looked up at Peter when she said this, and their eyes locked together.

"You're welcome," Silver said, as Cedric made his way out of the room. "Rest well."

She turned to walk out but saw that Peter looked like he had no intention of leaving. She grabbed his arm and half dragged him out of the room. As soon as the door shut, Peter seemed to come out of his trance. He shook his head slightly, almost as if to clear it. Silver punched his arm.

"Ow," he said, rubbing the place where she had hit him. "What was that for?"

"Just trying to knock some sense back in you," she said sweetly before heading up the stairs. Things were quiet on the main deck. They finally couldn't see the island they had come from. She made her way up to the helm and stood next to John. He nodded at her and then continued looking at the horizon.

They stood in silence for a few moments, before Silver said, "John? Thank you for everything you did today. I don't know what we would've done without you."

John inclined his head towards her, before saying, "Of course, Captain."

"I take it we're off to your client?" John asked, after a moment.

"Yes, I would like to get this orb off my ship as quickly as possible," Silver took a cautious look over her shoulder like she had been since they left the island. But there was no one following them, just the endless blue of the horizon where the ocean met the sky.

"We should be able to make it to them in a week or so if the weather keeps up."

John said nothing but continued steering. They stayed in comfortable silence for a while, in a way that two people who know each other so well can. The feeling of unease grew in Silver's chest. Hopefully, it was nothing, just her being paranoid. She couldn't help but feel that everything that happened was just a bit too easy.

A couple of hours later, Silver knocked softly on her door and walked in. Aisling was standing and looking out the window. Wearing the pants and shirt Silver had given her. She was so tiny they almost seemed to hang off of her. Silver quietly closed the door behind her and strode into the room balancing a tray of food and water.

"For you," Silver said, placing the tray on the table. "Did you sleep well?"

The girl turned to her, fixing her in her piercing stare. "I did, thank you. And thank you for the clothes and food."

"You're welcome."

They stood awkwardly for a few moments, eyeing each other. "Where is Peter?" the girl asked, looking over Silver's shoulder to see if she was about to walk in the door.

"He's probably got his ear against the keyhole," said Silver, rolling her eyes slightly. "I'll send him in, in a few minutes, but I was hoping that you might feel up to answering a few questions."

"Of course," said Aisling, and took a seat that Silver gestured to.

Silver sat down opposite her and crossed her legs leaning back. "Where did you come from?"

"I'm afraid I don't know," she said looking into her hands. "I don't have any memories until I was about eight."

"How's that possible?"

"I don't know. I didn't know that was a strange thing until just now."

Silver was silent for a moment gathering her thoughts. "Why were you in the tunnels? And do you know why you were hooked up to the stone?"

"I'm afraid I don't know that either. I may not be very much help in all of this," Aisling said, beginning to look a little worried. "They didn't tell me much, so it's hard for me to relay any information."

"They probably did it on purpose. That way in case something like this happened you wouldn't be able to tell us anything."

Aisling nodded. "I suppose that makes sense."

"Can you tell me about the bird people? Do you know anything about them?"

"A bit," she said, beginning to look uncomfortable. "But again, it's not very much. They call themselves the Cleansers. Part of their job is to get rid of the people who are sick. They come into towns where a disease has begun to spread, and then they eliminate it. At least that's what they told me. I'm not sure how reliable that information is."

Silver's blood ran cold at this information but she tried not to let it show. "What did they want with you?"

"Again, I'm not entirely sure. They performed a lot of experiments on me. I don't remember what exactly they did to me, I just remember the pain." Her eyes had begun to grow distant at some memory she was reliving. She looked so fragile, sitting there bent over herself. It made Silver feel enormous pity towards her. She leaned forward and looked into her eyes. "It's alright. You'll be safe with us."

Aisling looked up with fear clear in her eyes. "I'm not sure about that. I want to believe you, but you don't know the Cleansers as I do. They will stop at nothing to get me back."

"Well, you don't know my crew," Silver said, with iron in her eyes. "We'll keep you safe, and that's a promise."

Aisling still looked skeptical, but Silver didn't mind. She knew she'd be feeling the same if she had been in her position. They would prove it to her.

"Is there someplace we can drop you off? Anywhere you need to go?"

Aisling shook her head. "I don't have anywhere to go, even if I wanted to."

"Well, in that case, welcome aboard the Silver Shadow."

Days had a tendency to run together when they were at sea. Every day was pretty much the same, unless there was a storm or another ship that crossed their path. As each day passed with nothing to show for it, Silver became more uptight. It wasn't that she wanted bad things to happen, but she had come to expect them. It's what has kept them all alive to this point.

On top of this, Silver now had to find a new place to set up her office. Aisling had taken her chamber and hadn't wanted to leave. Silver didn't blame her, the poor thing had been through so much as it was, but it did make it difficult to find a place where she could relax.

She ended up just keeping busy. There was always something that needed to be repaired on her ship. It wasn't that the old girl was falling apart by any means, but the salty air took a toll on everything. The sea wasn't forgiving, and while everyone on board had been alright, they were never able to get everything fixed.

The current thing that needed fixing was a small hole that had begun in the mainsail. It wasn't a problem yet, but it would get bigger and bigger if she didn't handle it now. Gathering her supplies, she tied them to her waist and began climbing. It was a windless day, meaning travel was almost nonexistent, but it also meant now was a good time to patch up the sail.

Making it to the top, she walked across the mast, until she reached the small hole. Sitting so her legs hung over the side of the wooden railing the sail was attached to, she began sewing. The sun beat down on her, causing sweat to pool in her lower back. Brushing her short dark hair out of her eyes, she began humming to herself.

"I know that song," came a voice next to her.

She jumped, gripping the railing for dear life. "Peter!" she snapped, placing a hand on her wildly beating heart. "For the love of sailing, don't sneak up on me like that!"

"I didn't sneak," he said, unsuccessfully trying not to smile. "I made the normal amount of noise one makes when climbing a rope. It's not my fault you were too busy to pay attention."

Silver gave him a glare for good measure, and then got back to sewing. "Don't you have first mate duties to attend to?"

"Sure, but the most important of my first mate duties is checking on you."

Silver felt his eyes on her but she ignored him, intent on her task.

"So," he began, but that's as far as he got. Suddenly, there was a commotion on the main deck.

"What–" was all Silver got out before peaking around the sail. Aisling had emerged from her room, and the entire crew was surrounding her. "Great," Silver sighed, standing.

"I'll take over this," Peter said, taking her sewing from her.

"Don't you want to come and see her? After all, you haven't spoken to her since that first day," Silver offered. "I could always use backup."

"You can handle the crew," Peter said, turning away from her. "I've got this to finish."

Silver eyed him for a moment longer, unsure where this shyness had come from. Peter had always been the one to welcome new members on board, making sure they were comfortable and the like. It was odd for him to suddenly be so shy. Up until this moment, Silver never would have used the word shy to describe him. Shrugging it off, she grabbed a rope and swung down, right into the middle of the crowd.

All the talking abruptly stopped as she landed next to Aisling. "Alright men, don't we have work to do?"

"Aw, come on, Captain." This came from Biff, a young man in his late twenties, who was always ready with a smile. "We just wanted to welcome the newest member of the crew."

"It looks like you more than have. Go on," Silver said when no one made a move to go.

The other men grumbled, but took the hint and broke it up. There were a total of ten members including herself and Peter. Eleven if you included Aisling.

"Sorry about them," Silver turned towards Aisling. "They can be a bit overbearing and are terrible eavesdroppers," she said loudly, as Biff had begun moving closer to them with the guise of sweeping the deck. She shot him a look, and he sighed in the most dramatic way she had ever seen, before moving a far distance away from them.

"Come on," Silver led her to the small ladder that led to the helm. John gave them a nod as she led Aisling to the railing. "Sorry about that, we can speak freely here. John won't bite."

Aisling nodded, her eyes growing wide at the expanse of the sea surrounding them. "It's beautiful," she breathed, her eyes never pausing as she seemed to be trying to take everything in.

"It is," Silver answered, leaning next to her on the railing.

"Do you ever get used to it?"

Silver thought for a moment before answering. "To the beauty? No. There isn't a day that goes by where I don't feel my insignificance. But that's part of its beauty, isn't it? The vastness."

Aisling nodded before saying, "It scares me a little."

"Me too," Silver answered. They stood in silence for a moment, both of them lost in thought.

Silver felt eyes on her and turned only to catch a glimpse of two crew members hurriedly scurrying away. She rolled her eyes.

"It would seem you've made quite an impression," she started, her eyes flicking to Aisling who shrugged. "Is there a reason you came out? I'm glad you did," she hurried to add. "I was a bit worried you may stay in there the whole trip."

"I wanted to get some fresh air," Aisling said, turning her emerald eyes towards her. "And to ask you something."

Silver waited, trying to be patient.

"I don't have anywhere else to go. I–" her voice wobbled. Aisling took a breath to steady herself. "My family is dead. I would like to stay aboard if you'll have me."

She could feel John's presence behind her, almost like an anchor. This was going to be a hard request to fill. "Let me think about it," Silver said, finally, seeing hurt and disappointment rising in Aisling's eyes.

Aisling nodded and looked away. They stood awkwardly for a moment. Looking around for anything, Silver saw Peter sauntering across the deck.

"Peter! Would you come here please?" Peter stopped, looking up at her, his easy smile straining. Silver kept her eyes on him as he walked towards them.

"Why don't you give Aisling a tour of the ship? She hasn't seen everything yet, and frankly, you're the only one I trust to not try anything."

"Aye Captain," he said stiffly, very unlike his usual self. His eyes turned to Aisling briefly before jerking his head for her to follow.

For her part, Aisling followed him with her back straight as a board. She had gotten control of her emotions and was wearing a well-placed mask.

Silver watched them for a moment, and then heard John clear his throat. "Did you have something to say, John?"

"Yes," he paused for a moment. "May I speak freely, Captain?"

"Of course. I trust your opinion on things John, no need to ask."

"Then I want to know why you didn't let Aisling join the crew."

Silver sighed and leaned heavily on the railing. "We don't know anything about her. What if she's one of the bird people, or I don't know, a weapon of some kind."

"You've never denied someone before. You've been the first to help people who no one wanted. I just wonder what makes her different."

"I–" Silver broke off. "I don't know."

John gave her a knowing look that she felt without having to look at him. "I have work to do," she said, pushing back from the railing and walking down to the main deck. She felt his eyes on her across the deck until she made it to her chambers. Shaking John's comment out of her head, she sat down to get to work, but found her thoughts swimming back to the hurt look in Aisling's eyes.

CHAPTER FOUR

Peter

"This is the men's quarters." Peter led Aisling down to the array of swinging hammocks, where he and the other crew slept.

"Everyone sleeps down here?" Aisling asked, coming further into the room.

"Yes, except John and Sam. They have their own quarters."

Aisling was full of questions. She wanted to know what the rope was made out of, where they kept the food and how running a ship worked. He had been trying to answer all of her questions without getting too close. She was so innocent, which scared him a little. Not that she didn't know anything, but the feelings that had steadily begun deep in his gut were more than he could handle right now.

"Why do they have their own?"

"Seniority," Peter shrugged, keeping a safe distance between them.

"So, you sleep down here, too?"

He nodded, looking anywhere but at her.

"But aren't you the First Mate?"

"Yes, but the First Mate's job is to be the voice of the crew. How can I do that if I'm not with the crew?"

Aisling seemed to take this answer without another question.

"Come on," he nodded towards the door, and she followed him back to the hallway. "This is the kitchen," he said, knocking briskly before opening the door.

"Hello, Sam," he said, breaking into a smile as the other man clapped him on the back. Sam made a series of gestures. "Oh, this is Aisling."

Sam smiled and gestured a different set of hand motions. *Is she a new member?*

"Maybe, I'm not sure to tell you the truth," Peter glanced at Aisling, who was looking between the two of them with questions written all over her face. "Oh, right. Sam is mute. He had his tongue cut out. But he is the most wonderful chef known to man."

Sam gestured, *You flatter me.*

"No, it's true! You're amazing. Here, why don't we let Aisling decide?" Peter pulled out a chair, and she sat, a timid smile on her face.

Sam grinned and bustled about the room for a moment, before coming back with a plate of fresh tarts. They still had curls of white steam coming off of them. Aisling blew on one for a moment, before taking a very small bite. Her eyes widened, and she let out a small moan that went right through Peter like lightning. He concentrated on the floor counting to twenty before he felt back in control of himself. When he looked back up, he found that Aisling and Sam were having no problem communicating.

Peter let them talk while he tried again to shove down any emotions that had started rising again. Finally, he said, "Well, I should get back to my duties. Can you make it back by yourself?"

"Yes," Aisling turned her emerald eyes to him. "Thank you for showing me around."

Peter nodded and turned on his heel before he could get pulled into her gaze. He hoped that she would be off this ship soon.

"Land ahead captain!"

They had finally made it to the town where the supplier who was going to buy the orb lived. These past few days had been the longest days of Peter's natural life. Between avoiding Aisling and dealing with shoving down his own feelings, he was exhausted. The crew had been another monster to deal with. They wouldn't stop asking him questions about her until he snapped at them. He still felt bad about that, but he couldn't take it anymore. But even being this tired didn't stop him from being a part of the landing party with Silver.

Peter went to the area he shared with the other men to the supplies they had stacked in the corner. He grabbed a scarf and wrapped it around his face, covering his nose and mouth. Next, he put on thick gloves and boots. He grabbed his hat and made his way back up to the main deck.

When he got back on deck, Aisling turned, and instantly her face grew serious. "Is all of that for the disease?"

"Yes," he said, putting on his cap. The only skin showing was his eyes. "We aren't sure if this will even protect us, but it's better than nothing."

He saw her eyes cloud with worry, and he realized too late that maybe he shouldn't have told her all these things right before going out into the thick of it. "We've done this loads of times. We'll be safe."

She nodded, but the concern in her eyes still lingered. He wished he could say something to ease her worry, but as he was about to say more, Silver called everyone to get ready to board the boat that would take them ashore.

The streets were deserted, with only a few people hurrying from one place to another. They were all dressed similarly, with scarves and gloves, or whatever they could use to cover themselves. The spread of the disease had gotten worse and worse as the years went on. The survivors, thus far, had become accustomed to wearing protective covering. They weren't sure if it made any difference at all, but it was better than nothing.

This time it was just Peter, Silver, and John. Tom had wanted to come but Silver had forbidden it. Peter knew that he still felt bad about Tom getting hurt, even if it had been minor.

They walked quickly and quietly through the streets, following Silver's lead. After a few minutes, she stopped in front of a shabby shack in the middle of a crowded neighborhood.

There were a lot of neighborhoods that began popping up when the disease had gotten worse. They were lower-income and were for people who were no longer able to make a living while the disease was running rampant. It was a great idea in theory, but as the number of people who were unable to make a proper living grew, so did the neighborhoods, which made them crime-ridden and dirty.

Peter had no idea how Silver got her contacts, yet there was always work for them. As soon as they finished one job, there would be another one lined up and they were off again.

Peter didn't mind this sort of lifestyle. It was fun being able to see new towns, and he loved sailing. Only in the wee hours of the night, when his thoughts were unguarded, did he think that maybe he wanted something a bit more, a bit different.

He didn't want to live this life forever but he had no idea what to do about it. Silver wouldn't be leaving it, that was for sure, and she was the only family he had left. It wasn't like he was going to leave her behind.

He was pondering this as Silver knocked quietly on the door of one of the shacks in the center of the town. Then they waited. And waited. She knocked again this time a little louder and still nothing.

"Maybe he's not home?" Peter suggested.

"He's an old man," Silver said as she knocked again. "He wouldn't be stupid enough to leave his house in this town."

After a few more minutes of waiting, and getting tired of it, Peter leaned around her and tried the door. It was unlocked.

"Peter, we can't just barge into people's houses!" Silver hissed at him.

"We're not barging," he said, pushing the door open. "We knocked."

She rolled her eyes at him as he stepped inside first. Even through his mask, the smell hit him, sending him several steps back. It was rancid, like spoiled meat. He coughed and tried breathing through his mouth, which somehow still didn't help the smell.

"Does this guy know nothing about cleanliness?" he asked, still choking on the smell.

Silver came in, and he saw the confusion in her eyes. "It didn't smell like this last time. I wonder what he let go bad."

They came all the way in and had trouble seeing anything. The shack faced away from the sun, which meant there was no natural light, and there were no candles. Peter looked around at the tiny space. There wasn't much to it.

It was one-room and had faded wallpaper that must've been put up when the house was new. It didn't look like it had been taken care of in the past. There was a small area that looked like the kitchen and washroom combined. There were a few seat cushions scattered around the place. He glanced around looking for the source of the smell. He didn't see any rotten food. The house was somewhat taken care of, except for the grime that clung to everything.

Silver found an almost completely burned-down candle and struck a match. After a few tries, she was able to get it lit and she held it up trying to see.

There was a figure slumped in the corner. It looked like it might be human, but it was hard to see in the flickering light. Silver walked up to him and leaned down to shake his shoulder. She drew back quickly, almost stumbling over a pillow. "He's dead," she said, turning to the others.

As she said this, the front door to the shack opened slowly, squeaking on its hinges. They saw the beak before they saw the rest of the creature, and this time, it wasn't alone.

There were two of them, both in black cloaks and hoods. Their lifeless eyes took in the scene around them. "Hello again," came the familiar metallic voice of the one on the left. It must have been the one they met in the tunnels.

"Hello," Peter replied, in a pleasant voice like they were old friends meeting on the street. He was hoping his tactic of distraction might work again, however, he was concerned that there were two of them. Just the one had been hard enough last time. "Fancy meeting you here."

The creature chuckled with a sound like gears grinding together. "Funny human. Now, I believe you have something of ours."

The creatures slowly made their way into the shack, the space between them and the group growing smaller. Peter was trying very hard to keep his cool. He had no idea what these things' full powers entailed, and they were blocking the only exit. Maybe if he kept them talking, he could buy some time to figure something out.

"What do we have that's yours?" he asked, trying to sound innocent.

"Nice try," came the second one. It sounded very similar to the first one, but it had a different tonality to its voice. "We won't be tricked again. Give us the stone."

For a brief moment, Peter considered them. After all, without a buyer, what was stopping them from giving it to them?

"And what if we do? Will you let us go?" Silver asked as they slowly began backing away.

"Of course," said the second creature.

Peter met Silver's eye. While it sounded like a good idea, it seemed unlikely that the birdmen would let them go. After all, they already knew too much. They had a silent conversation in their heads. At Silver's nod, Peter knew they wouldn't give them the orb. After all, nothing good could come from giving crazy, experimental bird people a power orb.

They began to advance on the group, but they took their time. They knew the group had nowhere to go, but they weren't going to give them a chance to make a plan. They would be on top of them in mere moments.

Peter looked around frantically, trying to come up with something, anything that could get them out of this mess. He saw the pitiful candle in Silver's hand and had the worst idea of his life. But it was better than nothing.

He pulled his throwing knife from his belt and threw it at the one closest to them. The blade rang true and embedded itself into the creature's chest, right where his heart should be. The creature looked down at the knife, now jetting out of his chest.

"Nice try," he said, pulling it out with a hard yank. "But I'm afraid I'm made of–" a gunshot sounded through the room and the creature looked down as the hole where he had just pulled the knife from now had a bullet hole as well. Silver always had been an excellent shot. The hole started pooling the same strange black liquid on the floor by its shoes. It stumbled back a couple of steps but was still on its feet.

"You fools!" the creature cried as it regained its footing. "Your bullets may have taken me down before, but trust me that will not be the case now!"

Peter took the candle from Silver's unsuspecting hand and praying that the flame would hold, threw it at the creature aiming for the new hole in its chest. Time seemed to stop as the candle flipped end over end until it reached its mark.

"What–" the creature started before being completely engulfed in flames. The black liquid was exactly what Peter hoped it would be, flammable. The creature let out an inhuman scream, like steam whistling out of a pipe that is too hot. The creature trying to get away from the flames accidentally bumped into its friend who, also promptly caught on fire. This would have been great if they weren't in such a tiny enclosed space.

"Good work, genius!" Silver yelled while trying to back away from the two burning creatures. "They're blocking our only exit! Now, what do we do?"

"I'm working on it!" he yelled to be heard over the now two screaming creatures who were thrashing about the tiny shack. "I don't see you coming up with any brilliant ideas!"

Silver looked around the shack, her eyes finding a seam in the wallpaper. "John!" she said, gesturing to the wall. "I have a plan but I'm going to need some help!"

She pointed to the seam, and together the three of them peeled away the wallpaper revealing a small door. It had been plastered over but it must have been there in case of emergencies, which Peter thought this situation counted as one. Peter could feel the flames growing hotter on his back and knew they had just a few moments before the entire shack went up in flames.

John took a step back, running full force towards the door, hitting it hard with his shoulder. Nothing happened. John took a step back and did the same thing again. Nothing happened. On the third try, Peter, growing tired of not doing something, stepped back with him, and together putting both of their shoulders into it, broke free into the cool night air.

They ran away from the shack as fast as they could, following John's excellent navigating skills, and made it back to the docks out of breath. Just before they turned a corner, Peter looked back and saw not only was the shack they had just come from ablaze, but now the whole town was as well. People were running and trying to find water. A few people looked from their two-story windows but didn't make any moves to help. After all, the poor weren't worth anyone's time. They would probably die soon from the disease anyway.

CHAPTER FIVE

Silver

Silver came out of her chambers and took a deep breath of salty morning air. She hadn't slept well. The feeling of guilt was becoming a friend. All of those people who lost their homes. And it was all Peter's fault. Well mostly. She certainly hadn't come up with any better ideas, and his distraction had gotten them out of that mess.

She hadn't just abandoned the people either. As they ran, she called to all the animals to go and help, put out fires and save anyone who had gotten trapped. She had done all she could, at least that's what she told herself.

Making her way over to the railing, she leaned against it looking out over the water. She loved sailing and the feeling of the sun on her face. Maybe she hadn't done everything she could have for the people whose lives she potentially destroyed, but she hoped what she had done had been enough. Losing herself in these gloomy thoughts when she felt a tap on her shoulder.

Turning, she saw Tom looking at her sheepishly. "Yes, what is it?" she asked, trying not to sound too annoyed at him.

"Sorry for interrupting you Captain, but John would like a word with you." He scuttled off as soon as the words had finished leaving his mouth.

She was a little concerned that he was afraid of her, but she would have to worry about that later.

Climbing up the short ladder, she found John standing in his usual post by the wheel. She stood next to him and stared out to sea in the same direction as him. At this point in their relationship, she knew him well enough to know he would talk when he was ready to. They spent a few moments in comfortable silence, and then he said, "I wonder if I may ask a favor of you."

"Of course. You know, if there's anything I can do in my power to help you, I will."

"I… Well. Since the last buyer fell through, I wondered if we could take the stone to one of my colleagues. Since it may be part of a lost civilization, I think it could be of great use to him."

Silver pondered this for a moment. On one hand, the original deal had fallen through, so no one was relying on getting the orb. But on the other hand, money. They were always a bit short on cash, and going somewhere where they probably wouldn't get paid could be a problem. But John had never asked for anything from her before, so she was willing to take that chance.

"Yes, we can do that," she said, smiling.

"Wonderful, thank you," he gave her one of his rare smiles, but as he looked past her, his smile faded.

"What is it?" she turned and felt her heart sink, to her toes. There was another ship, and it seemed to be gaining on them quickly. Pulling out a telescope she always had strapped to her belt, she looked through it. The ship looked to be entirely made of metal, and to her utter dismay, had one lone figure on it, with a long cloak and a bird beak.

"John, we're going to have company."

Usually, when one is being chased by another ship at sea, it takes hours for anything interesting to happen. That was something Silver had a lot of experience with. However, this ship almost seemed to defy the laws of logic.

Although the other ship was larger, it was somehow making great time and was gaining on them much faster than Silver would believe to be possible. What would have normally taken days for a ship to catch up, the other ship had managed it in just a few hours. Silver kept her eye glued to her telescope, trying to convince herself of what she was seeing.

There were no rowers, so there was no reason for them to be gaining on them so quickly. Nothing about this sat well with Silver, and the more time that passed, the more and more worried she became.

"It's like a ghost ship, how is any of this possible?" she asked for the thousandth time.

John didn't answer, who was the only one within hearing distance of her. Finally taking her eyes off the other ship, she turned to him. "Do you have a plan?"

"Yes, there's a pass ahead. Our ship is small enough that we should be able to squeeze through it, but with the size of their ship, they shouldn't be able to."

"How far away are we?"

"Should be another hour."

"Let's hope we can hold out until. This ship's speed is ridiculous."

This hour could not go by fast enough. Even after lowering all the sails and doing everything they normally did to outrun ships, none of their normal tricks worked. Silver was pulled taut as a bowstring, and she felt her stress level rising with every passing minute.

The birdman was steadily getting closer and closer. By this point, he was almost in their cannon's shooting range. Silver didn't want to waste time shooting at them. What she wanted to do was get to the pass that John was taking them to. It had popped out of seemingly nowhere, just like the ship behind them. How John knew where this out-of-the-blue pass was, Silver would never know. It was almost like he knew the ocean the way someone knows the town they grew up in, like the back of their hand.

This wouldn't be the first time John had gotten them out of trouble by some random bit of the sea knowledge that no one else seemed to know about except him. She was halfway convinced that the ocean spoke to John in the same way animals spoke to her. Some magical power blessed him but she didn't have time to think about that right now.

Finally, they had reached the pass. The crew grew quiet as the rocks grew above their heads, blocking out the sky except for a small sliver. She looked behind at the other ship and saw that it had finally slowed its speed. No matter what kind of magic caused the ship to go so quickly. even it couldn't fit inside the narrow pass.

She kept her eyes on the ship until the rocks completely overtook the sight of the ocean. She let out a huge breath, relieved that John's plan had worked.

"Will they be able to surprise us at the exit?"

"They shouldn't. This pass is a shortcut. They'd have to go hundreds of miles around to make it, and we should be long gone by then."

"Finally some good news," she said, sighing out her breath.

"Well done everyone," Peter said, giving a solo applause. "We have outrun them thanks to John's excellent sailing!"

Silver rolled her eyes at him. "Don't celebrate yet, we still have to make it through this pass."

Aisling appeared from somewhere behind Peter. He turned and upon seeing her, his smile faded. He gave her a curt nod and turned away from her.

This wasn't the first time Silver noticed Peter giving Aisling the cold shoulder. He had been acting weird since she came on board, always leaving when she walked into a room. She opened her mouth to ask him what his problem was when suddenly he cocked his head to the side, "What's that sound?"

Silver strained her ears, but all she heard was the creaking of the ship and the gentle lap of the waves. Nothing out of the ordinary.

"I don't hear anything," said Aisling, also listening. "What does it sound like?"

Peter was quiet for a moment. Then he said slowly, "Singing. The most beautiful singing I've ever heard."

"I hear it too," said John. Then his face went white. "Silver, take the wheel."

"What?"

"Get all the men below deck," he addressed Peter, ignoring Silver's question entirely. "Quickly, we don't have much time." Peter rushed off and so he turned to Aisling. "It's time to put you to the test. Both of you need to protect this ship."

"John, what is–" Silver got out before he rushed off. She turned to Aisling and looked away quickly, unsure of what to say. She decided to just watch as all the men were herded by Peter and John to go below decks.

A couple of minutes passed in uncomfortable silence, only to be broken by the shuffling of men's feet and their faraway voices as they made their way below decks. Silver was growing more anxious by the minute. What was John playing at? She watched while in record time, all the men went below, except for Peter who was about to walk in the door, when the ship rounded a corner and he stopped dead in his tracks.

Silver watched in horror as he turned slowly, leaving the door open, and began to make his way to the railing. That's when Silver saw it. They were surrounded by strange creatures. They were shaped somewhat like women, in all the ways that mattered anyway. Their hair was long dark green like seaweed and flowing with scaly gray-green skin which Silver was seeing practically all of. They had two long legs that were covered in the same green scales ending in two long flippers.

Their eyes were huge and doe-like and they all turned to Peter, who in a trance, began to approach them. They must have been singing, for all of their mouths were open, revealing rows and rows of sharp teeth. But just like a dog whistle, they were singing at a pitch that Silver couldn't hear.

"Sirens, damn it," Silver said under her breath. "Aisling, Peter–" she broke off as she turned to the space that Aisling had been occupying just moments before. She was already down the ladder and was running to

Peter's side. Silver cursed again while keeping her hands on the wheel and trying to steer the ship away from the rocks.

"Keep him away from them!" she shouted, praying that Aisling would be smart enough to not engage with the creatures.

She wasn't. The first thing Aisling did was grab Peter and when he wouldn't budge, began addressing the creatures. Silver saw the creatures turn to Aisling, and their faces turned from innocent to furious in the blink of an eye. Silver cursed under her breath and tied the wheel to keep it steady then promptly slid down the ladder, making her way across the deck in a matter of seconds.

"Don't engage with them!" she yelled, but it was too late. The Sirens were gathering and began hissing, their bodies changing and morphing into a more and more grotesque shape the angrier they got. They were outraged now that there were two females, which Silver knew could only mean one thing: they were going to try and sink the ship.

She grabbed Aisling just before one of the Sirens reached up a webbed, scaly hand, almost pulling her overboard. "What are these things?" Aisling asked as she and Silver slowly backed away into the middle of the ship where they would be safer.

"Sirens," Silver answered grimly. "They lure men to their deaths and hate women. We can't be hypnotized by their songs, so they just try to kill us."

She looked over and saw the Sirens had slowly started luring Peter to the other side of the ship. As she and Aisling ran over to him, Silver saw that more of the crew was starting to emerge from below decks through the door that Peter had left open.

Cursing again, Silver saw a rope that had been coiled and hung on one of the many pegs she had installed for storage purposes. She ran up to the door and slammed it shut just as more of her crew had tried to emerge. She took a key from her breast pocket and locked it just to be safe and then hurried after Aisling who was struggling to keep Peter on the deck.

Silver shouted to get her attention and tossed her one end of the rope. Aisling caught it easily and without Silver having to explain her idea, began tying up Peter and the rest of the crew who had come above deck. Silver followed, and in no time, about a third of her crew was tied to the mainmast. All the men sat in a trance, their eyes glazed over and swaying in sync to the unheard music from the Sirens' song.

Silver was about to congratulate herself and Aisling when she saw the passageway making a sharp turn to the left ahead. Several other ship parts were scattered about, meaning this was all a part of the Sirens' plan. She raced across the ship back to the wheel, praying she would make it in time.

She untied the wheel, happy that one crisis was avoided. However, she realized too late that she had unintentionally left Aisling alone on the main deck with a few tied-up men, and now twenty Sirens who had just climbed up the side of the ship.

"This just keeps getting better and better," she said as she steered the ship around the corner.

When she looked back down to the deck, she was surprised Aisling wasn't doing too badly. She had found another rope that had a hook tied to the end of it, swinging it around herself in a perfect arch.

Anytime a Siren got close to her or one of the crewmen tied up, she would swing the rope around, hooking them in the center of their slimy chests. They let out a horrible scream and would turn into seawater. Soon the ship had several puddles, all thanks to Aisling's hard work. She seemed like she could handle it, but as more and more Sirens came aboard, Silver knew she couldn't hold out forever.

Silver used her inner eye to feel around for what kind of animals were nearby. Her subconscious brushed against something, and she pulled it towards her asking it for help. She heard something scuttle on the side of the ship, slowly making its way up to the deck. Praying it was something useful, Silver watched as something red and white climbed over the edge of the deck. It crawled like a spider, and it wasn't alone.

There were now a hundred crabs on the main deck with Aisling. At first, she didn't seem to know what to do with this new development. She watched with concern until she saw the crabs were fighting with her. Then, she looked up at Silver. She gave her a knowing look, and then abandoned the rope raising her hands. A strange, bright electric green energy shot out of her hands and was shooting the Sirens, instantly turning them into puddles. She now had a longer range and was able to get the Sirens on the rocks by the ship as it passed.

To say Silver was surprised would be an understatement. She knew there was something different about Aisling, but she never imagined she had powers like this. Silver was impressed and thought that perhaps she and Aisling weren't so different after all.

Between thc crabs and Aisling, soon the Sirens learned their lesson and wouldn't come aboard. They kept singing though, still hoping for a snack.

Silver expertly steered the ship around the broken pieces of the other ships that weren't as lucky as them, and finally, she saw the light at the end of the passage. As they neared the exit, Silver heard all of the Sirens let out an inhuman scream. The passageway around them began to shake just as the back of the ship passed through. Suddenly, the tunnel collapsed, blocking the passageway so that no one could get out if they tried to go through there again.

Silver released her hold on the crabs, and they crawled sideways off the ship and back into the ocean. Aisling sat down heavily on the deck, clear exhaustion on her face. Silver tied the wheel again to keep it steady and walked over to where Aisling was sitting.

"Are you alright?" she asked, sitting down next to her.

Aisling nodded, still trying to catch her breath. "I haven't used my powers like that in a long time." She looked up at Silver curiously. "So, you can control animals?"

"Not so much control. It's more of if I'm polite, they usually do what I ask. I've never tried it with crustaceans before, so that was new to me."

They sat together quietly for a few moments, catching their breaths. Silver began to feel the exhaustion that normally happens anytime she used her powers. It was a kind of tiredness she could feel in the marrow of her bones. The kind that felt like she could sleep for days after. It didn't happen often, and only talking to animals was fine. But calling a hundred crabs or so would do it. Aisling and Silver sat together in silence as an understanding grew between them.

"This may go without saying, but you've more than earned your keep. Sorry, I didn't trust you before, but if you want it, you can officially become a member of the Silver Shadow."

"What? It only took slaying a few Sirens then?" Aisling asked, but there was a light that danced in her eyes.

"I should have trusted you earlier. I just–"

"No need to apologize. I would have felt the same. I'm just glad to have proved myself."

"Me too. Our crew is better with you being a part of it."

Both girls grinned at each other like schoolchildren. Silver could feel an understanding growing between them. A kinship that only happens when finding out someone shares a part of you.

"Um, can someone please tell me why we're tied up?" came Peter's confused voice just as there was a knock from the door that led below deck.

"Well, duty calls," said Silver, reaching out a hand to help Aisling stand. She handed her a small knife and said, "Would you mind releasing the boys?"

"What happened?" Peter asked as Silver turned to go unlock the door.

"Oh, you know," came Aisling's mischievous voice. "We just saved the ship by ourselves. No big deal."

CHAPTER SIX

Peter

Peter didn't know the specifics of what had happened, but he did know that somehow Silver and Aisling had become sort of friends because of it. For this reason alone he was grateful to thc stinking Sirens who almost had him for lunch. He did feel bad he wasn't any use to anyone, and may have made more work for them, but he decided the two girls' newfound friendship was well worth any trouble he may have accidentally caused. After all, he was under the Sirens' spell, it's not like he wanted to make more work for them.

For now, he had bigger worries. When it came to the rest of the ship, their supplies were beginning to run low.

They still had enough for the time being, but it was obvious to everyone that their meals were getting more meager. The crew was aware of this, and while most of them were happy just to have a job and be sailing, those two things lose some of their shine on an empty stomach.

Peter could tell Silver was worried. They were supposed to get supplies from her last buyer but that hadn't worked out as well as they were planning. Then with the whole Siren thing, they hadn't had much time to plan out where they were going to stop for more supplies.

Also, in the crazy times they were living in, people were less likely to sell food to travelers. People were suspicious of strangers. If someone traveled into your town who may have the disease, they could carry it in and infect everyone, so people steered clear of the Silver Shadow crew. Because of this, they had very specific buyers that would usually trade them for something that they had acquired or sometimes in great desperation, they would have to "borrow" the supplies they needed.

This wasn't ideal or the way they preferred to run their ship, but it did happen on occasion. Peter was worried this might be the kind of occasion they had to get more creative when it came to acquiring their supplies.

There was a port town that was relatively close to where they were currently sailing. Silver didn't have a contact there, but Peter did. They had met a long time ago when he and Silver were still kids. There was only one point in their childhood when he and Silver had gotten separated. It was the worst year of his life.

"You're looking like you're remembering something unpleasant," came Silvers's voice, pulling him out of his thoughts.

"Well, that would be accurate then," he said, looking over at her and smiling. "But I'm alright. You brought me back out of my unpleasant thoughts."

"Good," she said, smiling back. "By the way, this trip might be a little odd."

"How so?" Peter grabbed one of the scarves and began wrapping it around his face.

"For one thing, John won't be joining us. He has a friend in the area who wanted to take the orb. See if they can find out anything about the ancient civilization that was lost."

"Alright. That's not too odd though."

"Well, there's another thing…"

"Oh no, I know that tone of voice," Peter turned to look at Silver who was keeping busy, clearly avoiding eye contact.

"What tone?"

"The one where you tell me something I'm not going to like." Peter reached over and snatched one of the scarves she had been admiring. "Come on. Spit it out."

"Aisling wants to come. And I told her she could."

"What?" Peter froze, his heart began beating wildly in his chest. "Why would you do that?"

"Because," Silver put her hand on her hip. "She has been stuck in a cave or this ship and hasn't ever seen the outside world. She got left behind last time, so it's only fair she can come this time."

"Last time was dangerous," Peter growled.

"Well, this time won't be. Come on, it's only Francis."

"Which is why you should've asked me first."

"Oh, you're being ridiculous," Silver threw up her hands and walked away to gather more supplies.

"I'm being ridiculous?" Peter felt his stomach begin to bubble as anger filled him.

"Yes, you are. I don't get what's with you. You're always so welcoming, but then Aisling comes aboard, who we bring on the ship at your request I might add, and then you act like she's not even here! Do you have any idea what that does to her?"

"I don't understand why it's any of your businэss."

"Maybe because I'm the captain. And I'm worried about you."

"Well, don't. That's not your job."

"Of course, it's my job."

"No it's not," Peter snapped, causing Silver to turn and look at him. He had been itching for a fight. "You don't have to look out for me. I can take care of myself."

"Can you? Because I don't know what's going on with you lately. You hardly eat, or sleep and are acting strange."

"Stop! This isn't your job! You've tried to take over responsibility for me since mom died but you aren't my mom!"

As soon as the words were out of his mouth, he wished he could take them back. He saw a hurt flit across Silver's eyes before being replaced with anger.

"No," she said, slowly turning away from him. "I'm not."

"Silver–"

"Fine. I'll back off. But don't expect anything else from me." She pushed past him and was out the door before he could call her back.

Letting out the anger that had built up inside, he kicked a box sending it flying across the room.

Peter led the way through the near-empty streets. As the two girls trailed behind him talking quietly. He hadn't had time to make up with Silver. When he got to the deck she was already helping Aisling get ready, and now here they were.

The town was pretty much unchanged since the last time they had been here. There was an abandoned marketplace, with stalls completely grown over by greenage. The market places had stopped and were no longer a good way to get fresh food. Although it wasn't that long ago when they went out of business, it seemed like a lifetime had passed since the days you could go and easily buy the food you needed.

With the progression of the disease, people had stopped leaving their homes as much, meaning they needed a new way to get food. People had taken to eating special vegetation they could grow themselves. It was a strange green plant in the grass family that didn't need much water or sunlight, which were two things people didn't get a lot of.

It was easy to grow and most people mixed it with some kind of spice that was supposed to be good against the disease. There was no proof of this, of course, but when people were desperate, they were willing to try anything. They usually ate this sort of grass soup with the spice.

Although more and more people were staying home, it didn't seem to stop people from dying. Perhaps fewer people were dying from the disease, but they were developing other problems. Those who weren't sick were well on their way to becoming sick. The lack of sun and the weird soup were causing issues. Since that's all anyone was able to eat, it meant they weren't getting the right nutrients and their bodies were suffering because of it.

The whole thing was a big mess, in more ways than one, and had progressively gotten worse as the years went on without a cure.

Peter led the way through the maze of huts that lined the outskirts of the city. Although they were similar to the huts that they had been to in the other town, each town's houses were a little different. These were on the outside of the city, while the other ones had been a little farther in. They were about the same size and shape, with a rounded top to help the rainwater runoff. But these were made out of different materials that were local to this Island.

They walked through the small outer city, keeping their heads down. It was quiet. They only passed a couple of other people dressed similarly to them who hurried about their day. Since this whole thing had started, people were less and less likely to stop and talk, which made getting information or directions challenging. Lucky for them, they didn't need any of those things. Peter knew exactly where he was going.

They reached the outer edges and were getting to the inner city. It had normal buildings made out of stone and other materials that would have been used before the outbreak. These homes weren't extravagant by before-outbreak standards, but they were very nice compared to the hovel that most of the population lived in. They were also incredibly expensive, so if you lived in one of these homes, you were considered upper class.

Keeping their heads down, the small band followed Peter down a twisting cobblestone street. He led them through an alleyway and stopped at the back door. He knocked, and they waited. Peter felt the sweat trickle down his back. The heat from the sun reflected off of the windows in the area, making it hotter than usual.

The door opened, and there was Francis just as Peter remembered him. "Hello beach scum," Peter said with a grin, knowing the mask covered his face. "Got a minute?"

Peter had missed Francis. It had been a few years since they had seen each other, so they wasted no time in getting reacquainted. It felt just like old times.

Francis led them into his living room and served tea. It had been a long time since Peter had good quality tea, and Francis didn't disappoint. He held his cup and inhaled, the aroma of strong black tea and steam filling him with memories spent in the all-boys school where he and Francis met.

Francis sat across from him, grinning like a schoolboy. "It's so good to see you. Even if you do look a little worse than the last time we met. Are those ants crawling all over your face? Or is that your sad excuse for facial hair?"

Peter grinned, rubbing his face sheepishly. He hadn't had time or resources to shave in a while, and his face was looking a little shaggy. The complete opposite of Francis, who was neat as a pin, face freshly shaved and in an expensive-looking waistcoat and crisp black trousers.

"I prefer to think of it as ruggedly handsome," he said, taking another sip of his tea. "It's much better than looking like I have a stick up my–"

"Are you two done flirting?" Silver interrupted crossing her arms. "Sorry for the interruption but you boys could go on for a while." She looked over and winked at Aisling who was looking more and more confused by the minute.

"Oh, I had no intention of wasting your valuable time, Captain," said Francis with mock horror. "Is that what I'm supposed to call a woman who runs a ship? Perhaps there is another name for it?"

"Watch it," Silver said, over the top of her cup. "You'll lose more than your dignity if you keep that up."

Francis laughed heartily at that. "How I've missed you both," he said, crossing one leg over the other. "No one else had the guts to talk to me like that. I feel like everyone tiptoes around me, afraid I won't be able to take a joke."

"Then they don't know you very well," said Peter. "After all, everything you are made up of is a joke."

"Alright," said Silver, when she saw Francis open his mouth to reply. "As much fun as this banter is, I have a crew in desperate need of supplies."

"Well, you've come to the right place," he said with a sweeping gesture. "What is it you need?"

As he and Silver talked business, Peter tried to look anywhere but where Aisling was. He had tried to sit as far away from Silver as he could, which unfortunately meant sharing a loveseat with Aisling. And now that Silver and Francis were distracted, he had nothing else to contribute.

"Are you alright?" Her voice pulled him out of his thoughts.

"Yes," his eyes flickered over to her. "Why do you ask?"

"No real reason. You just seemed off."

He had no idea how she seemed to be able to read him so easily. But he shook it off. "I'm alright thanks."

She nodded, and then he tried again to look anywhere else. But he felt his gaze shift to her on its own accord. She was sipping her tea like a royal, her back straight as a board and with a thoughtful look on her face as she looked around the room. He noticed she had a bit more color in her cheeks now, which was good. Now she didn't quite look like death. As he was thinking this, her emerald eyes flicked over to his. He jumped, nearly spilling his tea, before hastily looking away.

"Well, now that's over with, do tell me about yourself," Francis had finished up his conversation and was now leaning towards Aisling. Peter knew the flirty look that Francis was giving her. He had seen it work on many girls and boys over the years of knowing him.

Before he could open his mouth to dissuade Francis, Silver beat him to it. "Aisling's not interested in you." Silver sprawled in her chair, like a king sitting on his throne.

"I wasn't even going there!" Francis turned to her, as if offended. "I was just asking about her."

"Well maybe she doesn't want to tell you." Silver examined her nails, unbothered by Francis's complaining.

"She's also sitting right here," Aisling spoke up. "And can make her own decisions."

Silver's eyes snapped to green ones, and there seemed to be a kind of conversation between the two women spoken without words. Peter looked over at Francis, who shrugged.

"I apologize. I didn't mean to speak for you," Silver broke the silence. "You're more than capable of handling yourself. Francis can just be a bit forward is all."

"I take great offense to that," Francis said, stiffly.

"No, you love it," Peter broke in. "After all it's kind of what you live for."

"How did you all meet?" Aisling asked, breaking whatever comeback Francis was going to say.

"Well, that's a bit of a long story. Let me think of where to start," Francis answered, taking another sip, seeming to buy himself some time.

"We met at an all-boys school about ten years ago. This was our first time away from home, and both of us were having a hard time." He took another sip of tea and continued. "Peter and I shared a room. It was randomly assigned, so we had no say in the matter, and I was anything but excited to share a room with an orphan, while my parents had sent me to a commoner school to teach me a lesson. I had every intention of hating him, but that didn't work out."

"The first night we spent in the school, we were awakened in the middle of the night by a strange noise. I couldn't quite put my finger on it but it sounded like a strange scratching on our window. This would've been a weird occurrence even if our room wasn't on the fourth floor. So, I crept towards the curtains with Peter right at my heels."

"I pulled back the curtain to reveal a man crouched on the window sill. He must have scaled the whole building to get to our room, and he was trying to pick the lock on our window."

"Several things happened all at once here. The lock he had been fiddling with broke, and he pushed the window open. Peter had a– well…" Francis looked over at Peter, a question in his eyes as to how much to tell her.

"I had a feeling," he said, struggling for words on how to describe his gift without freaking her out. "I felt like the man was going to pull Francis through the window. So, I took the curtain that was still in my hand and wrapped it around the man, preventing him from being able to get to Francis."

"What happened after that?" she asked, literally on the edge of her seat.

"Well," Francis took over, lowering his voice and moving in closer. "The man was trapped in the curtains. The more he struggled, the more tangled he became. I was feeling pretty happy about the whole thing, until I realized too late what was about to happen. The man frantically struggling, didn't realize he was pulling the curtain off of the rod. With a huge ripping sound, the curtain detached from the window."

Aisling gasped and covered her mouth with her free hand. "How horrible."

"Yes, it was," Francis nodded solemnly.

"Except it's not true," Peter said, breaking the spell Francis had put Aisling under.

"While Francis was somewhat accurate in the telling of that story, I remember the ending differently," Peter answered.

"How so?" asked Silver, with a curious look on her face.

"Well, the man did indeed almost grab me and our young Peter here, did wrap him in the curtain," Francis continued the story. "However, the man did not fall out the window to his death. He did fall out the window, but he was so tangled up that he was just sort of swinging there. We had made such a racket that one of the teachers came running into our room right at that moment, and quickly and efficiently ushered us out of the room."

"Why would you change the ending like that?" Aisling asked, not in anger, just curiosity.

"I suppose I have a flair for the dramatics," he said with a flourish, ignoring Silver's snort from behind him.

"But it wasn't what happened," Aisling pressed on.

"That's true. But you have to admit, mine was a better story," he finished with a grin.

They got everything they needed loaded into the ship, but they had to do it under the cover of darkness and without making much noise.

Desperate people make desperate decisions, and an ambush was always possible, even with Francis's guards. You could never be too careful in these crazy times.

After quickly and efficiently getting all their supplies on board, Peter walked back to where he knew he could find Francis, his favorite place in the world: the beach. While he and Silver felt most at home on the water, Francis felt more at home on its shores. It wasn't that he hated sailing but he had a near-death experience in the ocean, so he preferred to stay out of it. He always said that he had cheated the ocean's grip once, and he didn't want to take any chances on that again. Yet, he still loved the beach and couldn't get away from the ocean even if he wanted to. It was a strange kind of irony to be attracted to the thing that almost killed you.

Peter stood next to him, and they watched the way the moonlight reflected off the small waves. It was a comfortable silence, one they had shared many times throughout their friendship.

Francis looked over at him and said, "You must have been pretty desperate if you came to me."

"What's this now? Can't a man come to see his friend without him thinking there was a problem?"

Francis gave him a knowing look, and Peter knew there was no point in hiding it. "Fine, you win," he said, throwing up his hands in mock surrender. "We have run into some problems recently."

"What kind of problems?" Francis asked, concern written on his face. Peter briefly explained about the birdmen, and the battles the group had undergone ever since that island. Francis listened intrigued, not interrupting or making any sound.

Once Peter had finished, Francis was quiet for another minute before saying, "You all have been through all sorts of adventures, haven't you?"

"Trust me, I would much rather have less adventure in my life. I think I've filled up several lifetimes' worth of adventure."

"Yes, you certainly have," said Francis, looking away again and gazing out over the ocean.

"Come on, Francis," he said, bumping his shoulder with his own. "Don't look so gloomy. I thought you liked your life here."

"I do," he replied, smiling a sad sort of smile. "I would just like to have an adventure like you, that's all."

"Maybe you don't need to wait to be given one," said Peter, quietly. "Maybe it's time for you to get out from under your parents' shadows. Make a life of your own."

"It's not that simple."

"Why not?" Peter asked, excitedly. "Answer this, Francis, what's holding you here? It's not your parents. It's you."

He was quiet again, not in anger but in contemplation. "I don't know," he said finally. "I'll have to think about it."

"You always say that."

A ghost of a smile touched his lips. "I suppose I do."

They were quiet again, each lost in their thoughts. "Well," Francis said, breaking the silence and holding out his hand. "It is always a pleasure."

Peter took his hand for a handshake. "It is. I'll try not to let so much time pass before I come back over."

"Don't worry. I know you're busy," he said. Peter made it two steps before Francis said, "Also you might be needing this!"

Time slowed as Peter turned around. Francis had taken a scabbard out of nowhere and threw it towards him. It sailed end over end before hitting Peter across the face, causing him to lose his balance and hit the sand hard. Time sped up again, and this time, Peter was ready for it and caught the sword.

He unsheathed it, the metal singing as it slid effortlessly across the scabbard. Peter held it up to the fading light, watching as the metal sparkled. There wasn't anything fancy about it, no jewels or special carvings, which suited Peter just fine. Peter had never been much into the showiness of swords. He was only looking for one thing, which was balance. This sword was perfect.

"How did you know?" Peter asked as he sheathed it.

Francis shrugged. "I couldn't help but notice you didn't have a sword on your belt. I typically have a few on hand. Think of it as my gift. You know, for saving my life that one time."

"Right," was all Peter said, shaking his head. "Well, thank you."

"Anytime," Francis said, with a grin.

Peter nodded and was about to walk off again when he heard, "I like her by the way."

Peter whirled around, having no idea what he intended to say. "I don't know what you're talking about."

Francis laughed and said, "Yes you do. Although, maybe tone it down on the whole obsessed looks."

Peter sighed, his heart squeezing. "It's that obvious then?"

"Maybe only to those who know you," Francis gave him a thoughtful look. "I'm not sure if she knows it though, especially if you brush her off."

"Right," was all Peter managed to get out. He wasn't sure if he wanted her to know. Sometimes, he felt like his feelings were a deep well, one that even he didn't know the depths of. That scared him a bit.

"I can't help but wonder why someone who's usually so confident would take this long."

"Aisling's different, she's... she doesn't know much. I don't want to push her or hurt her."

"Well, that's up to you then. But I think she may be stronger than you think. Also, that may not be fair to her."

Peter hadn't thought about this. He had been so busy trying to protect her from his feelings that he had never thought about how she may be feeling.

"Good sailing to you!" Francis said, waving and not seeming to need an answer.

"And good fortune to you," Peter said, back.

"Don't let any bird men get you!"

Peter rolled his eyes, and with one more wave goodbye, he turned and walked towards the ship. Talking with Francis had put him in better spirits, but he knew there was something he needed to do before he could call it a night. He hopped aboard just as the ship was pulling away from the dock.

"Oi!" He called up to Biff, who was trying to look innocent. "I almost got left behind! Whose idea was it to set sail?"

"That'd be the captain," Biff answered, trying and failing to look busy, weaving a large rope in front of him. Biff was someone who could weave the rope in his sleep, so he wasn't fooling anyone.

"We tried to stop her, but you know how she gets," this was from Gwane, a man in his mid-twenties who came off the same island as Biff. The two of them were a bit of a pair, in more ways than one. They were shunned from their town for their relationship, so they had come aboard looking to start a new life. Gwane had a strong build with light hair and light eyes, the complete opposite of Biff, who was slender and had dark hair and eyes. But they were well suited to each other, complementing each other.

"Right," Peter rubbed his eyes, exhausted all of a sudden. He doubted that any of them tried to stop her. Frankly, Gwane and Biff worshiped the ground that Silver walked on. "Any idea where she is?"

Both men pointed up to the helm, where Silver's hair was blowing softly in the ocean breeze. Peter turned back to say something else to them, but both men had their heads together talking quietly. Peter knew he was unlikely to get anything else out of them. Sighing, he made his way to the helm.

Silver was indeed there, but so were John and Aisling. The last thing he wanted was an audience. Silver said something that made Aisling laugh, and he stood there for a moment enraptured. Usually, Aisling only had a detached look about her or one of curiosity. He had never seen her smile, and it lit up the space around her, almost like she was one of the stars that were shining around them.

He swallowed, remembering how to use his legs, and finished climbing up the stairs. He cleared his throat and six eyes stared at him. "Silver, can I talk to you?"

Silver heaved a huge sigh, like what he was asking of her was painful, and the last thing she wanted to do. Always the dramatic one of the two of them. She jerked her head around the helm to the small space in between the helm and the sea below. It was a workspace, but when the twins discovered it when they were young, it had become their hiding place.

"What is it?" she asked when they were alone.

"I... well," Peter cleared his throat again, hoping that the action may give him the words he needed. "I didn't mean what I said earlier, and I wanted to say I'm sorry."

Silver's eyes shifted to his own. "Is that it?"

"What more do you want from me?" Peter rubbed the back of his neck, feeling his face flush.

"You say one of the cruelest things you can to me, and then you just expect me to forgive you when you say sorry?"

"I've been under a lot of pressure–"

"And I haven't?"

"What else do you want from me?"

Silver turned away from him, not in anger like he had expected, but in contemplation. "You'll do anything to make this up to me?"

"Yes," he answered, without hesitation.

"Then I'll save it."

"What? You can't save it!"

"Says who?"

"Says... well says me."

"Do you want to be forgiven or not?"

Now it was Peter's turn to sigh. "Fine."

"Good," Silver gave him the first real smile that he had seen in days. He pretended to be grumpy, but they both saw through it.

When he settled down to sleep for the night, he was glad he and Silver had made up, even if there was a favor to her hanging over his head. But sleep didn't come to him for a long time. Francis' words came back to him, and he couldn't stop the thoughts circling in his head.

CHAPTER SEVEN

Silver

Now that their supplies were stocked, Silver felt much better about her role as Captain. She knew none of the men would say anything to her face, but she did worry that they might talk when she wasn't around. She needed to prove that she was capable of taking care of her crew no matter the cost. She would do whatever it took to take care of them.

She had missed Francis and Peter's antics. When they were kids, Francis wasn't her favorite person. She may go as far as to say she hated him. She had no idea what a rich kid like him was doing with a kid like Peter. They had come from nothing, no family, no money, no use to anyone. Yet, here was this rich spoiled kid who was used to getting whatever he wanted.

At first, she was worried that he was taking advantage of Peter somehow, or maybe bullying him. She also felt like he was taking her place as his best friend. She didn't want anything to come between them.

But that was a long time ago. Now that she was older, she could see what a good friend he was to Peter as well as a good contact for supplies. Anytime they needed anything, somehow he always found a way to get it to them. He always tried to get her to take the supplies for free, but she didn't feel right about it. Now that she was running her crew, she needed to be able to pay for the supplies. She didn't want any kind of special treatment, even if it was from a friend.

Silver was pulled out of her thoughts by a knock on the door. At her call to come in, John stepped into her room.

"Hello, John," Silver said with a smile, gesturing to his preferred chair in front of her desk. "I'm sorry we didn't get a chance to talk after we docked. How did everything go yesterday?"

"Not as well as I had hoped," he placed the wrapped orb carefully on her desk before sitting. "Turns out that this orb was never a part of the ancient civilization. I won't bore you too much with the details, but the old civilization disappeared like they had been wiped off the face of the earth, maybe a hundred years ago. There one day, and gone the next."

"That's so odd," Silver took the orb and unwrapped it, careful not to touch it. "There was never a reason found as to why they disappeared?"

"Not that historians have been able to find. Because of that, their ancient text is very hard to come by, and I don't have much practice reading it. So looking at this orb, and maybe even the doorway we walked through, I mistook these writings for the ancient civilization because they're similar in shape. But that's not what we're looking at here."

"This shape here," he leaned forwards to point to one of the faces of the stone. "Is what should have given it away. It's an arcane symbol. One that combines magic with science."

"Fascinating," Silver leaned closer to get a better look. "And you still don't know what this thing does?"

"Arcane is not a language I'm familiar with," John shrugged.

"Well, this may make it harder to find a buyer," Silver wrapped it back up.

"Or not," John said in a thoughtful voice. "People like all sorts of things, it may just be difficult to make sure it doesn't fall into the wrong hands."

Silver opened her mouth to ask more, but suddenly there was a knock on her door. It opened without her saying anything to reveal Peter.

"Hello, Captain," said Peter with a salute before stepping fully into the room.

"You know, typically people wait for a reply before they come barging into someone's chambers."

"Don't worry. I knew nothing interesting was happening in here. Twense," he said, tapping his finger to his head.

"What's that?" asked John from his position at the table.

"Don't ask," Silver said quickly, as Peter opened his mouth to answer. "Is there a reason you came into my chambers?"

"Oh right," said Peter leaning lazily on her table. "There's an island ahead."

"Peter, we pass islands every day," said Silver, exasperated.

"True," he said, grinning. "But we don't usually come across too many islands of this sort."

"Peter, get to the point."

"The point is," he said, slowly drawing it out as long as possible. "This island has a man tied to a tree."

Silver was on another rowboat. She had to admit that her curiosity had gotten the better of her, but she couldn't just leave some poor man marooned on an island. And the fact they had tied him up was cruel. There was little chance of surviving a marooning as it was, so to tie someone up meant you wanted to take away any chance they had of surviving. It would have been kinder just to shoot them, honestly.

Peter had opted to stay on the ship, figuring that a man who was tied up wouldn't be of any danger to Silver. So it was only her and John who made their way on their tiny rowboat to the incredibly small island. It only had about two palm trees on it, which didn't provide much shade or food. It didn't look like there was any wildlife either, just the two trees and some sand in between. The whole thing was only about twenty feet across and wide, so it was a miracle her crew had even spotted it. If they had been a bigger ship, they probably would've missed it entirely.

She helped John pull their small boat to shore. Keeping her hand on her pistol, she walked forwards and approached the tree. As she grew closer, she saw the man's ankles were shackled.

He had black pants and a billowing white shirt that she couldn't help but notice was cut just a touch too low, showing off his muscled chest. He had long pale white hair that went down to his shoulders. His hands were tied up over his head and was slumped forwards with his head bowed, making his silvery hair hang down and cover his face.

"Hello?" Silver asked as they approached. "Are you alright?"

The man lifted his head, and Silver stifled a gasp. He was gorgeous. There was something about his perfectly symmetrical, angular face that made him the perfect kind of handsome. He had high arched eyebrows that were the same color as his hair and long eyelashes that were so light they almost seemed to disappear. His eyes were what drew her in, they were a pale icy blue that seemed to almost see into her soul.

He grinned, showing off perfectly straight white teeth. "It seems that a dark angel has come to my rescue."

His voice was deep and was surprisingly smooth, considering he was tied to a tree, and who knew how long he had gone without water. At the sound of his voice, she felt the world rock to the side. Maybe she didn't have her land legs yet. Getting a grip on herself, she moved a bit closer and asked, "Are you hurt?"

"No, but I wouldn't mind if you did the honors," he grinned a mischievous grin, which sent a shiver down Silver's spine. "I can think of several things we can do with me tied up like this," he purred, giving her a suggestive look.

Silver turned on her heel. "Come on John, we're leaving." She briskly began walking back towards the boat.

"Wait!" she wasn't sure if it was the desperation in his voice, but something about it made her turn. "Please," he said, seeming to drop the mask he had been wearing a moment ago. She took a good look at him and saw parts of his skin that were bright red and sunburned. She took in his cracked lips and pity washed over her against her better judgment.

There was a distant connection she felt with him. Something that drew her in and made him feel familiar, even though she was sure she had never met this man before in her life. She sighed and walked back over to him. It wasn't right to leave someone in need here, even if they were annoying.

"We're taking him with us," she said, addressing John. The man grinned a victory grin.

"Leave his hands tied," she said and watched in satisfaction as the grin was wiped off his face.

John got to work, and Silver walked back towards the boat hoping, she wasn't making a terrible mistake.

"Didn't we agree not to bring dangerous people on the ship without talking to each other first?"

"Peter, he's not dangerous."

"You brought him on the ship in handcuffs! That doesn't scream safety. Not to mention we know nothing about him, is that wise to bring him aboard? What if he was sick?"

Silver rubbed her temples that were beginning to ache. "Peter, if he had been sick, he would have died already. It looked like he had been on the island for at least a couple of days. Plus, I didn't see you worrying about Aisling being sick when you marched her aboard."

"That's a completely different situation," he said, grumpily.

"No it's not and you know it," she said, satisfied with her victory. "Besides, Cedric is looking at him now. Speaking of which, I should probably go down there and see how it's going."

She turned and walked out of her cabin, closing the door on Peter's scowling face. She knew he wasn't happy about this whole thing, but it was his fault to begin with. If he hadn't made that motto of "no person in need left behind" then they wouldn't be in this mess.

Also, if he had an opinion on it, why didn't he just come to the island in the first place? He probably thought it was going to be some grungy pirate, not a gorgeous, strange young man who looked like he could handle himself. Oh well. It was her ship, and Peter will have to accept it.

She walked in just as Cedric was making his way out. "How is he?" she asked as they passed in the hallway.

"He's fine, besides a little dehydration. It looked like he had been on the island for a couple of days. Any longer and he may not have made it."

"Did he talk to you at all?"

Cedric shook his head. "I'm afraid not. I asked, of course, but he wouldn't say a peep."

"Thank you, Cedric," she said, and he gave a slight bow as he left.

She pushed open the door and walked in. The man almost seemed to glow in the darkness, his white shirt blending into his hair. His hands were still bound in the strange cuffs they found him in, but they were placed in front of him instead of above his head. He was braced against the floor, with one leg up while the other was tucked under him. He lifted his head and caught her attention with those icy blue eyes.

He grinned, "Well, I see they sent you in to check on me. Glad you came alone this time."

"No one sent me," she bristled. "I'm the captain of this ship. I'm the only reason you're here."

Understanding lit up in his eyes. "A female captain, interesting." He continued to grin, his teeth seeming to glow in the dark space.

"I have some questions for you," she said, deciding not to let his attitude bother her, and walked farther into the room.

"Of course, whatever the captain desires," that grin never left his face, making Silver want to get rid of it for him.

She squared her shoulders and began. "Why were you on that island?"

He shrugged easily. "Who can say?"

"You can. They left you there without any way of survival. Whoever left you there wanted you to die and wanted you to suffer. I want to know why."

"Ah, well you're an observant one." She couldn't tell if that was sarcasm. "Yes, the people who left me there wanted me dead."

"Why?"

"Let's just say they were afraid. Don't look so surprised," he said, causing Silver to wipe her face clean of emotion. "Trust me, I can be terrifying when I want to."

She looked at him slightly skeptical. It's not that he didn't look strong or anything, but he didn't look like he could be terrifying. But if there was one thing Silver had learned in all of her years at sea, no one was ever entirely what they seemed.

"What is your name?"

"I'll tell you what," he said, leaning forwards. "How about you ask a question, and I'll ask one. After all, it's only fair."

"Very well," she said, after a moment of thinking it over. She knew she was playing a very dangerous game, but she needed information from him. Plus, she reasoned, if he became a member of the crew then he would need to know about her anyway. Although, his chances of being invited to join were getting slimmer the longer she talked to him.

He leaned back, that grin never far from his lips. "Let me think of a good one," he took several minutes while Silver tried not to fidget. "What made you become a pirate?"

"We aren't pirates," she said, automatically.

"Sure, merchants, explorers, whatever it is you call yourself. We both know what you are. Now, answer the question."

"I love the ocean and love adventure. Now back to you, what is your name?"

"Nathaniel Valentine Felix the third, at your service," he said, with a mock bow in her direction.

"Are you an aristocrat then?"

"Nuh-uh," he said, holding up one finger in his chained hands. "My turn. What is your name?"

"Silver."

"What, no last name?"

"If I had one, I was never told. And that's two questions. Are you an aristocrat?"

"Yes."

"Care to elaborate?"

He looked thoughtful for a moment before answering, "No."

She groaned in frustration. She was getting nowhere with this. "Well," she said, brushing off her pants and standing. "While this has been so much fun, since you aren't cooperating, I'll be going now."

She turned her back on him and began walking towards the door. She had taken two steps before she tripped on something she knew hadn't been there when she came in and began falling forwards. She was jerked back by strong arms wrapped around her shoulders, with one chained hand circling her neck. She stood very still and felt his breath tickle her ear as he said, "I'm not quite finished yet if that's alright by you."

She sighed, more annoyed than scared. "Well, I don't seem to have much of a choice in the matter. Oh wait," taking him by surprise, she threw her head back, hitting him in the nose and causing him to let go. She whirled around to face him with her gun placed on his temple. "I do have a choice."

They stood in tense silence for a moment, before he began to laugh. "Well done," he said, not seeming to be bothered by the fact she held his life in her hands. She felt his arms still wrapped around her, they seemed to have settled on the curve of her back. She was pressed against his chest and felt the steady thump of her heart in her ears.

"Release me," she demanded, realizing they were at a bit of a standstill. Additionally, her pounding heart wasn't helping the matter.

"Hmm," he purred, tightening his grip and pulling her even closer. "I kind of like the way this situation has gone,"

Using her thumb, she cocked the pistol and placed it firmer against his head. His grin widened, "Very well," he said, slowly lifting his arms above both of them. "After all, I have a feeling this won't be the last time you'll be in my arms."

As soon as his arms went over her, she took a step back, keeping the gun pointed to his head. "I sincerely doubt that," she said, not trying to hide the venom from her voice.

He shrugged, hardly bothered by her conviction. She looked down, trying to see what she tripped on when she saw something that made her heart momentarily stop. There was a white boa constrictor snake tail wrapped around one of her ankles.

She followed it with her eyes, her heart in her throat, trying not to panic. If there was a snake that big on her ship, it could be tricky to fight in such close quarters. She followed it, attempting to keep her breath steady.

The end of it was wrapped around her ankle and slowly, but oddly going up, almost as if it was climbing the wall behind Nathaniel. Bracing herself for a fight, she swung her other foot around and kicked it with all of her strength, trying to get it away from her and Nathaniel.

To her surprise, Nathaniel cried out and fell to the ground in the direction of her kick. He hit the ground hard, barely catching himself with his chained hands. Silver's brain was trying very hard to process what it was she was seeing. At first, it looked like the snake had eaten Nathaniel's legs, but that couldn't be right because he wasn't crying out in pain, other than the pain she had caused him thus far.

Just then the tail began to change, if she hadn't seen it with her own eyes she wouldn't have believed it. What was once a long snake tail slowly morphed into two strong human legs in black, form-fitting pants. Silver stared, unmoving and unblinking for several seconds.

"Silver, I–" she held up her hand, cutting him off.

"I need a moment to process this," she said, and Nathaniel stayed quiet, still sitting on the floor where he had fallen because of her earlier kick.

She straightened up, determined this changed nothing, even though it changed everything. “Well,” she said, briskly. “I apologize for kicking you.” She leaned down and offered him a hand up. When he didn’t move, she continued, “But I’m not sorry for head-butting you. You deserved that.”

He took her hand cautiously, she saw that his mask was back in place, even though she had seen it drop just moments before. “Well, my secret is out now,” he said with his infuriating grin. “I suppose you mean to dispose of me like the others tried to?”

Ah, now she understood. “It’s easier to be behind that mask you wear than being yourself, isn’t it?”

His eyes clouded over briefly, and she saw just a glimpse of his true emotions. But the mask was back before she could be sure of what she had seen. At least she knew she had hit a mark.

“Now to answer your question, I don’t plan on trying to or having you killed.”

She saw confusion and something else in his icy eyes. Was it hope? Or cautiousness? She couldn’t be sure, maybe a strange mixture of the two, but for the first time in this newfound relationship, she felt like she had the upper hand. This wasn’t something she was going to give up lightly.

“What are you going to do with me?” he asked, this time doing a better job of keeping the easy grin in place. She doubted she’d be able to surprise him again.

“It’s my turn to ask a question,” she said, before placing a grin of her own. “Would you care to have dinner with me?”

His smile widened at that and responded in a most gentlemanly way, “Why I could think of nothing that would delight me more.”

“You know, when you invited me to dinner, I expected something a little more intimate.”

Silver was sitting at the table in her chambers with Nathaniel next to her, his arms crossed over his chest. Peter was there with Aisling who was taking up the other half of the small table. Silver smiled inwardly, knowing she had him right where she wanted him.

"What do you mean?" she asked, sweetly as she poured him a drink. "There are candles and everything."

Peter mirrored Nathaniel's position perfectly, but he wasn't being as subtle about it. He glared at Nathaniel, annoyed at every move he made. Silver didn't know what to do about that, he was just going to have to get over it.

Nathaniel picked up his glass, inspecting the amber liquid carefully. "It's not poisoned if that's what you're worried about," Silver said, continuing to fill everyone else's drink at the table.

"Well, I wasn't worried about it until now," he said, that ever-present grin flashing across his features.

Silver rolled her eyes but took a big mouth full of her drink. The liquid burned her throat, leaving an almost metallic flavor in her mouth before settling heavily in her stomach. She had taken a big swig, but if you wanted to hang with the men, you needed to drink like one.

"Nicely done, however, there is no telling as to whether my actual cup has been poisoned. If you'd do me the honors?" He offered her his cup with long, slender fingers.

"No one is going to poison you, Nathaniel," she said, but she reached for his cup anyway.

Before she could grasp it, Peter leaned over abruptly from the other side of the table and took the cup in his hand. He took a huge swallow and handed it back roughly, splashing some of the liquid over the side of the glass.

"Well," said Nathaniel, as he wiped his hand up to the lip of the glass, trying to disperse the liquid. "Now you've gone and made my cup dirty." He delicately wiped his hand on a napkin that was left by him on the table. "Silver, darling, would it be too much trouble to ask you for another?"

"What's wrong, Prince?" Peter asked in a nasty tone. "You were fine with Silver drinking out of your cup. You've got a problem with drinking after men?"

"Oh no," he purred, grinning his Cheshire grin. "Trust me when I say, I've done more with men than you ever have. I could show you sometime what to do with a cup and–"

"Enough," Silver said, interrupting. She held her hand up to Peter, who began to rise from his seat seething.

"Your loss," Nathaniel shrugged, hardly bothered. "Now you," he said, leaning towards Aisling. "You're a picture of loveliness. How would you like a lesson in something more interesting than a dinner party?"

Peter jumped to his feet, causing the plates on the table to rattle. His face was flushed, and his hands were clenched into fists at his side. "Peter, sit down," Silver said, standing as well.

She glared at him until he sat begrudgingly. "Now," she said, taking her seat once he did. "Peter, don't let him get under your skin. He's trying to get you riled up, which you are playing right into his hand," she said, holding up a hand, silencing him when he went to speak.

"Now, Nathaniel, if you continue this behavior, you will endure the rest of the meal with a muzzle. And no," she said, at the grin that spread across his face. "I do not want to know what you can do or have done with a muzzle. With that out of the way, I would like to eat dinner and discuss what I have brought you all here to discuss. Does that sound possible?"

She waited, fixing Peter with a hard stare until he sighed and nodded gruffly.

She looked at Nathaniel, who held up his hands in surrender. "I will do whatever my dark angel commands of me. Whatever she commands," he said grinning.

"Good," she said, pulling her food towards her. "Let's eat, then get down to business."

CHAPTER EIGHT

Peter

Peter glared at Nathaniel throughout the meal. He knew that he had been baiting him, but couldn't help his reactions. If he ever talked to Aisling like that again, he would show him what a fist meeting a face can do.

What was Silver playing at? They had entered into a dangerous game, and he wasn't happy about it. When he and Silver had a moment alone, he was going to give her a piece of his mind.

Aisling and Silver talked among themselves in a way only girls could. Peter was glad that they were at least getting along. They had become fast friends. Something happened when they were fighting the sirens, something Peter had no memory of at all. Although he had asked, neither of them had answered his questions. Oh well, if they wanted to keep their secrets then that was fine by him.

Once the tense meal was eaten, Silver broke the silence. "Well, I am certainly feeling better." This statement was greeted with silence. Even Aisling sat quietly with her hands folded delicately in her lap. Silver sighed, seemed to brace herself then said, "Look we need to talk. Nathaniel has… well… we will call it a gift. Nathaniel, will you show them what you can do?"

Nathaniel sat with his arms crossed over his chest, looking upset. "It's not a party trick. I can't just do it whenever I want."

"I don't believe you," Silver countered, leaning forwards. "You can trust us. We won't hurt you."

He rolled his eyes. "Trust me, you hurting me is the least of my worries. I would be more than happy for you to hurt me," he grinned at her.

"We can always put you back below deck, and this time," she said sweetly. "I won't forget to tie up your feet."

"As much fun as that does sound," he said, stretching his arms above his head. "Your wish is my command."

Right before Peter's eyes, Nathaniel seemed to almost melt, and in the blink of an eye, a white cat was sitting on the chair, calming licking its paw. He stared at the cat, his brain trying to catch up to what his eyes were seeing.

Then, right when he was almost convinced there had always been a white cat on board, the cat morphed again, and Nathaniel was sitting in the chair with his arms crossed. He didn't look happy.

Peter was speechless, which even he would admit was no easy feat. He felt his mouth hanging open and shut it with a snap. He couldn't believe what he had just seen. He looked over at Aisling to see how she was taking it.

She was looking at Nathaniel with a thoughtful look on her face, her head cocked slightly to the side. She didn't look freaked out, or like she was going to run from the room screaming, which was sort of what he felt like at that moment. Rather, she looked more curious than anything else.

"Thank you," said Silver, smiling at Nathaniel in a way Peter could only describe as grateful. "Now, if you'd explain."

Nathaniel looked over at her, surprise clear in his eyes. "Excuse me?"

"You heard me. I would like you to give us an explanation."

"What do I get in return?"

"How does not getting thrown in the ocean sound?" Peter snapped. Nathaniel was trying his patience.

Nathaniel shrugged. "The ocean wouldn't bother me. I would be perfectly happy living out my days as a shark."

"So, you can keep up the shape indefinitely?" Silver asked, ignoring Peter.

Nathaniel sighed heavily, resting his chin on his hand on the table. "I liked this better when we were doing a question for a question."

"How about this," replied Silver in a reasonable voice. "You answer our questions about your gift, and we will tell you about ours."

"What?" Peter exclaimed, heart dropping to his toes at her words. "We never agreed to this!"

"Oh, I think this is perfectly fair trade," Nathaniel said, grinning wickedly. "Especially if it upsets young Peter here."

"I am not young! I'm twenty-two, probably the same age as you!"

"Ah, but you see, there's a thing called mental age, and trust me," he said leaning forwards. "I have far more experience than you in most things."

Peter stood. "Sil, Aisling, can we discuss this over there?" he said gesturing to the other end of the room.

Now it was Silver's turn to sigh. "Fine, let's make it quick. Stay put," she said, speaking to Nathaniel.

"Oh I wouldn't dream of moving now," he said, smiling. "After all, this just got a lot more interesting."

The trio moved to the corner of the room, as far away from Nathaniel as possible, and awkwardly huddled up.

"This is ridiculous!" Peter whispered angrily towards Silver. "How can you possibly agree to tell him all of this? We don't even know him! What if he's working for the birdmen?"

"Is that how we're referring to them now?" Silver asked, mildly.

"Just answer the question!"

"Fine, no I don't think he's working for the birdmen."

"Silver," he said exasperated. "You're driving me crazy!"

"No Peter, you are. You've been acting like a child all night and you know what, I'm beginning to believe what Nathaniel said about you is accurate."

Peter was hurt, but he wasn't about to show it. "I don't know what you mean," he said, stiffly.

"Look," said Silver, rubbing her eyes. "I think Nathaniel can help us. His gift is incredibly useful, and I feel like we should give him a chance."

"I can think of several reasons not to do this."

"Oh really? And what might they be?"

Peter knew she had him in a corner, but he wasn't about to tell her that. "How about the fact we know nothing about him."

"That's not true. We know his name, we know he came from a rich family, and we know people were trying to kill him."

"And none of those things concern you?" Peter asked, exasperated.

"No Peter, they don't. And you want to know why? Because every member of this crew has some reason as to why we shouldn't trust them. The rest of the world didn't trust them, no one else gave them a chance. Now here we're with someone who has been in the same predicament as us. Why wouldn't we give him the same chance as everyone else?"

Peter was silent. He knew she was right, and the only thing he had against Nathaniel was his attitude. "Fine, but I still don't like him."

"I'm not asking you to, I'm asking you to trust me."

"That I can do," he said, begrudgingly.

"Good," she said, and without waiting for him, she turned and walked back to the table. Aisling gave him a small smile as she walked past him.

"Have a good meeting?" Nathaniel asked pleasantly once they were all back seated.

"Fine thanks. Now, who do you want to know about first?" Silver said, taking a deep drink of her cup.

"Wait a moment," he said, genuine surprise crossing his features. "Do all of you have gifts?"

"Is that what you want to waste your question on?"

"No, no that's alright. Hmm let me think," he said, eyeing everyone around the table. "Why don't we start with you, love?" he said, gesturing to Aisling. "You've been pretty quiet this whole evening. I'd like to know what you can do."

Peter felt his temper rising again but quickly swallowed it back down. He knew Nathaniel was trying to rile him up, especially when it came to Aisling. He couldn't give too many of his feelings away, or Nathaniel could use them against them.

"Very well," she answered in her quiet voice. "I can generate a kind of energy and can release it through a point in my body."

If Peter hadn't been so frustrated at the situation he would've been upset. How could both Aisling and Silver not think of mentioning this to him? He hadn't asked, but still. This seemed like a kind of important thing to mention.

"So, basically what you're saying is you can shoot electricity out of your fingertips?" Nathaniel asked, curiously.

"That is it essentially. It's easier to release the energy out of my hands, but if I get stressed or upset, I can release it from virtually anywhere."

"Well, that is an interesting concept," he said, looking at her with a seductive look. "Now say that you wanted to release it from–"

"That's enough," Silver interrupted, just as Peter began to rise out of his chair.

"You're both no fun," said Nathaniel pouting. "Very well, what do you need to know?"

"What're the limitations of your gift?"

"Oh starting with this one, are we? Fine. I can transform into any animal. But I can't change into another human or anything. They're always the same silvery-white color, no matter how hard I try to change it. I can't stay in the same form for more than twenty-four hours, and apparently, I can't transform with magical handcuffs."

"Magical how?"

"Nope, it's my turn," he said, holding up one slender finger. "How quickly you forget. Now, what is your gift, my dark angel?"

"I would prefer it if you didn't call me that," Silver said, stiffly.

"No promises," he said with a shrug. "Now your answer please."

"I can speak to animals. Usually, they find me, but I can also call them and ask them for help or just talk. My gift extends for a few miles but not across continents. Satisfied?"

"Not in the slightest," he said, thoughtfully. "However, you did answer my question; it's your turn."

This game was making Peter's head spin. He sure hoped Silver knew what she was doing because he was beginning to lose patience.

Silver thought for a moment before asking, "Why were you left on that island?"

This question seemed to take him by surprise. He let out a breath slowly, seeming to not want to begin.

"I'm waiting."

"I know," he snapped, "I'm gathering my thoughts."

"Come now. It shouldn't be that hard to explain why someone wanted to kill you."

"Fine. They didn't like that I could transform into other creatures. At first, they did. They used me for all sorts of things, then the experiments started. Can't say that was a pleasant experience that I'm willing to revisit. There, I have answered your question."

"Not really," said Silver, leaning back. "But you may now know Peter's gift. Go on Peter."

Peter took a deep breath and then said, "I can see briefly into the future. I can't always control it or know when it's going to happen, but if I or someone I love is about to get hurt, I can usually see what is going to happen and try to stop it."

"Interesting," Nathaniel purred. "So, could you stop me if I did this?"

The world slowed as Peter saw Nathaniel grabbing a dinner knife off the table and throwing it at him. The knife embedded itself into his shoulder, barely missing his heart. His brain snapped back into the present.

He lunged over the table and pinned Nathaniel's wrist, right as he was reaching for the knife. "Yes," he answered inches away from Nathaniel's slightly shocked face. "I can stop you."

Nathaniel seemed to gain control over himself. "Interesting. Well, I don't know about everyone else here, but I am exhausted." He wiggled out from under Peter's grip and reached his arms over his head, faking a huge yawn. "Shall we call it a night?"

"Just a moment," said Silver, taking the floor once again. "One more question."

"Oh love," he said, smiling sadly at her. "You don't have anything else that I want to know. I think we are done here," he said standing.

"I think I do have something that would interest you."

"Oh and what, might that be?"

"Sit down and then I'll tell you."

"Sil," said Peter in a warning. He had a bad feeling he knew where she was going with this, and he wasn't sure this was a good idea at all.

She shook her head at him, and when Nathaniel sat, she continued. "Now, the people who experimented on you, what did they look like?"

"I don't know, I never saw their faces. They wore masks with bird beaks."

Silver and Peter exchanged glances. "Well, then you and Aisling have come from the same place."

"What do you mean?" he asked, genuinely seeming like he was trying to understand.

Silver rose and got the stone out of its lockbox. "Do you recognize this?" Silver unwrapped the stone, careful not to touch it.

Nathaniel had frozen in place. He didn't even seem to be breathing once she pulled it out. "Where did you get this?" he asked, in a quiet voice.

"We found it. Now, since you and the stone have been acquainted, what can you tell us about it?"

Nathaniel was quiet for a moment, and this time no one tried to rush him. He took a deep breath and began, "That's a powerful device, I don't know entirely how it works, but I do know that the people who I work– well… worked for, wanted to use the stone to gather power."

"It's some kind of storer that can suck someone completely out of their powers and turn it into pure energy. Now I can only guess what they wanted with it, and thankfully they never hooked me up to it. But that thing can drain people's powers, and if left in their hands, I dread to think of what the world would become."

It was so quiet at the table you could hear the gentle creaking of the ship. Now that they finally knew what the thing did, it made them all incredibly nervous. "Well, what do we do with it now?" asked Peter, finally breaking the silence. "Destroy it?

Silver was quiet for a moment. "That may be the most logical answer."

"And how do you plan on doing that?" asked Nathaniel, leaning back with some cockiness coming back into his tone. "If it has any power in there destroying it would release that energy, then we'd have a much bigger problem on our hands."

"Can they track us with this?"

He was quiet for a moment as he thought it over. "It's possible. But there's no way of knowing for sure."

"So, we can't destroy it, even though it could be leading them straight to us? And somehow we need to make sure it doesn't get into the wrong hands, so selling it is out of the question. What're we supposed to do?" Peter asked, feeling his temper rise.

"Oh, looks like we've upset him again," said Nathaniel, in a belittling voice.

"Don't start with me, or I'll make sure it's the last thing you do," Peter said dangerously.

"Enough," said Silver standing. "Now I do think that is quite enough tension for one night. Let's all go to bed, and we can continue this discussion in the morning."

"I wouldn't be opposed to sleeping in an actual bed. Especially," Nathaniel said, fixing Silver with a long pointed look. "If I had someone to keep me warm."

Peter finally cracked. He stood and before Nathaniel even had a chance to react, his fist hit Nathaniel's face with a satisfying crack. Nathaniel flew out of his chair and hit the floor hard on his side.

"Peter!" Silver shouted. "That was uncalled for!"

"Well, I couldn't handle him talking to you like that anymore! He's ridiculous!"

"What is with the violence in this family?" came Nathaniel's voice from the floor.

"Peter, I understand your frustration," said Silver, visibly trying to keep her cool. "But that does not justify punching people. As Nathaniel has already pointed out, I can, and have, taken care of myself. Now if you'd kindly, apologize to Nathaniel."

Peter ground his teeth, anger burning in his stomach. Nathaniel picked himself slowly up off the floor and Peter said, "I'm sorry for punching you."

Nathaniel grinned until Silver said, "And now you Nathaniel."

He looked over at her in mild shock before the grin returned to his features. "Very well," he said bowing to Peter. "I sincerely apologize for the upset." He straightened and stretched again before saying, "Well, if no one else needs anything, I think I will be heading to a cold empty bed."

He brushed past Peter and out the door, seeing himself out. Silver sighed and looked at Aisling. "Thank you for dealing with him. I know he's a lot but–"

"A lot! He's insane! Why are you letting him talk to you like that?" Peter was outraged. All that pent-up anger was starting to bubble over.

"Peter," Silver said, enunciating each syllable. "Listen to me carefully. Nathaniel is a rare shapeshifter. This means we can use him to help on some of the more complicated missions. So that does involve being nice to him. However, I have already kicked his legs out from under him, insulted him, and threatened him with a gun. That being said, he knows his place. If you hadn't reacted so badly, he probably would have stopped. Next time, I trust you to be the mature adult that I know you can be. Are we clear?"

Peter took a breath, still feeling the anger trying to rise but he swallowed it down. "Crystal."

"Excellent, now if you don't mind, I think we girls need to get some sleep. So off you go."

Peter turned on his heel and tried, unsuccessfully, to not slam the door on his way out. If there was one thing he hated more than being made a fool of by someone else was being made a fool in front of everyone else. And by his sister for that matter.

Silver knew him better than anyone else in the world, which he thought meant she wouldn't use that against him. She knew he hated it when she treated him like he was somehow younger than her. He was the older one! It wasn't like she had that much wisdom on him.

He paced angrily, hands crossed behind his back. "You know, you'll wear holes in the ship if you keep this up."

His head shot up and looked into the eyes of the person he least wanted to see. Nathaniel was leaning lazily against the railing, his pale hair gleaming in the moonlight. "Oh great," said Peter, throwing his hands in the air. "If it isn't the sex king himself!"

"That's not fair," said Nathaniel, a frown growing between his eyebrows.

"That's a perfectly fair statement considering everything that happened in there!"

Nathaniel looked thoughtful for a moment before shrugging. "Just trying to keep things interesting."

"Is that what you call it? That certainly clears up matters," Peter shook his head and turned to go.

"Wait, Peter, please let me explain."

Peter should have kept walking, but there was something in his voice that sounded oddly familiar to him. It was a kind of vulnerability that he had heard in his voice on the occasion. He turned and crossed his arms over his chest, "I'm listening."

"Look, I know we got off on the wrong foot."

"That's putting it lightly," Peter grumbled.

"But," said Nathaniel, ignoring his comment. "I like your sister. She… intrigues me."

"In what way does she intrigue you?" asked Peter, eyeing him with suspicion.

Nathaniel grinned. "Not in that way. I mean she is beautiful, so maybe someday if I'm lucky, but believe me that isn't my intention. Or rather my only intention."

"You aren't helping your case here."

"Look," he said, running a hand through his long silver hair. "This is difficult for me. I haven't had the best experiences with, well, people in general, so I tend to be a little dramatized."

"So, all that stuff you said in there isn't how you truly feel?"

"Oh no, that's how I really feel. It's just a bit over the top is all."

Peter pinched the bridge of his nose. "Nathaniel, if you're telling me these things to try and get me to feel sympathetic to you, it's not working."

"Well, it's the truth, and if you're telling me you don't feel that way then you're lying. Besides, I've seen the way you look at the redhead. You can't tell me your only intention is to be friends forever."

Peter sucked in a breath and let it out slowly. As infuriating as he was, Nathaniel had a point. "I would prefer it if you didn't talk to her like that in front of me."

"Understood. I will certainly try not to, however, old habits die hard as they say."

"Also, while we are on the subject, no spying on them."

"On who?"

Peter rolled his eyes. "God, on either of the girls! What if you turned into a bug and watched them?"

"I would never do such a thing," he said, in mock offense. "However, that isn't a terrible idea now that you've put the idea in my head." He grinned his signature grin, making it difficult to tell if he was joking or not.

Peter glared at him until he finally said, "Oh, very well no spying. Trust me, the last thing I want to do is get on your sister's bad side."

"Good," said Peter, feeling satisfied with his answer for once.

They stood in awkward silence for a moment, each waiting for the other to go first.

"We seem to have reached an impasse."

"So it would seem," Peter answered. "I still don't like you."

"And I think you're hot-headed."

"Well, that may be the best we can do," Peter held out his hand. "To new beginnings."

Nathaniel pushed off from the railing and took Peter's hand in his own. "To new understandings."

CHAPTER NINE

Silver

Silver walked out of her chambers and breathed in the fresh, salty air deep into her lungs. She was preparing herself for a conversation with Peter. She hadn't meant to make him feel inferior last night, especially in front of Aisling. They had already been fighting so much.

Last night had been rough in the sleep department. She was somehow not able to get comfortable. She knew it was her guilty conscience keeping her awake and she intended to make it right. Even if it did involve a few deep breaths to steel herself.

Taking one more breath, she turned to go find Peter. "Silver!"

She turned back around to see Nathaniel coming up to her with his typical grin in place. He still had on the white, flowy shirt that was cut too far down and fitted black pants.

Her breath caught in her throat, and she felt her heart skip a beat. He was so handsome, even with the bruise that was blooming across his cheek. Getting control of herself, she placed a pleasant uninterested expression on her face. "Good morning," she said when they were close enough to talk to each other without shouting.

"It is a good morning," he said, lazily leaning against the railing next to her. "I may even be so bold as to call it a beautiful morning." He turned his head and looked directly at her as he said this. She felt her heart give a little flutter, which she pushed back down.

"Is there something you need?"

"Yes, actually there was," he said, continuing to look at her. Her stomach gave a strange lurch. She was used to getting unwanted attention from men, but somehow, this didn't feel unwanted.

"Do I have to ask you what it is or are you just going to tell me?"

He grinned. "Very well, I wanted to let you know I spoke to Peter last night."

"About what? Did he punch you again?"

"Trust me, the next one of us to get punched will be him."

"I don't know, as I recall, you didn't stop me when I put a gun to your head."

"Well, see, here's the difference," he said, leaning closer to her. "I wanted to see what you and your brother were made of. I gave you an opening, and you took it. The same can't be said for most people."

"I think we just caught you by surprise."

He shrugged. "Think what you will, dark angel. My time will come, and then you'll see how strong I am."

Silver rolled her eyes. "Sure, Nathaniel. Now, what were you saying about Peter?"

"Oh right. Peter and I had a little chat last night, and I think we've come to an agreement."

"Oh? What sort of agreement?" Silver did not like the sound of that, especially coming from Nathaniel.

He grinned. "Oh you know, we agreed to become partners, commandeer the ship and leave you on the nearest deserted island we come across."

"Well, now that I know your plans, I will kindly be throwing you overboard."

"Oh come on! Can't I at least walk the plank? Isn't that what pirates do?"

"We aren't pirates," said Silver firmly. "We're merchants."

"Just keep telling yourselves that."

Silver rubbed her right eyebrow trying to get rid of the twitch she felt coming on. "Nathaniel," she said, speaking with as much forced calmness as she could. "If you don't tell me what you and my brother agreed on, I will personally make sure you can't walk for a week."

The grin stretched over his face, a glint in his eyes. Before she could stop him, he leaned towards her, his lips brushing her ear. "I would love to know in great detail exactly how you were planning to accomplish that, but you know if I'm not walking, I'd prefer to be on my back with you."

He leaned away just as quickly, leaving her whole body tingling. She glared at him, then turned and began walking away. Before she had taken two steps, she felt his hand grab her wrist and he twisted her around with inhuman strength to face him. She used that momentum to bring her other hand around to strike him. He caught her hand easily and pinned it behind her.

"Nathaniel," she said through gritted teeth. "I will take those magic handcuffs of yours and throw you into the sea if you don't release me this instant."

He pulled her closer to him, and she began to panic. He didn't look playful anymore. There was a hungry, almost animalistic look in his eyes, and he wasn't letting go. "Nathaniel," she said in her most authoritative voice. "Release me."

His grin slowly began to melt off his face, and she saw something there, something vulnerable that she had seen once before. "I–" he said, looking like he was the one trapped, not her. He released her and took several stumbling steps back rubbing his right arm, in rough jerky movements. "Please forgive me," he said, seeming to gain a little control over himself. "Sometimes I lose control and… well. I'm sorry."

She looked at him curiously. "Nathaniel, are you alright?"

He let out a breath in a rush and continued to rub his arm. It was almost like he didn't realize he was doing it. "I'm better now thank you for your concern."

"What do you mean to lose control?"

"I… I'm not sure if I'm ready to talk about it," he said, looking away. The bravado was gone and in its place was something strange, almost broken. His shoulders had a hunch to them now, and he seemed to almost cave in on himself.

"Alright," she said, keeping her distance. "This will have to be discussed at some point, but I'll give you the time you need."

"Thank you, that is most kind," he said, not meeting her eyes. He shook himself and said, "Your brother and I won't be hitting each other, anytime soon anyway. We've found a sort of understanding. While we aren't friends by any means, we have agreed to be civilized. I thought you might be happy to know."

Silver was surprised by this but pleased. "Thank you for telling me, and for making an effort. I know he can be hard-headed sometimes."

He smiled a small smile that didn't quite reach his eyes. "Well, that's all I had, Captain. I'm sure we will talk again soon."

Before she could say anything else to him, he turned on his heel and walked away. She could've gone after him, but she didn't want to push him. She would give him some time and maybe soon she would've gained his trust enough for him to trust her. But for now, she couldn't worry about him. On to the next problem of the day: breakfast.

Silver opened the door to the kitchen and the smell of baking filled her lungs making her stomach grumble. Sam turned and seeing her, his face lit up. He rushed over to her and led her to the table. He knew she knew where everything was but he enjoyed fussing over her, even if it made her a little uncomfortable. She didn't want anyone on the ship to feel inferior to her or like they had to wait on her. She wanted them to respect her as their leader, but she would help with the chores just as much as the rest of the crew.

Peter and Aisling were already seated on opposite sides of the room. They both seemed to be trying so hard to ignore each other that they didn't seem to hear Silver come in.

"Good morning," she said, smiling that they both jumped at the sound of her voice.

"Good morning," Aisling replied, smiling up at her but continuing to ignore Peter.

"Your future seeing skills must be waning, Peter," Silver said, as Sam placed a steaming plate in front of her. "Thank you, Sam."

"What do you mean? There's nothing wrong with my sight."

"Well, it just seems that you would've foreseen my coming in, or at least heard me." She turned slightly to get a better look at him, enjoying the look on Peter's face. "You've been distracted, Peter."

"Well… I mean…" Peter stumbled over his words, trying to figure out a good comeback.

"Lucky for you, I'm taking the distraction away," she added when he looked like he was about to argue. "Aisling and I are due for some quality time." She looked over and smiled at her, a smile which Aisling returned readily. "As long as that's acceptable to you?" she asked, addressing Aisling.

"Oh yes! I would like that," she said shyly.

"It's settled then," Silver said, to a very disgruntled Peter.

They finished their breakfast quickly and after thanking Sam numerous times, the girls went up into Silver's chambers.

Silver sighed as she sat in her chair, and Aisling sat in the one opposite. "You, know, you have quite a hold on him."

"A hold on who?" Aisling seemed generally confused.

"Come on, Peter of course."

"Oh no, he hates me," Aisling said, a crease beginning between her eyebrows.

"No, he doesn't."

"Yes, he does. Otherwise, why would he leave as soon as I walk into a room? He won't talk to me, even when I try talking to him, and he only answers me with short answers when he does talk to me. I have no idea what his problem is."

"Aisling, it's because he likes you," Silver offered the other woman a candy that she always kept in her desk drawer. "My brother is many things, but hateful he is not. He doesn't always know what to do with his feelings, so he may react badly. Especially if he thinks you'd turn him down, or that you'd be intimidated that he's more experienced. He wouldn't want to push you."

Aisling didn't seem to know what to say to that. She looked lost in thought.

"As much fun as this is, I didn't ask you to come here to talk about your love life," Silver said, making Aisling's head pop up with full alertness. "I had the most interesting conversation with Nathaniel this morning."

"Oh? Then are we here to talk about your love life?"

"My what now?" Silver asked in shock.

"You can't deny that he's incredibly attractive."

"Of course but–"

"And he certainly seems like he would be passionate in everything he did."

"Maybe *too* passionate."

"Or not. Maybe just the right amount of passion. Besides, you can't deny you're attracted to him or that you've thought about what it would be like to be with him."

Silver felt her mouth hanging open, so she shut it with a snap. She pinched the bridge of her nose and said, "Look, I also didn't come to discuss my lack of love life either."

"Oh, I don't think it's lacking," said Aisling cheerfully, enjoying herself. "What was it you said? Subtlety is not your strong suit either."

Silver let out her breath in a huff. "Nothing is going on between Nathaniel and me."

"Just keep telling yourself that," Aisling replied.

"Anyway," said Silver, trying to steer the conversation back to her original intent. "Nathaniel was acting weird…"

She continued to explain what happened on the railing that morning. Aisling stayed silent for the entire thing, listening intently. When she had finished, Aisling was quiet for another moment or two.

"So, you want to know what I might know about this?"

"Sort of," said Silver leaning forwards. "I was hoping you might know what the Cleansers might have done to him. He seems to have some kind of trigger that makes him act like… well… Nathaniel but a more intense version of himself."

Silver wasn't sure if she was making any sense at all, but she knew there was something off. She found herself pacing the small chamber, she didn't even remember standing but she must have during her explanation of the problem.

Aisling answered bluntly, "You want to know what kind of experiments they did on us."

"Yes," said Silver, sighing again. "I'm not trying to be insensitive, but I need to know if there is something about you two I should know about."

"I'm not sure if I can explain," said Aisling, seeming to steady herself. "I don't remember exactly what was done to me. There was a lot of pain, and I always ended up passing out from it. I'd wake up the next morning in my bed, making me think that it had all been a dream. I don't know how different our experiences were. I never saw anyone else at the house where I grew up, but who knows how many other people he experimented on."

Silver stopped pacing. "He? He who?"

"The man from the house I grew up in. His name was… Let me think." She was quiet for a moment. Then she snapped her fingers, "Barron Loch, that's right. I grew up with him. He was the one who turned me over to the Cleansers."

"You never mentioned him before."

"Well, I hadn't thought about him in years. I had somewhat of a normal life… well as normal as a girl who was experimented on and imprisoned could've been, I suppose. But I spent so long with the Cleansers that I had forgotten my childhood until now."

"How old were you when all this happened?"

"Well, I was turned over to the bird people when I was about twelve, I think. I only remember my childhood from age eight, so from the ages eight to twelve I spent with the Barron. I don't have any memories before that."

"He seems to have some kind of tic," ventured Silver, watching Aisling for a reaction.

"What sort of tic?"

"Well, he was rubbing his right arm, almost without realizing he was doing it. Could it be some kind of trigger?"

Silver could see worry brimming in Aisling's eyes that she didn't even attempt to hide as she thought this over. "I'm not sure," she finally answered. "I wouldn't put it past the Cleansers to do something like that."

"Is it something we need to worry about from you?"

Aisling's eyes flashed. "Even though I may not know entirely what has been done to me, I can tell you right now, nothing like that would work on me."

"I didn't mean to cause offense," replied Silver, holding up a hand in surrender. "I just needed to know where we stood."

"I understand. And you didn't offend me. Just remembering all this is hard for me."

"I'm sorry. I'm not trying to cause you pain," said Silver, gently. "Let's talk about something else. What–" Silver broke off as something brushed against her subconsciousness. She couldn't tell what it was, but it was huge and was heading straight towards them. "Aisling I–"

The ship took a violent shift to the side, causing both women to topple from their chairs. They landed on the floor with a huff, with Silver's chair dangerously close to landing on her. She rolled to avoid it and was on her feet in an instant. She looked over and saw that Aisling was standing again as well, seeming to have done a similar kind of maneuver to avoid a collision with the chair. They looked at each other for a moment before dashing off to the deck simultaneously.

The deck was in utter chaos. Men were running from one end of the deck to the other, carrying buckets of water that the ship had taken on, ropes, and weapons. They were yelling instructions to be heard over the chaos of moving bodies. Somehow in the twenty minutes since being below deck, the ship had come under attack.

Silver began to run to the main deck where John was at the wheel. Just before she reached the ladder to hoist herself up, the ship violently swayed to the right and before Silver knew what had happened, she found herself airborne. She heard Peter yell her name right before the cold water closed over her head.

Well, damn it, she thought as she began to sink. She was a strong swimmer, but even her powerful strokes were no match for the rocking, swirling waves that were pulling her down instead of up. She thought this might be the day when the ocean took her. She was just beginning to come to terms with this notion when she felt strong arms around her waist.

Before she had much time to react to this new development, she felt her body shoot up and her head broke the surface. She took big gulps of air, the stars slowly fading from her vision. She turned to see who her savior was and saw Nathaniel without his customary grin, his face full of concern. "Are you alright?"

She nodded, trying to catch her breath when she looked down to see a massive scaled tail where Nathaniel's legs were supposed to be. "Are you a merman?"

He blanched at her. Whatever he was expecting her to say, wasn't that.

"You have a fishtail," she said trying to explain herself.

"Are you sure you're alright? Didn't swallow any saltwater?" he asked, his concerned expression deepening on his handsome face.

"I don't think so," she answered as he began swimming them back towards the ship. The current must have taken her farther than she thought.

"As stimulating as this conversation is, I don't think now is the time to be talking about this."

"What?" she asked, turning towards the ship, then she happened to see what had caused the massive rocking of her ship. "Oh, right then."

There was a huge horrible sea creature attacking her ship. It looked exactly like the kind of monster she had read about in children's stories, but she was not prepared to see something as horrifying in person.

It was about three times the size of her ship. It looked to be serpent-like, with a long scaled body that was slowly wrapping itself around the ship. The scales weren't like the ones that belonged to a fish. They weren't smooth; they looked rough, almost like the scales she had seen on alligators. It had these large scales jutting out of the top of its back, making a row of incredibly sharp and hard armor. This must've been what was pushing against her ship, which she saw to her horror was much lower than it should've been and was quickly taking on water.

They had made it back to the ship where some of her men, led by Peter, had lowered a rope ladder. Nathaniel pushed her gently towards it, and as she grabbed it she turned to see him swimming away from her. "Wait! Where are you going?"

He turned back towards her and called, "Well, someone has to battle this monster. Why don't we give it someone closer to its size?" his grin was back in place, not comforting her in the slightest.

She frowned, but knowing she probably wasn't going to be able to stop him, "Be careful."

"Oh, my dark angel, don't worry. This, after all, is my area of expertise." The last thing she saw was his grin as he slid below the surface. She turned back towards the ladder, her stomach in knots.

She scrambled up, jumping over the railing. Peter was on top of her the moment her feet touched back on the deck. "Are you alright? Are you hurt at all?"

"Peter, calm down," she said, waving him away. "I'm fine! And I think we have bigger problems on our hands right now."

She looked around taking stock of the damage. The creature had its body completely wrapped around the front end of her ship. She watched in horror as she saw the scales slowly moving forward, meaning it was trying to break apart the ship.

Her men were running around carrying buckets of water that they were dumping overboard, as well as swords that they were unsuccessfully trying to use on the creature. The scales were too hard; the swords were bouncing off of them.

Silver turned to the others who were surrounding her with Peter. "Any idea what this thing is?" she asked, addressing John as she began walking purposefully towards the weapon storage.

"Unfortunately no," he said, matching her pace easily. "Even in all of my research, I've never heard of anything like this beast."

She nodded, continuing her brisk pace. "Silver you can't possibly be thinking about fighting it!" Came Peter's voice from pretty close behind her. "You just fell overboard!"

She turned and walked up to him until their boots were practically touching. "I will do what I believe is best for this ship, and if my men are fighting then you or anyone else won't stop me from joining them."

"Silver you're in no condition to fight," he replied just as firmly as the tone she had used with him.

"I am perfectly fine, and as my second, I need you to trust me," she said, placing a gentle hand on his arm.

He nodded but did not look happy or like he fully trusted her. She sighed, knowing there was nothing she could say to convince him otherwise. But frankly, she didn't have time, she had a ship to save.

CHAPTER TEN

Peter

Peter watched Silver go, leading the crew in the way only she knew best. He wasn't sure why he had tried so hard to stop her. Deep down he knew she was up to fighting, but something about seeing her surprised face as she fell over the railing had undone something in him. And Nathaniel of all people is the one to come to her rescue. He shook himself, now was not the time, he had to protect Silver.

"Stay safe," he said, turning to Aisling.

She crossed her arms over her chest. "I can take care of myself."

Peter threw his arms up in the air. "Not you too! What is with the women on this ship?"

"Maybe the women on this ship know what their limits are and don't need anyone else to tell them what they can and can't do," she said gently, looking up at him and capturing him with those emerald eyes.

As her eyes met his, he was completely put under her spell. The ship gave another tremendous rock to the side, nearly knocking Peter off of his feet. "The men on this ship are a little superstitious and may not take kindly to, well, your abilities."

Aisling did nothing but stare at him. "I'm not asking you to stay out of it, just please stay safe, can you do that for me?"

She fixed him with her intense stare before giving a curt nod. "Thank you," he said while taking the sword from his belt and charging into a battle that was already raging.

No one had seen the creature's head yet, which was concerning. The thing had come out of nowhere, hitting the ship and then wrapping its ugly body around the front of it before anyone had even been fully aware of what was going on.

Peter ran up to the other men who were desperately trying to pry the huge serpent-like body off of the ship. He took his sword and began doing the same, hoping that if enough of them were trying, together they could pry it off.

He heard a huge splash off to his right and emerging out of the water, he saw what must have been the creature's head. It was roughly the size of a rowboat. It could easily fit three or four men in its mouth at one time. It had two orb-like eyes the size of shields on the front of its face. Its snout was long, similar to that of a large crocodile, with teeth jutting out at different points of its lips. Its mouth was shaped in a wide grin and opened to reveal three rows of teeth. To Peter's horror, he realized too late the creature had turned to face Aisling, who was staring wide-eyed at the creature and backing away.

Without thinking, Peter yelled and raced towards them. Time slowed as the vision began to unfurl around him. He saw the creature turn towards him and in a lightning-fast movement, he saw the rows and rows of teeth descend on him. Right before they snapped him up, time began moving again. Just like in his vision, he saw the creature turn its head towards him, but this time Peter was ready. He continued running, picking up speed and at the last possible moment, he twisted his body letting the creature fly past him and bury its head into the deck of the ship.

The creature jerked once then twice but stayed in the same position. It must have been going so fast that its massive fangs got stuck in the wooden deck. Not knowing how long it was going to stay that way, Peter rushed forwards and with a flying leap impaled his sword in the creature's eye. The creature let out a wailing screech, then blood and jelly-like liquid began flowing all over the main deck. Wrenching his sword free and taking a step back, he slipped in the mess and began sliding to the railing. It hit him in the stomach, knocking the wind out of him. He stayed there for a few moments, gasping like a fish out of water trying to get his breath back.

The creature, still screeching, managed to pull itself free from the deck and was waving its head around. Blood flying out of its eye, drenching the crew and leaving wet puddles all over the deck.

"Fire!" Peter heard Silver's voice call through the noise. There was a massive boom as the cannons released one right after another. She must've been waiting for an opening. The cannonballs hit the creature moving it with the impact, but the cannonballs bounced harmlessly off of its armored body. It did less damage and only seemed to confuse the creature.

Peter, wary of the slippery puddles, rushed to the rest of the crew who were still frantically trying to get the massive tail unwrapped from the front of the ship. It seemed like all they had been able to do was loosen it, but it was still wrapped around tight. The cannons were on a cycle, so there was constant fire coming out of the ship, which unfortunately made keeping their footing on the now slippery deck quite difficult.

There was another roar, and to his horror, Peter saw another creature rise out of the ocean. It was just as large as their assassin if not larger, with big, icy blue eyes. It looked like a dragon out of a children's book, with scales that went up to its back in spikes. The only thing that was missing was wings. It opened its mouth and let out a bone-rattling roar, leaving most of the men on deck to cower and cover their ears.

Peter almost joined them, but there was something off about the white dragon, something strangely familiar. The realization hit Peter with a jolt, it was Nathaniel. Maybe he had his uses after all. Most of the men had abandoned the tail and were seeking cover below. Sighing, but not surprised at the crew's behavior, Peter kept on the mission still trying to wedge his sword in between the deck and the tail.

He heard another shriek coming from the monster. Turning, he saw that Nathaniel had his jaws around the creature's head, fangs pressing into the already wounded eye. He turned back to the task at hand and felt someone at his elbow.

"Move back!" Aisling shouted to be heard over the noise.

On instinct, Peter jumped back, somehow managing to miss a particularly large puddle of liquid. Aisling's hands began to glow green and with a sound similar to a thunderclap, green electricity shot out of her hands and directly onto the sea monster's tail. Finally, the tail loosened and with another screech from the monster, it unraveled and slid off the side of the ship. This made the ship rock violently, causing Aisling to run into Peter knocking both of them over. Peter wrapped his arms around her using his body as a cushion, and they hit the deck hard.

This time they weren't so lucky, and they landed right into the puddle of gunk. Peter got the wind knocked out of him again, and they began sliding dangerously fast across the deck, picking up speed as they went. Aisling was frantically grabbing at anything she could to try and slow them down to no avail while Peter was just trying to catch his breath, again.

They continued to slide picking up speed until they reached the railing. It just so happened that they were heading straight for the one part of the ship that was broken by the serpent, leading directly into the rocking waves below. Peter dug in his heels, keeping his grip on Aisling until his foot struck what he was hoping for, the rope that raised the sail.

Aisling screamed right as they reached the edge of the deck. Just as they were about to fall over the edge, Peter felt the rope tighten around his ankle. They slid off the deck, Peter's leg jerked making him grunt as the rope pulled taunt, leaving him and Aisling suspended upside down.

He wasn't sure how long the rope would support them, but luckily they didn't have to wait long before he felt the rope being tugged up. Strong hands pulled Aisling up first, at his commanding, then him up and over the side of the ship.

When Peter was finally upright, he saw Silver looking at him intently. "You alright there?" she asked, concern clear in her eyes.

"Fine," he answered, as he felt a shooting pain in his leg when he tried to stand. "Well, mostly," he said after being unable to put more than a little weight on it.

Calling two men over, they hoisted him to his feet and half carried him into Silver's chamber with Silver and Aisling close behind him.

"What happened?" he asked Silver when they set him down. "Where is the sea monster?"

"I'm not entirely sure," she answered, tending to his wounded leg. "They both swam off after Aisling zapped him."

Just then, John came in with Cedric in tow. "What's the damage?" Silver asked, standing to face him. Cedric came over to Peter to fully inspect his leg.

"I'm afraid it's not looking good, Captain," he said slowly, almost as if he was afraid to continue. "There has been massive damage not only to the front of the ship but also to the bottom where the creature ran into us."

"How are we currently still afloat?"

John opened his mouth to respond just as the ship rocked again. Everyone grabbed onto something so they wouldn't go toppling to the floor. Then the ship began moving much faster than it had ever moved on its own.

Everyone collectively looked at each other and ran up the stairs. "Hey wait!" Peter called to their backs, but no one paid him any mind and continued on their way. Cursing, he hoisted himself off the bed and slowly hobbled to the door.

When he finally made it up to the main deck, everyone had made their way to the front of the ship and were trying to see where they were headed. Something was off about the way the ship was moving. It was racing across the sea against the wind. Something was pushing them.

Peter hopped over to the back end of the ship and looked over. There was a pure white sea creature that Peter could just make out under the water and it was pushing their ship. It looked like Nathaniel had survived the battle.

At the speed they were going, it was kind of an incredible feat he was pulling off. Now that Peter was higher up he could see the damage the ship had taken, and it honestly shouldn't have been floating. There was the huge hole that he and Aisling fell through at the front end of the ship, not to mention all of the scratches and scrapes both sides of the ship had undergone. Peter could only imagine the amount of water the ship had taken on. However, with the exact speed Nathaniel was managing it was creating a kind of barrier against letting any more water come into the ship.

Peter leaned over a little farther, trying to see what kind of creature Nathaniel had turned into to be able to go this speed but he wasn't able to see anything more than it was a large white creature. He heard a shout and looked over his shoulder to see Silver running up to him.

"How did you get up here?" she asked when she reached him. "Never mind," she said, not letting him answer. "Let's get you back below. It looks like we're heading for a town."

A few hours later, Peter felt the ship slowing down. He was "resting" in Silver's chambers completely by himself. Really what he was doing was standing on his good leg, looking out the small window on the back wall. He wasn't good at lying down and doing nothing.

The ship so far was holding together and looked like it would hold up until they got it repaired. He knew he was going to get left behind when they went ashore, which he wasn't particularly happy about. He was just trying to figure out a way to convince Silver that he needed to come when there was a knock on the door. It swung open before he could so much as look at the bed he was supposed to be laying in.

"Aren't you supposed to be resting?" asked Cedric as he walked in.

"I am resting, see? I'm not doing anything."

Cedric gave him a disapproving look and helped him back to the bed. "Now then, if you wouldn't mind?"

He began his inspection professionally and with pursed lips. He disapproved of injuries as a general rule. Even though without any injuries on the ship he would be without a job. This logic didn't seem to bother him, which made him give anyone who got hurt the disapproving look.

Peter sat still and let Cedric have his way knowing he wasn't going to get any information out of him until he was satisfied that Peter wasn't in danger of losing his leg. It didn't hurt that badly, Peter had been gravely injured before, and he knew what that felt like. He would never forget the deep-rooted pain and him swimming in and out of consciousness. That was rough.

The ship came to a grinding stop causing both Cedric and Peter to jolt and almost tumble to the floor. "Good gracious!" exclaimed Cedric as he righted himself.

"It feels like we may have crashed into something," Peter said, jumping out of bed and hobbling to the door.

He felt Cedric's hand on his shoulder stopping him with surprising strength. Although he shouldn't be surprised in hindsight. Cedric had been a medical doctor during the last war, and Peter had seen him lift full-grown men twice his size and carry them to safety. "You need rest," he said firmly, steering Peter back towards the bed.

"No, I need to see what's happening!"

"Peter," he said sternly, still keeping his grip on his shoulder. "I will go see what's going on. If you're on that leg too much you'll hurt yourself."

Peter grumbled but let Cedric direct him back to the bed. He was the doctor after all. "Please come back and tell me what's going on," Peter said, feeling like he was a child again and hating it.

"I will come back with a full report," Cedric replied gently. "Or send someone else in to report back to you. Hold tight." Cedric turned on his heel and left the room quickly, leaving the door cracked behind him. Peter laid on the bed straining to hear anything that might give him a clue as to what was going on above deck.

He was trying to be good and listen to Cedric but he couldn't help it. He needed to know what was going on. Standing, he limped slowly over to the door to try and get to a better spot to listen. Just as he pressed his ear to the keyhole, something moved it and he felt something brush against his leg. He looked down and jumped almost out of his skin. There was a white cat slowly winding itself against his good leg.

"God Nathaniel! Can you give me some warning next time?" he asked, looking at him with narrowed eyes.

The cat gave him a very un-cat-like grin, baring its little fangs. "That's creepy," Peter said, wincing slightly. "You could've just turned back into a human you know?"

Nathaniel seemed unbothered by this statement and began licking his paws delicately. Peter sighed, "Well, I'm glad you survived. I wasn't sure there for a while."

Nathaniel blinked up at him, giving him a look of understanding. Just then, the door opened fully and smacked Peter in the face, almost knocking him to the ground.

He barely caught himself on the wall. Groaning, he put his hand to his head. "Ouch," he said, coming out from behind the door to see Silver's shocked face.

"Peter? What're you doing out of bed?"

"I was just trying to find out what the hell was going on! Then you come barreling into the room."

"First of all, it's my room. Second of all, if you had been in bed like you were supposed to be then this wouldn't have happened, would it?"

Nathaniel was making a hissing, choking sound that Peter assumed was a cat form of laughing. "Oh, that's rich coming from you! Imagine if you had been standing there, you wouldn't be laughing as you flew across the room. Then who'd be laughing?"

"Is that…?" Silver trailed off on seeing the white cat.

"Nathaniel, yes," said Peter, still rubbing his head and making his slow way back to the bed. "Give me a hand, would you?"

Silver helped him wordlessly back to the bed, not taking her eyes off the cat. Once he was settled, she leaned down until she was at the cat's level. "I'm glad you're alright," she said softly. Then she cocked her head to the side as if listening, as she did when she was hearing animals talk to her.

"Can you hear him in animal form?" Peter asked, curious.

"It would seem that I can," she answered, not taking her eyes off Nathaniel's cat ones.

Peter was silent for a few moments until he couldn't stand it anymore. "While this is a fascinating discovery, can you please tell me what is happening above?"

Silver finally turned to him, her eyes clouded over with a look that said she was still thinking about whatever Nathaniel had been saying to her. She shook her head as if trying to clear it, then replied, "We're in a small town. It looks like they'll be able to repair the ship for us. I'm hoping we're going to have enough to cover the cost of it."

Peter nodded, aware of the crew's meager funds. He had been hoping they would be able to go to another island to find something worth trading, but thus far they had only been running around avoiding bird people and now sea monsters. Hopefully, nothing else would get in their way and maybe the people of this town would take pity on them.

"Where's Aisling?" he asked.

"She's helping the men with the repairs. Luckily, she was unharmed in your dangerous maneuver."

"That's a positive," Peter answered, his heart quickening at the memory of her being so close to him. He could almost still feel her in his arms.

"Well, I'd better get back out there," Silver said, seemingly unaffected by Peter's emotional distress.

"Have fun," Peter grumbled as she made her way to the door.

"Stay in bed," she ordered, turning back to him as she opened the door.

"Wouldn't dream of doing otherwise," Peter replied, giving her a mock salute.

Silver rolled her eyes and closed the door behind her. As soon as she was gone, Peter made to rise again but was stopped by something furry and white that hopped onto the bed next to him.

"Oh, that's very good. Did she leave you to guard me then?" he asked the cat.

Nathaniel just looked at him with his large pale eyes. Then very catlike, he stepped on Peter's chest. "Ouch! Watch the claws!"

The cat just looked at him, and then gently rolled himself into a ball cuddled on Peter's chest. "You know this won't stop me. I could still get up if I wanted to."

Nathaniel just blinked at him and settled down more. Peter sighed, knowing that he probably should just stay put or Nathaniel could very well claw him or something. After all the excitement he was feeling tired. He closed his eyes and drifted off feeling the weight of the cat on his chest.

CHAPTER ELEVEN

Silver

The repairs on the ship were going much smoother than Silver had thought. The people of this town didn't get many visitors, especially not a barely floating ship that came hurling at them from across the sea. They were more than happy to help, which put Silver at ease. You never knew with a small town you happened upon. Sometimes, if you were desperate, they would take advantage of you, which had happened to Silver more times than she was comfortable confessing.

She stood at the main deck overseeing the work that was being done. Then was, almost knocked to her feet as something heavy landed on her shoulder, practically knocking her over.

Regaining her balance, she looked over to see what it was that had disturbed her. "I see you've made yourself comfortable," she said. Nathaniel in cat form was sitting on her shoulder. She felt his tail wrap around the other side of her neck for the stability, she figured. "I take it I won't have to worry about Peter?"

"He's sleeping," replied Nathaniel, looking at her with his big pale eyes.

His eyes were strange in his cat form. They had changed to look more cat-like with the extended pupil but, there was something still human about them.

"Thank you."

"For what?" asked the cat.

"Let's see where to start?" she said and began ticking off a finger one by one. "How about saving me, fighting the monster, and pushing us to safety?"

"I only did what anyone with my powers would've done."

"You don't know that," said Silver, not understanding where this modesty was coming from. What she had known about Nathaniel thus far was he was anything but modest. She felt the need for him to know how much he had done for them. "Someone with your powers might have just saved themselves. I don't think we would've made it without you."

Nathaniel shrugged in a decidedly not cat-like way and looked away towards the people working below.

"I am curious, of all the animals to pick, why a cat?" Silver asked.

"Cats are small and go unnoticed by most," he said, matter of factly. "People often underestimate cats. They're powerful hunters and master escape artists. I don't know," he said softly. "I just find myself attracted to the cat form."

"I see," she said, even though in truth she wasn't sure that she did see. "Why not turn back into a human afterward?"

His eyes grew cold. "I don't enjoy being a human. Too easy to lose control."

"So, in a weird way, this is your true form?"

He looked at her thoughtfully, his eyes losing their coldness. "I've never thought about it that way, but I suppose so. I've never felt much like myself when I'm a human. I somehow always felt slightly better as a cat."

"Well, if it's any consolation, I think I like you better as a cat," said Silver smiling. There was something raw about him in this form. There wasn't the ever-present mask or the grin he always hid behind. Maybe they could get along better like this.

Just then, there was a commotion from the lower decks. Silver's head snapped around until she found the source of the noise. One of her men was arguing loudly with the head of the suppliers from the town. Knowing nothing good could come from this, she made her way over to them.

"Gentlemen," she said when she was in range. "What seems to be the problem?"

"Captain, this brute is going back on our agreement!" exclaimed Biff. He was usually the one in charge of fixing the majority of the ship. He knew how much things should cost for fixing it and was put in charge of negotiations.

"Manners Biff," she chastised him. "Now why don't we discuss this like civilized people?" she asked, addressing the man before her.

He was tall and thick with a bald, shiny head. There wasn't anything particularly different about him, but he had an air of arrogance that Silver picked up on right away.

"Well now," he said with a horrible grin. "I knew this crew was funny but having a woman as a captain, I didn't even know you people could be civilized." His eyes traveled up and down her body.

While she had been used to people not taking her seriously because of her gender or crew, at least most people weren't so forward about it. Instead of cowering and covering herself from his disgusting gaze, she stood up straighter and glared at him. "We most certainly can be civilized, however, I am beginning to wonder if you can."

Anger flashed in his eyes, and the smile wiped clean off his face. She may have taken it too far, but he was asking for it.

"Why don't we discuss the payment," she continued. "We agreed to 10,000 was my understanding."

"Well, you understood wrong," he said, crossing his arms over his chest. "We want 30,000 and won't take any less."

Three times the amount they agreed on, goodness. "We won't do that," she replied calmly. "We'll do the 10,000 we agreed to."

"Not anymore. See, we agreed to the 10,000 when we thought an actual Captain was running this ship. We won't take anything less than 30,000 from the likes of you."

Biff let out a cry in outrage, and Silver held up a hand to stop him. "Are you any good at dueling?" She asked pleasantly as if they were discussing the weather.

"Am I? I'm the best in this town!" he boasted, puffing out his chest like a stuffed turkey.

"How about I make you a deal?"

"What sort of deal?"

"I challenge you to a duel, with swords. If you win, I'll pay 30,000. Now if I win, we pay 10,000."

"You!" he exclaimed looking shocked. "How can a woman fight?"

"Well, if you are afraid to lose to me, then we can just pay what we originally agreed to now."

"Fear has got nothing to do with it."

"Then are we in agreement?" she held out her hand to shake his.

He nodded, ignoring her hand in a blatant sign of disrespect. He turned and began shouting at his men to get him a sword, and Silver turned to Biff. "Never stoop to their level, Biff. We can be civilized even if they will not."

"Yes, Captain," he answered. "But the way he treated you! It was disgusting!"

"Agreed," she said, turning back towards the ship. "Well, let's go ahead and bring him to his knees, shall we?"

Biff nodded and ran off to assemble the crew. "Are you sure you know what you're doing?" asked Nathaniel, who was still perched on her shoulder through all of this.

"Yes," she answered, calmer than she felt. "This isn't the first time this has happened."

In less time than you'd think, Silver was in a circle of men facing "the brute" as Biff had dubbed him. She had dueled on several occasions, unfortunately for much of the same kind of reasons. The fact she was a woman made a lot of people not take her seriously.

Although Peter was the better swordsman, and she preferred the no-nonsense of her pistol, she knew the benefits of challenging someone to a duel. They wouldn't refuse for fear of their honor, and she was a capable swordsman, which usually took them by surprise. She was pretty good about sizing up her opponent before the fight, but she was unsure with this one.

They stood at the ready, swords drawn and placed in front of them. At John's mark, they began.

The man was fast, much faster than Silver thought was possible with his stocky frame. He lunged first, and she twisted to the side, just barely avoiding his attack. He got his footing and pressed his advantage, not letting up his attack for even a moment. She continued to dodge completely on the defensive, feeling like she was barely keeping up.

Predicting her next move, he moved right and then swung his sword to the left, cutting her arm and drawing blood. She hardly felt the pain but knew that now was the time to use her secret weapon. She changed hands, her sword now in her left and dominant hand, and pressed forwards, fighting with new strength.

She didn't usually have to change hands when fighting, so this man was good enough to need it. She pressed forwards with new vigor, taking the brute by surprise. With the last bit of fancy swordplay, she twisted her sword around his, disarming him. His sword flew blade over handle, which she gently caught in her right hand.

"I believe," she said panting and holding both swords at his throat, "That is the end of our duel."

His face was red, and he was shaking with rage. "You insolent wench! You cheated, the deal is off!"

"I didn't cheat," she said calmly. She was used to this kind of behavior from a defeated foe. "We have all these witnesses to prove so."

She looked around at the shocked faces of the men he employed and the gleeful ones of her crew. "Did any of you see any foul play?" When no one answered immediately she said, "Speak up!"

Still, no one answered. "There you see?" she said, turning back to the brute.

He wasn't taking this defeat easily. In one swift movement, he charged at her, for what Silver would never know since John stepped in his way before he could do anything. The man barreled into him as John put out a hand, grabbing the other man's hand and spinning him around while pinning the man's hands behind his back.

"I believe," said John, addressing the crowd in front of him. "That our duel has come to an end. Now if you'd all get back to work, and we shall be on our way."

There were laughs and cheers, mostly from Silver's crew, but she was surprised to see some of the other members of the brute's workers cheering as well. With that, the group disbanded and after John returned from escorting the man off her ship, he turned to Silver. "Why don't we get that arm checked out?"

Silver looked down, having completely forgotten about it, and saw her shirt completely soaked with blood. "It's just a scratch. It doesn't even hurt," she said as her arm gave a painful twang.

John inclined his head, "Even so, I would still like Cedric to take a look at it. For my peace of mind."

Silver conceded, and they walked below deck together but not before Aisling caught up with her. "That was some incredible swordplay! I've never seen anyone fight like that before!"

"Thank you, Aisling," she answered, genuinely pleased at the younger girl's reaction. Sometimes she forgot that Aisling was younger than her and Peter because she was always so stoic. But when Aisling was bouncing around her like an excited puppy, she showed her age. Silver didn't mind at all, she found it rather flattering that Aisling was impressed by her skill. After all, the girl could shoot electricity through her hands.

They continued below with John leading the way, and Silver and Aisling bringing up the rear. They walked into Silver's room right as Peter was sneakily trying to get off the bed. He looked up sheepishly at being caught, which quickly turned to worry as soon as he saw Silver and all the blood.

"She's alright," said John, always the mediator as they came into the room. "Just a scratch," he said with a grin back in Silver's direction.

"What happened?" Peter asked, the panic only slightly out of his voice.

"There was a sword fight and–"

"And Silver was amazing! It looked like she was losing. That's where she got the cut. But then she changed hands and flipped his sword over his head catching it with her other hand! It was incredible! Then he looked like he was going to charge her, so John took care of him," Aisling finished happily.

"Oh," Peter said, seeming to try to make sense of all the words that just came spewing out of Aisling's mouth. This was the most she had probably said in front of him. Which was good, Silver thought to herself. This meant that maybe they could open up to each other.

John sat Silver down on the chair by the window and rolled up her sleeve to show the cut. It was shallow but it was long, going from her shoulder down to her elbow. Luckily, Peter was distracted by Aisling, or he probably would have thrown a fit.

With an amused look, John leaned down to Silver and said, "I'm going to get Cedric, push this against the cut," he handed her a small cloth. Silver nodded, the pain of the cut throbbing slightly as she did as he said. "Oh, and Silver? Good fight," he gave her a wink and then was out the door.

Peter had completely missed this interaction as his attention was completely on Aisling, who had continued to talk animatedly. Silver was glad for this because it gave her a minute to gather her thoughts.

She was happy with the way the fight had gone but this kind of behavior happened quite a bit. Her crew was of all ages, shapes, and colors. This often led to people being less than accommodating or even being hostile towards them. Usually, this was something she could take care of by talking and being civil, but sometimes it did lead to some sort of violence. For some, being civil wasn't enough, and the only way to make people listen was through speaking a language they understood. Silver could handle it but it always left her slightly shaken.

The table she was sitting by moved slightly, and she looked over to see Nathaniel, still as a cat sitting there looking at her. "Where have you been?" she asked, quietly to not disturb Peter and Aisling's conversation across the room.

"Around," he answered. "Are you alright?"

She took a deep breath and let it out slowly, before answering. "I think so," she answered when she was sure she could answer him truthfully.

The cat nodded, seeming to understand. "It was very impressive."

She looked at him, trying to discern any sarcasm but he looked genuine. Well, as genuine as a cat can look. "Thank you."

They sat in silence for a little bit before Silver asked a question that had been bothering her. "Nathaniel, how long are you planning on staying as a cat?"

His tail flicked back and forth showing irritation. At least she thought so, you can never tell with cats. "For right now, this is how I'm most comfortable."

"If this is about this morning–"

"No," he interrupted. "It's more than that. I can't stay in control when I'm in human form. For now, this is how I'm choosing to be."

"Very well," she answered, dropping it. She knew there was probably more to it than he was letting on but she wanted to respect his space.

Just then Cedric bustled in with all of his medical supplies.

"For goodness' sake!" Silver exclaimed. "It's just a scratch, all of that isn't necessary."

"It is better to be safe than sorry, Captain. I, for one, would like to see you live long enough to get to a ripe old age. The only way this will happen is if we take every precaution. Now if you don't mind?" he finished his lecture and got to work on cleaning and bandaging her arm. She sat as still as possible, not wanting to upset him into another fit of lecturing.

After a few short moments, he had her arm all wrapped up, making her feel like a mummy but she didn't complain. "Thank you, Cedric."

"You're welcome. Now if only you and your brother," he said, shooting a look at Peter before looking back to her. "Would stop injuring yourselves, I think we would be a very happy crew indeed."

"Oh but then Cedric, you wouldn't have anyone to fuss over," Silver teased as she stretched her arm, getting used to the feeling of the bandages.

He looked as though he was going to retort when he seemed to notice Nathaniel for the first time. "Since when have we had a cat?"

Silver froze, realizing she didn't think of any stories to cover this up. "Must've wandered aboard at some point," she said, in what she hoped was a nonchalant way.

"Hm," he said, leaning forward and pushing his spectacles up to inspect the cat further. Nathaniel decided at that moment was the perfect time to begin licking himself thoroughly. "Yes, well," said Cedric, wrinkling his nose and straightening back up. "And where did that other fellow go? The new one, I think his name was Nathaniel."

Silver's heart dropped, right when she thought she was out of the woods. "He's around here somewhere, I haven't seen him since this morning."

"Well, let's try to keep an eye out for him. I'd hate for him to slip off the ship when we aren't looking."

With that he turned and walked out of the room, carrying all of his unused supplies with him. As soon as he was out of the room, Silver felt herself sink with relief. It was going to be harder than she thought to explain how a cat was on board and what happened to Nathaniel. Some of her crew members might start asking questions as well unless she came up with a convincing story.

She decided not to worry about it at the moment. After all, she was safe and so was her crew so, all was well as far as she was concerned. She looked over at Nathaniel and said, "You know, I think I like you better as a cat."

He cocked an eyebrow at her, which was impressive in cat form, but said nothing in reply. They sat quietly together as Peter was distracted by Aisling's chatter off to the side, both lost in their thoughts.

CHAPTER TWELVE

Peter

The next couple of days passed by quickly for Peter. He spent the first day resting and waiting for his injured leg to heal, which it did by the second day. Feeling good as new, he was up and back to his usual antics. His main job when he was back on his feet was to oversee the ship's repairs.

While he and Aisling had a moment together when Silver had been injured, he had gone back to avoiding her. He still didn't trust his feelings, and after being so close to her, and touching her, he didn't think it was a good idea to try and get close to her again.

Luckily, repairing the ship was no small feat. It took a team of strong men and several days to get all the repairs done, even though the ship was on the smaller side. Aisling was in awe of everything they did, and he saw her asking all the crew about everything they were doing.

"How are things going?" Peter asked, slapping Biff on the shoulder.

"They're going well! Especially since Silver showed everyone we weren't to be messed with," Biff smiled at the memory.

Just as Biff was saying this, Gwane snuck up behind him and grabbed the other man around the waist. Biff jumped, almost knocking Gwane over, who just held on and laughed.

"Well, hello to you, too," Peter grumbled as Gwane laughed.

"You scared me! What if I had lashed out not knowing who you were?" Biff asked Gwane, who just shrugged.

"Then I probably would have deserved it," Gwane kissed Biff on the cheek, already forgiven.

"You should be more careful, Biff. More aware of your surroundings," Peter said, continuing the teasing. "I am always aware of my surroundings. You won't see people sneaking up on me easily."

"What're you all doing?"

Peter jumped and turned. Silver was standing directly behind him. Aisling was standing behind Silver and looked like she was trying unsuccessfully not to laugh.

Peter cleared his throat to be heard over the two men who had burst into laughter. "We're watching over the repairing of the ship. I think things are almost done."

"That's excellent news," said Silver, smiling. Both Biff and Gwane gave a wave and got back to work. It was just then that Peter noticed the white cat that was sitting on her shoulder.

"Do you go anywhere without him?" he asked, referring to Nathaniel.

Silver looked at the cat, almost seeming to forget that he was even there. "Well, he likes sitting there, and I don't mind his presence. He has a lot to tell me, and it's easier to hear him when he's closer to my ear."

"Ah, well, as long as he doesn't watch you change or anything."

"Peter!" exclaimed Silver, her cheeks growing red at his words.

"Come now Peter, we both know Silver wouldn't do that," said Aisling.

"Thank you, Aisling," Silver answered.

"And for all of Nathaniel's bravado, I honestly don't think he would either."

The cat inclined his head towards her in a movement of gratitude. "We all need to trust each other."

"I'm working on it," Peter grumbled, feeling attacked by everyone.

Just then, there was a commotion from the workers. The group looked over and saw there were a group of county guards heading towards the ship. There was a group of maybe ten or so, which was unusual in the best of circumstances.

County guards were what they sounded like. They were guards that were supposed to keep the county safe from invaders as well as deal with petty crimes in the area. They usually weren't trained as much as warriors if at all, and if there was an issue two or max three would show up. The fact there were about ten of them made everyone on the ship wary.

As they got closer, Peter saw they were led by a middle-aged man who was balding and looked like he spent most of his time eating. He was grinning triumphantly and was leading the guards directly to their ship.

Peter looked over at his sister, who had a look of concern on her face. John had materialized out of nowhere and was standing at Silver's side, quietly showing his strength.

The man practically skipped up the pier. The guards followed in his wake.

"We meet again," said Silver pleasantly, her stance showing nothing but ease. "Is this a courtesy call or did you have something else in mind?" she not so subtly rested her hand on her pistol that was always strapped to her side.

"I have come to take you into custody," the man said joyfully, crossing his arms over his chest.

"What're the charges against me?"

He handed her a letter that she opened slowly. "We come with the following charges against you and your crew: disturbance of the peace, piracy, you've stolen property from me, and," he said with a flourish, "For stealing this ship from its rightful owner."

Peter cried out in anger and pulled his sword from his belt. "Silver has done no such things," he growled, his vision turning red.

"Doesn't matter if she has or not," said the man with an evil grin. "It's my word against hers, and frankly no one will believe a woman. We're here to take her away."

Silver finished reading the letter and calmly folded it. "To address these allegations against me: I have not disturbed the peace any more than any other ship in this port. The only thing I stole from you was your pride, and this ship was given to me by a very dear friend who is no longer with us. That being said, I'm afraid that I won't be going with you."

"That's not an option," he said, grinning all the more broadly. "You'll either come willingly, or we'll take you by force."

Silver looked at John who gave a slight nod, and then at Peter whose grip tightened on his sword. "Well," she said, addressing the group before her. "I'm afraid we don't have an option." With that, she pulled out her sword and charged the guards who weren't expecting this sort of full-frontal attack. Peter, who was itching for a fight, jumped right in front of the ringleader.

"Ah, well, it looks like the brother of the swine has come to defend his poor sister," said the man with a belittling grin.

"Oh, trust me, she can take care of herself," he answered with an easy swagger in his movements. "This fight is for me."

"Oh really?" said the man, still cocky.

"You see," Peter began as the two of them began circling one another. While his leg wasn't perfectly healed, it was well enough for this. After all that time sitting still over the past couple of days made him twitchy and ready for a fight. "I have a problem with people who have money and power and use those two things against people who are different from them. When rich white men come with false allegations and guards to do their dirty work, see that does something to a man."

"Let's hope you're as good as your sister. I won't go down without a fight."

"Trust me," said Peter with a grin. "She is better at many more things than me, but sword fighting is my specialty." With that, he lunged and the fight began.

While most people may have used talking as a way to stall, Peter knew everything he needed to know about the man before him. He could tell from his movements that he was quicker than he looked, but favored his right leg ever so slightly, something someone less observant may not have noticed. He also had some form of training from a school, although it wasn't very good.

Peter pressed his advantage, making the man on the defensive for the entirety of the fight. It lasted mere seconds before Peter easily twisted the sword out of the other man's hand and caught it easily. The man looked shocked then turned red in anger, shame filling his features.

"Well, that certainly was quick," said Peter, twirling the other man's sword around like a toy. "How about the best two out of three?" he threw the sword back to the man, which he almost didn't catch, then the battle began again.

This time Peter held back, letting the anger from the man fuel his movements. He only raised his sword to defend, not to attack back in return. He could hear the sounds of the battle with the guards across the deck, but they sounded as if they were somehow far away; he kept his attention on the man.

He twisted and hit the man behind with the flat end of his sword, not going for harm but humiliation. "Come on now, surely you can do better than that," he said, as the man came barreling towards him, which he avoided easily. "Now you're just getting sloppy."

The man was starting to run out of steam, which Peter saw as good a time as any to begin his final attack. He hit him fast and with precision, leaving the man completely unprepared for where his next attack would come from. Blood began to drip from the man's arms and face as Peter's wicked sword cut into him.

"One cut for every insult you have given me and my sister," said Peter as a blur as he danced around the man. Once the man was barely holding onto his sword through exhaustion and blood loss, Peter finally unarmed him again.

The man fell to his knees gasping for breath. He looked up at Peter with a hatred that went beyond the embarrassment of losing. "Well, finish it, then!" he shouted.

"No, I don't think I will," said Peter in an utter calm almost like he hadn't just had a sword fight but had been discussing the weather. "See, there is something I need from you."

"I would rather die than do anything for a pig like you," the man spat.

Peter was inches away from his face before the man had time to even draw another breath. "That may still be an option," said Peter in a dangerous voice. "However, killing you will bring me no pleasure, and you are far more useful to me alive." He leaned back and held both swords to the man's throat. "Now here is what you're going to do: you'll drop all allegations against me and my sister, you will turn from your ways of sexism and deceit, and in return, we'll never visit your village again."

"And if I refuse?"

"Well, you've got a long swim to think it over," answered Peter with a grin.

The man flinched, a look of pure horror on his face. The guards were gone and the ship was currently a few meters away from the port. The crew around him cheered and began to haul the man up and over the side of the ship. The man screamed as he hit the water below, causing everyone aboard to laugh.

Silver came up to Peter and threw her arms around him in an embrace. "Thank you," she whispered in his ear, emotion heavy in her voice.

"Anytime," he said, giving her a squeeze before releasing her. "It's a good thing they had just finished repairing the ship, or else this story might have had a slightly different ending."

Silver laughed and shook her head. She gave his shoulder one more squeeze before walking away. Peter watched her go, glad that he was able to defend his sister, even though she was perfectly able to defend herself.

CHAPTER THIRTEEN

Silver

Silver was sitting at her desk in her chambers. She seemed to be spending a lot of time there these days. It wasn't exactly that she was hiding from her crew, but she was hiding from her crew. She was embarrassed about what had happened. It wasn't because of her gender but she hated that these kinds of things happened way more often than she ever wanted them to.

She heard the soft patter of paws as Nathaniel jumped up on her desk. "What's wrong, Silver?" he asked, blinking his cat eyes at her.

Silver sighed, but knowing he wouldn't stop asking, she answered, "I'm just lost in thought I guess."

"Those kinds of interactions happen often, don't they?" he asked, seeming to read her thoughts.

She nodded and looked out the window, unable to face him or anyone right now. "If the crew had a different captain this wouldn't be an issue."

"The crew wouldn't be here if they had a different captain."

Her eyes snapped back to his. There was no sarcasm or hints of deceit in his eyes, only genuine concern and seriousness. "You put this crew together. You gave them a new life and reason for living when no one else would. Can you honestly tell me that someone else would've given them that?"

Silver was quiet. She didn't want to answer him, even though she knew in her heart he was right. "Look," he said, never breaking eye contact. "What happened was handled, and those who handled it were happy to do it because they love you."

She felt tears prick the back of her eyes, and her throat closed over. How embarrassing to now be crying because of the words of a cat. He was more than a cat which they both knew, but still. Crying was not something Silver was comfortable with.

She looked back towards the window, trying to hide her tears from him. She heard a soft noise, almost like a sigh, and felt something soft on her chin turning her head to face him.

Bright blue eyes stared into silver ones as she realized with a gasp that he had somehow turned human again. "People are going to reject things they don't understand because that's easier than growing. The only way to change the system is by being different. We'll get there someday, but Silver, you can't let them get you down. Keep fighting. Don't let anyone make you feel ashamed of who you are."

The tears were falling now, she could feel them making trails down her cheeks as his words washed over her. He wrapped his arms around her, and she let the tears fully take her, shedding them for all the hate she had experienced and how utterly exhausted she was for people treating her in such a hostile way.

They stayed there for several minutes, his steady heartbeat against her cheek, and her arms wrapped tightly around him, fully allowing herself to feel everything. After the tears had stopped, she stayed in his embrace not wanting the moment to end. But like all good things, he pulled back, breaking the spell.

"Thank you," she said, shakily once he was a few steps away.

"You're welcome," he answered, continuing to look at her. His handsome face was riddled with concern, but she felt much better. Sometimes tears need to be shed for the healing to happen.

He was so handsome. She had almost forgotten his face that looked like it had been shaped by angels. Sounds dramatic, but she found herself slightly tongue-tied for the first time being around him. It had been so long since she had seen him as a human, that now she didn't know what to do with it.

An uncomfortable sort of awkwardness settled over the both of them, each for their separate reasons. He cleared his throat. "I guess I'll leave you to your thoughts, Captain," he said, and before she could object, he gave a small bow while turning into a cat before her eyes, speeding out of the room.

She stood but didn't reach him in time before he left. Crossing over to the door, she closed it softly. What was that? Maybe the moment they had was all in her head. Maybe he had just been waiting for her to stop crying before he felt like he could leave. After all, he had been the first one to pull away.

Sitting back down, she looked out the window, feeling somehow better and worse at the same time.

Silver wiped the sweat pouring off her face with her shirt sleeve. While there was a nice breeze blowing off the water, the sun was hot today and was beating down on her. She did her best to keep the Silver Shadow in shape, but the briny air wasn't good for anything over long periods.

Her ship still needed constant maintenance. While it was something she could always pass off to someone in her crew, she enjoyed the hard labor. It kept her hands busy, and it was good to have something to do. The only thing was, she wished it kept her brain busy.

As of late, her thoughts always seemed to turn to Nathaniel. She hadn't seen much of him since their last conversation. She knew he was still on the ship because she would occasionally hear snippets of conversations from the crew discussing how a white cat had snuck aboard. If she was being honest with herself, which she wasn't, she would admit she missed him.

Whether as a cat or a human, she missed his conversations and his presence.

A huge shadow blocked the sun from her for a moment. She didn't even have to turn to know who was standing behind her. "Hello John," she said, without turning. "Thank you for being my sun shield."

She heard him chuckle as he knelt beside her. "You could've someone else work on this," he said, leaning down to check her handy work. She had been trying and maybe failing to fix one of the railings that had begun rotting. It was one of the many things that hadn't quite gotten done after their last repair.

"I know," she said, leaning back, rubbing the tense muscles in her neck and shoulders. "But I would rather do it."

John nodded, not questioning her. "Quite a bit of our repairs were rushed."

"Yes," she answered, rolling her shoulders. "We could always use some new supplies, and it may be time to find a new buyer for the stone as well."

"I may be able to help you there."

Her head snapped up, and she looked at John. "You can?"

"There's an island. Its location is secret. But it has buyers who may be interested."

"Where would this mysterious island be?"

When he didn't answer right away and wouldn't meet her eyes, Silver's heart sank. "John? Please don't tell me it's where I think it is."

"We need supplies. Come on Silver, you're not still afraid of the place are you?"

"No," she answered too fast, and they both knew it.

"That was a long time ago."

"I know but that doesn't–"

"You were much younger than. And you weren't the captain of your ship."

"Sure but–"

"Silver," John's voice was soft, but it stopped her in her tracks. "We need help."

For John to say that must've meant they were in much worse shape than she had thought. She debated a moment longer, with John sitting next to her, not saying anything.

"Fine," she huffed out a breath. "But I want you there beside me. I don't know what's going to happen."

"I wouldn't have it any other way, Captain," he added with one of his rare smiles.

CHAPTER FOURTEEN

Peter

"We're doing this?"

"Yes, Peter."

"I mean. To see *him.* I thought you hated him."

Silver gave a long exasperated sigh. "No Peter. I don't hate him."

They were gearing up to go ashore. Much to Peter's dismay.

"Didn't he throw you in jail?"

"Just the once," Silver answered, not meeting his eyes.

"Isn't once enough?"

Finally, Silver looked up at him, her silver eyes had an edge to them, but they were also tired. For a moment he saw how worn down she really was. How long had it been since he had looked at his sister? He could see the slight bend in her shoulders like she was carrying the weight of the world. But there was something else in her eyes, something that he had only seen in wild animals who had gone too long without food: desperation.

"It's that bad then?" he asked. Silver looked away from him again, enough of a confirmation. "Right then," Peter squared his shoulders. "I'll have John stay with the ship. After, all as the first mate, I–"

"Peter, I don't know if–"

"Are we ready?" asked John as he peered in from the above deck.

"Yes, although I believe Peter had something he wished to tell you," Silver said, trying to keep a straight face.

John looked over at Peter expectantly. Peter swallowed. It wasn't that he was afraid of John, even if the man was twice his size. But when John had decided something, it was like trying to move a mountain.

"I wanted to ask if you were ready," Peter mumbled as he pushed past him. Silver's laugh followed him out.

The landing party gathered on the main deck. It currently consisted of himself, John, and Silver. Although Peter had thrown a fit, they had left their weapons in Silver's chambers. While this had made Peter feel all the more vulnerable, and he hated it, he did as he was told. Silver always had a reason for what she did, even if he had no idea what she was thinking.

"But I don't understand," Aisling was saying to Silver. "Why can't I come? Did I do something wrong?"

Peter kept his eyes forwards, keeping his eyes on the other people who were moving around the docks and away from Aisling.

"It's just too dangerous," Silver was saying.

"We just defeated a sea monster," Aisling argued.

"Right, but this is a different kind of threat. Sea monsters are one thing, but the people who frequent this island are not people you should involve yourself with. This is just to keep you safe."

Peter saw a white flash over to his right, and there was Nathaniel, still in cat form. He was sitting on the railing blinking up at him.

"What?" Peter asked, in a rough voice.

The cat looked over at Aisling and then back at him.

"You heard Silver, it's not a good idea for her to come."

The cat seemed to raise an eyebrow at him. If cats even had eyebrows.

"I'm not going to let you make me feel guilty. If Silver says no, then that means no."

Pushing back from the ship's railing, Peter walked down to the platform. He felt the cat's eyes boring into his back, but he didn't turn.

Silver joined him shortly after, followed by John. "Ready?" she asked, just as three more people swung down.

"What're you three doing?" Peter crossed his arms over his chest.

"What?" asked Biff, trying unsuccessfully to look innocent.

"Can't two people go and show a younger pup around?" Gwane swung an arm around a sheepish-looking Tom.

Silver sighed heavily but gave in. "Fine, be back in an hour."

"Aye, Captain!" Biff gave an overly dramatic salute and the three of them turned.

"Keep him safe!" Silver called.

They gave a wave over their shoulders. Tom was still under Gwane's arm, and as Peter watched them, he saw Biff wrap an arm around Gwane's waist before they were swallowed up by the crowd. He hoped they would keep an eye on young Tom.

"Well, then. Shall we?" Silver asked, leading the way through the crowd.

The Island of Lidon was interesting, to say the least. Besides being a pirate town, they also were somehow protected. This was the one place the disease hadn't spread. No one wore face coverings or any sort of protection. And even though people came and went, no one seemed to get sick.

Lidon was above all, a place to share stories, trade, and get into whatever mischief anyone could desire. There was only one rule here: don't upset the Kri siblings. They were a brother and sister duo. Similar to how Peter and Silver were, which is why they had become friends.

Had, being past tense. Peter still didn't entirely know what happened, but the brother had thrown Silver in their family dungeon a couple of years ago.

Just as he was thinking this, he saw a flash of red over his right shoulder. Turning, he saw Aisling hurrying behind a clothing stall. Breaking off from Silver and John, Peter made a beeline towards the stall.

As he got closer, he saw a flash of white, meaning Nathaniel was also off the ship. His stomach began to bubble as anger filled him. By the time he got over to the stall, he was full-on angry.

"What the hell are you doing?" he asked, causing Aisling to jump. "Both of you," he glared at the cat who only blinked in reply.

"I wanted to see the town," Aisling answered. "Everyone else got to go."

"Right, but Aisling, you aren't like everyone else."

Hurt danced across her eyes before being replaced with anger. "You think I'm weak. That I can't fend for myself."

"Well, you didn't grow up like us and–"

"So what? That makes me somehow inferior to you?"

"No! It's–"

"Look I already know how you feel about me, so you don't have to spell it out. But I thought Silver saw my worth. I just wanted to help."

To his horror, he saw big fat tears beginning to fill her eyes. It wasn't the tears that scared him, women or men crying didn't bother him. But it was the fact that Aisling felt like he didn't like her, and she had to pull her weight. He saw the same need to prove herself that he had.

She turned away from him, with one angry jerk of her head. He sighed, rubbing the back of his neck, trying to figure out what to say.

"Well, what do we have here?"

Peter turned, keeping Aisling behind him as he turned towards the new voice.

"Why hello," Peter said, in a well-practiced casual voice. The man in front of him was tall, much taller than Peter's five feet eight inches. He was wearing normal clothing, except for the insignia on his vest. It was of a snake making a figure eight, with no ending or beginning. "What are the odds? We were just coming to see your bosses."

The other man didn't look amused or at ease. "You'll come now," was all he said.

At the sound of footsteps, Peter turned to see another appeared and stood behind Aisling. "Right, we'll just follow you then, shall we?"

Both men said nothing but one stood in front of them and the other behind them, leading them out from behind the stalls. Just as they were passing the first stall, Peter saw a flash of white, before disappearing behind one of the large stalls behind them.

The two men led them through the town. Peter kept his eyes peeled, but saw no sign of John and Silver. Maybe if they were lucky they hadn't been caught like Aisling and himself.

They reached a huge mansion. At first glance, it seemed like any other nice house that was in this neighborhood. But the closer one got, the more the details would pop out.

The large, black iron gate iron bars that looked strange and uneven at first turned out to be writhing snakes that were enchanted to move. They slithered through and around each other, blurring the grounds from view.

As they passed through the gate, Peter saw a strange simmering, meaning that there was another enchantment to keep people out. He had once witnessed someone who didn't have permission to enter get eaten by the metal snakes. It wasn't pretty.

Once through, he noticed the green grass and hedges were cut to look like snakes. These didn't move, but that didn't make them any less intimidating. The mansion itself had a black roof, and black outlining but the walls themselves were a deep purple. The front door was black as well as the dark snake knocker, which also slithered around the door in a perfect figure eight.

Before either man reached for it, the door swung inward, revealing a long, dark hallway. Everything inside the house was black trimmed with purple, opposite to the outside. Because the dark interior made everything dim with shadows that pulled long over the four of them.

They were led to a large, purple door on their right, and one of them knocked. At the stoic "Enter," that followed, the two men opened the door and unceremoniously pushed Peter and Aisling into the room.

The room was wrapped in deep purple velvet drapes that hung on the walls, blocking any windows or forms of light. There was a small raised dais in the far corner, and there were the two Kri siblings, draped across the two chairs that were on the raised platform, looking like kings.

"Well, fancy meeting you here," Peter began, before feeling a well-aimed kick in his back. He fell to his knees as the person behind him gripped his hands behind, restraining him. "You will not speak unless they give you permission!" the voice behind him spat.

"Now, now, Diamond," Peter couldn't see anything from this vantage point, but he would recognize Flora's deep, smooth silk voice anywhere. "Is that any way to treat our guests?"

The person holding him loosened their grip enough that he could lift his head. Flora had gotten up from her throne and was slowly making her way towards him. "Ah Peter, it's been a while."

Flora was beautiful, with long, dark hair that hung down her back to her waist, and dark eyes that could swallow you up. With full lips and fuller hips, she was a beauty. Peter had a crush on her, but that was a long time ago.

"And it looks like everyone is here!" She turned away from him as he was able to get a glimpse of John, who was tied up with a nasty purple bruise blooming across his face, and Silver, who was kneeling next to him.

"I believe we banned you," came the rich voice of Daz Kri, the leader. He had the same dark eyes and hair as his sister, but was a huge man, well over six feet tall and built like a bull. He was still lounging on his throne, with the look like a tiger who was about to pounce. "So, why would you show your face here again?"

He was addressing Silver who looked stoic in her kneeling position. "We have something you might be interested in."

"Oh? And what could you possibly have that would interest me?"

"It's an orb, one that could be charged enough to power your whole island."

The silence at these words stretched for what felt like a century, but was in reality, was only a few moments.

"An orb, you say?" Daz scratched his chin thoughtfully. "And I would imagine you'd want something in return for this magical artifact? Payment I would imagine?"

"Only what you think it would be worth," Silver answered.

Daz let out a huge booming laugh, which did nothing to ease the rising tension. "It's a pity what happened between us," he glanced at Peter and seeing the look of surprise on his face he continued. "Oh, you didn't know? Yes, we were quite close, to your sister and I. Until she stabbed me in the back. I had gotten word of a very rare artifact being moved in an unassuming ship. They thought if they didn't look threatening, they may be able to make it to their town. But Silver here heard about the artifact and the unassuming ship, went behind my back and took it from me," his eyes were blazing with an unreleased fury.

"And now she comes waltzing into town, like she didn't steal from me, and wants to sell me an artifact? Does that seem like a fair deal?"

"We didn't mean offense. We only thought you could use it," Silver answered.

"Docile doesn't suit you. And I don't think we'll be making a deal."

"Didn't the Cleansers tell us about an artifact that went missing?" asked Flora, coming back to stand next to her brother.

Peter's heart dropped. "You know the Cleansers?"

"But of course, how do you think we've avoided Arak so far? It's not by luck. It's by a deal. Now then," Daz rose from his chair, the platform making his already impressive form even larger. "As I recall, they were also missing a redhead," Daz's eyes found Aisling who had been left standing behind Peter.

Peter wrenched out of Diamond's hands, jumped to his feet and rushed Daz. Lucky for him, no one had been expecting this. He threw his fist which connected to Daz's jaw. Daz's head was thrown back, with a satisfying crack. Then Peter felt hands on him, restraining him and dragging him off the platform.

"I see you have just as much fire as your twin," Daz said, rubbing his jaw. He gave a nod to one of the people holding Peter. Someone forced his head down, exposing his neck. There was a small pinch on the back of Peter's neck as something stabbed into his skin.

Just then there was a loud commotion in the hallway.

"What the hell is going on?" asked Daz, as he gestured to one of his goons. They opened the door only to go down.

"Sorry we're late," Nathaniel stepped into the room, with his customary grin in place. "Took a while to find someone who could let us in."

Behind him were a scared but excited-looking Tom, Gwane, who was cracking his knuckles, and Biff, who looked ready for a fight.

After that, it was pure chaos. The guards holding onto Peter released him, to join in the fight. Biff tossed him his sword, giving him a grin before racing off to punch one of the goons in the face. Peter fought his way to where he last saw Aisling, who was doing pretty well for herself, blasting anyone who came close to her with her strange, green energy.

Both Daz and Flora had disappeared, and in a moment, Silver and John were by Peter's side. "Let's go!" Silver shouted above the ensuing chaos.

Their troops ran for it. As they passed the door to the mansion, Peter noticed it seemed to have been blasted open, the snakes were no longer slithering around. Before he could think too much about it, he heard gunshots from behind him, which pushed him to run even faster.

Back through the city, they ran, with John leading the way, and Nathaniel and Peter taking up the rear. "Thanks for that," Peter panted as they ran. "Did you break the enchantment? How did you know where to find us?"

"I knew they worked for the Cleansers," Nathaniel answered as they ran, hardly seeming winded at all. "When I saw them take you, I figured you could use some rescuing."

They rounded the corner and were surprised to see nothing or no one blocking their way. Making it to the ramp, they ran up to the ship, which had already been prepped to sail. Catching his breath, Peter leaned on the railing, watching as the island began to get smaller and smaller. No one was following them.

"Does anyone else think it's weird that they aren't pursuing us?" he asked to no one in particular. He turned to see that Cedric was fussing over John's bruise and everyone else was going about their normal sailing tasks. Feeling something brush his leg, he saw Nathaniel back in cat form, looking up at him with concerned eyes.

"It probably doesn't mean anything, after all, we shouldn't question some good luck, huh?" he smiled at Nathaniel who just continued to look at him. Shrugging, he began to make his way over to the rest of the group.

As he was walking, he felt himself stumble. It felt like the whole ship had been pushed to the side by a large wave. No one else seemed to have felt it but him, so he shook himself off and continued his way on board.

After a few more steps, there was another rocking that brought him to his knees. His head felt heavy, like someone was packing bags of sand in it. The deck of the ship swam before his vision, causing him to collapse. He heard someone call his name, but dizziness had taken over and was pulling him under its spell. He tried to fight it for as long as he could, but after struggling in vain for a few moments, the darkness overtook him.

CHAPTER FIFTEEN

Silver

Silver paced outside of her chamber. She was unsure why they always end up using her chambers for injuries, but this was the least of her worries. Aisling leaned against one of the walls with her arms crossed over her chest, looking uncharacteristically grim. Silver couldn't stand still. She felt twitchy, like a caged animal, waiting for any news.

Suddenly, the door to her chamber opened, admitting a serious-looking Cedric. "Well?" she demanded before he had even taken one foot out the door.

Taking his time, he closed the door and faced her square on. "It's not good, Silver."

Her heart plummeted, feeling as though it had been plunged into ice water. She knew the news must be bad if he was using her name instead of her title. "What do you mean?"

He took off his spectacles, cleaning them and no doubt stalling for time. Replacing them on his nose, he spoke, "Silver, I'm sorry, but he has it."

"Enough of this," she said, not even trying to hide the panic in her voice. "Speak plainly. I want to hear you say it. What does he have?"

"Arak. The disease," he answered with defeat clear in his voice.

"No," Silver whispered, feeling her knees give out from under her. Aisling caught her, with surprising strength.

"How?" Aisling asked, addressing Cedric. Silver felt like they were underwater, but she was able to make out what they were saying.

"There is a small incision in the back of his neck," Cedric said with medical coldness. "It seems to have been injected into his neck. With that direct of an infection, it took quickly."

Those damn Kris, Silver thought, remembering them sticking something in the back of Peter's neck. If only she had been faster, or smarter. Despair began to cover her like a wool blanket.

"Mourn when there is something to mourn," Aisling whispered in her ear. "For now, let's hope."

Silver shoved back from her, her confusion and pain coming out in anger. "What do you mean to hope? There's nothing to hope for! My brother is–" her voice caught, but she pressed on. "My brother is dying. What is hopeful about that?"

"I've heard of a place," said Aisling slowly, and calmly. "A place that brings healing. It… it might be just the thing to cure him."

"Cure him? Have you lost your mind! There's no cure! That's the whole problem with this disease! If you have it, you'll die! End of story!"

"You're wrong," Aisling said with an utter calm that Silver found infuriating. "The Cleansers talked about a place. A place that could bring the cure of this disease. A place of healing. It's one of the places that they were desperate to find, but were unable to."

Against her better judgment, Silver was beginning to feel a small hope blossom in her chest. "And you know where this magically healing place is?"

"No," Aisling held up a hand to quiet Silver's outcry. "But I know how we can get there."

"Stop speaking in riddles!" Silver said, throwing her arms up in frustration. "How can you possibly know this?"

"I–" Aisling broke off, finally starting to show some kind of emotion in all of this. She took a breath to steady herself, then said, "There's something about my…gift I haven't told you."

"Oh really? And now is a good time?" said Silver, her frustration coming back in a whoosh.

"Perhaps not in this hallway," she answered, making a meaningful head gesture in Cedric's direction.

Silver, who had completely forgotten about Cedric during this exchange, addressing him said, "Thank you, Cedric, I don't think we'll be needing you right now."

"I don't mean to disregard you as Captain," he said seriously. "But this conversation is getting interesting, and I feel you may need my expertise in the subject of this disease."

"Fine. Does anyone else need to join this meeting?" she asked sarcastically.

"I think John should be there and Nathaniel as well," he had the answer ready as if waiting for her question.

She pinched the bridge of her nose. Nathaniel was the last person she wanted to see right now. "And where will we have this meeting? The usual place is otherwise occupied."

"How about the kitchen?" suggested Aisling. "I'm sure Sam is trustworthy and would like to be kept in the loop."

"Fine," Silver said again, feeling like she was losing all control in this situation. "I want the rest of the crew left in the dark on this," she said, thinking there was no need to start a massive panic. "Shall we meet in half an hour?"

Everyone agreed to this and scuttled off to find the other members of their meeting. Silver stayed behind and looked over at the closed door. "Hang in there, Peter," she whispered. "Hang in there."

Half an hour later, Silver found herself seated at a small table with a cup of untouched tea in front of her. She faced the small group in front of her, consisting of a calm-looking John, Cedric, and Aisling as well as Sam, who had seated himself next to a surprisingly human Nathaniel.

John was sitting next to Cedric with the bruise now clear on his face from where the man had punched him.

She had often wondered if something was going on between Cedric and John. It wasn't so much that they were obvious, more of just a leaning in towards one another. But now was not the time to be thinking about this. She sighed, knowing they were waiting for her to start this meeting.

"Well," she began, tired and feeling wrung out like an old rag. "Let me get straight to the point: Peter has Arak, and Aisling thinks there may be a cure for it."

She gestured to Aisling while the rest of the group sat in tense silence. "I have a rare gift. I can see things when I am in a meditative state," Aisling began slowly. "This isn't something that happens all that often, and I can't control when I will get a vision."

"What are your visions usually of?" asked John, curiously.

So they don't think she's mad, that's good to know, thought Silver filing that information away for later.

"Usually of places, or specifically one place," Aisling answered. "It's a stunning forest, the light filters down through the trees. I can hear woodland creatures rustling around, and there's a clearing ahead of me.

"When I break through the trees, I see a large fire burning and a man sitting on a log. I can't see his face because his back is turned to me. But there is something about him that feels so familiar. I've felt this way since the very first vision, that familiarity. I don't know if I can explain it better than that, but I've always wanted to go there. I just didn't know how to, until now."

"What do you mean?" asked Silver.

"Last night, I had another vision, this time it was different," explained Aisling slowly. "A pure white dolphin came to the deck of the ship."

Silver's eyes flashed to Nathaniel, who kept his eyes fixed on Aisling.

"The dolphin took me across the sea to a forest. In this forest, there was a pure white stage waiting for me. I jumped on his back, and he took me to the clearing. I think…" she trailed off, then taking a deep breath said, "I think this was a sign and I was hoping you might've some information for me," she said, addressing Nathaniel.

Nathaniel's arms were crossed over his chest, and although he was sitting in what seemed to be a relaxed matter, Silver could tell he was tense. "I don't know of any white animals. I'm not sure I'm the right person to talk to."

"But if there are other white animals then, maybe they're part of your people!" exclaimed Silver, remembering too late that both Cedric and John were in the room. She cringed, glancing over at them out of the corner of her eye to see their reaction. Or rather lack thereof. Neither reacted at all to her words. Leading her to believe that perhaps they knew more than they let on.

"It's possible," Nathaniel conceded. "I've never met anyone else like me."

"Well then, what do we do now?" asked Silver.

"My only other idea involves you," answered Aisling calmly. "I was hoping you could reach out and find the dolphin."

"I've never tried for a specific animal before," said Silver, her stomach clenching at thc thought. "And how do you know that this man will even help you? Or that he heals? Have you seen him do any healing in your visions?"

"No, but anytime I go there in my head, I feel rejuvenated. It's a place of healing, I can feel it."

"So, we're basing this entire operation on finding a magical dolphin and a feeling?"

"Do you have any better ideas?" asked Aisling, her temper finally starting to rise.

Silver took a breath to calm herself before saying anything she would regret. "Have you heard of any place like this?" she asked John.

He sat quietly for a moment, thinking before answering, "Yes, actually. Many books talk about a place of healing in an unknown forest. The problem is, no one can find it. The stories always involve people coming across it by accident, or the forest somehow finding them."

"And the man? Are there any stories about him?"

He was nodding before she finished her sentence. "Yes, in the forest there is usually a man. He has many different names depending on what story you're reading but there are two things that are the same. The forest and the man. Usually, the man has some kind of healing powers, but that power isn't in all of them."

"Thank you, John," she said, feeling a little better about the validity of Aisling's vision. "How much longer does he have?" she asked, turning to Cedric.

"Not long, I'm afraid," he said, stiffly. "Two, three days at most. His eyes have already grown black."

Silver pinched the bridge of her nose, feeling the weight of responsibility pushing down heavy on her shoulders. Everyone was sitting quietly, waiting for her decision on this. "Alright," she said finally. "I'll do it."

Another half-hour passed while they made preparations. Everyone else had enormous faith in her ability to find the white dolphin. She, on the other hand, had less faith in herself. She had never called on one specific animal before, so she had no idea how this was going to work.

She made her way to the deck of the ship and leaned on the railing, feeling the cool night breeze on her face. She could almost feel the salt as the soft wind played with her short hair. Feeling a presence next to her, she opened her eyes and turned to see John standing quietly beside her.

"I thought you could use some company," he said, in a voice just louder than the breeze.

"I don't know if I can do this," she admitted, turning back to face the horizon.

"Well, not to worry. I have enough faith in you for the both of us."

She turned back to him in surprise. "Why?"

"I've seen you do some amazing things. Both you and your brother," he said leaning against the rail next to her. "You both have amazing gifts, and they've never failed you up till now."

"How long have you known?"

He smiled down at her. "You and your brother may think you are sneaky, but seagulls don't often fly down from the sky to talk to a small girl."

She smiled back, remembering the time that a seagull had told her a storm was coming. She had rushed to tell the captain, even though the sky had been clear the whole day. John had been the navigator of that crew as well. "I hadn't realized you had been watching me," she said, a little sheepishly.

"I'm the reason the captain listened," he said with a laugh. "Poor Captain Reynolds. He had no idea about your powers, but he saw something in you."

"What did he see in me?" she asked, feeling very fragile. "I don't feel like I should be the captain of this ship."

"Come on, now," he said, placing a hand on her shoulder. "He saw the same things I do: your courage in the face of adversity, your clear headedness in an emergency, and your ability to lead. Gift or not, these are the things that make a good leader, and you've got them all and then some."

She felt tears making tracks down her cheeks at his words. She had no idea that Captain Reynolds had felt that way about her and said those things. She didn't feel worthy of his praise or his confidence, and she wasn't sure what she had done to earn them.

Taking a deep, steadying breath, she wiped her face and squared her shoulders. Whatever adversity she faced next, whatever this meant for Peter's future, she would stick to her guns. Her instinct had never done her wrong before. She hoped this time wouldn't be any different.

"Thank you, John," she said, as she hastily brushed the tears from her face.

"You're very welcome," she heard a smile in his voice, and with one last squeeze to her shoulder, he walked away back towards the wheel.

She looked out over the horizon, closing her eyes she reached out with her mind. She felt sea urchins down below and a small school of fish. She passed over each of them, continuing her reach further and further, not exactly sure what she was searching for, but trusting she would know it when she felt it.

But there was nothing. She didn't even know what she was looking for. How was she supposed to find a specific animal? All these doubts swirled in her head like the ocean currents, clouding her ability to even try. Maybe she shouldn't try. Who was she kidding, anyway? She opened her eyes, frustration making her grind her teeth.

But then John's words came back to her. He had faith in her. Her crew did too. But most importantly her brother was relying on her.

Taking a deep breath, she shut her eyes and concentrated.

Just when she was reaching a distance she had never tried before, she felt a little spark coming from the west. She reached out, closing in on it. She could feel that this was indeed a dolphin. She wasn't sure if it was the exact dolphin she was looking for, but this one felt different.

She called it to her, and the dolphin responded, turning its course and heading directly towards her. She held onto it, afraid if she let it go it wouldn't come, tracking its progress across the sea until she heard something break the surface directly below her. She opened her eyes, afraid of what she might see.

Sure enough, there was a large, white dolphin, blinking up at her with kind brown eyes. It gave a little noise of triumph, and before she knew what was happening, it went back under and came shooting out of the water, doing a perfect backflip before landing back in the water with a splash.

"Well done!" came Aisling's voice as she jogged up to her. "You've found him!"

"So I did," Silver answered, noticing that she had a bag packed and looked like she was going on a trip. "Hang on, why are you dressed like that?"

Aisling looked down at herself, almost as if noticing how she looked for the first time. "How else would I dress when going on a trip?"

"I'm going with Peter on this one. End of story."

"No," Aisling answered calmly. "You're not. I'm the one who had the visions. I'm the only one who knows where to go."

"I thought the animals did all the steering," argued Silver. "Besides, he's my brother, and I'm the one who is making this decision."

"Silver, someone has to still run the ship."

"John can do that."

"And navigate at the same time?"

"Well, Cedric can help him."

"You know she's right," Silver whirled to see Nathaniel leaning up against the railing, still in human form. He pushed off and walked over to them. "Both the captain and the first mate can't leave the ship. It'll be utterly defenseless. Come on, Aisling will take good care of him."

Silver looked from Nathaniel to Aisling and back again. They were both giving her encouraging smiles, but she was having a hard time letting go. "But he's my brother," she said, sounding pathetic in her ears.

"He's more than that," said Aisling, gently. "I will protect him with my life, do you not trust me?"

"No, I do. It' just–"

"Then let him go," Aisling said, coming closer and putting her arms around her in a hug.

Silver leaned into her, letting her warmth and courage fill her up. "Be safe," Silver whispered before releasing her.

Just then, Cedric came out wearing a mask and pulling Peter onto a small bed. He was strapped to it with a couple of ropes, not to the point of hurting him but just to keep him secure. Luckily, the crew was sleeping, so no one saw any of this. Silver didn't want to cause any of the crew to panic.

Before they lowered him into the water, Silver wrapped her face in a mask and leaned down towards Peter. His breathing was coming in shallow gasps, his body shaking and covered in a light sheen of sweat. She knew this was risky, but she couldn't just let him leave without saying something.

Pressing her masked lips to his forehead she whispered, "I'm cashing in on that favor you owe me. Get better and come back to me."

Fighting tears, she stepped back and took off the mask before hurling it into the ocean. She watched it bobbing on the surface for a moment before it sank. Gaining some control over herself, she turned back to the group.

Aisling hoisted herself over the railing and scrambled down the rope that she had just tied there. Together, Cedric and Nathaniel lowered Peter's makeshift bed slowly into the water below. The Dolphin was sitting very still and allowing Aisling to secure the ropes around its neck. Once everything was in place, and Peter's bed was bobbing along behind them, Aisling looked up one more time. She gave a wave before wrapping her arms and legs around the dolphin, and they were off.

Silver watched them go, sending up a prayer to whichever deity was listening, *please please, please, keep them safe.*

Several days passed. The crew noticed Peter's absence, but everyone was too afraid to ask what happened. Silver tried to smile at all of them and continue as normally as she could. She felt the loss of Peter as well. It was almost like there was a piece of her that was missing.

She and Peter had been separated only once before when they were children. This one somehow felt different, more final. She at least knew she was going to see him again back then. This time she wasn't too sure.

There still was no word from Aisling, not that Silver had expected anything. Although she thought she was doing a pretty good job of hiding her feelings on the outside, internally, she was as taut as a bowstring. The more time that passed, the tighter she became until she thought she might break from the strain.

She had taken over the wheel, giving John a much-needed break when she felt a presence over her left shoulder. "Hello, Nathaniel."

"How did you know it was me?" he asked, coming into her peripheral vision.

"Who else would awkwardly stand just out of my line of sight without saying anything?"

She heard him chuckle before saying, "You caught me."

"Is there something you need?" she asked when the silence had stretched past the point of being comfortable.

"Yes, actually," she glanced over at the sound of his strained voice. "I wanted to ask… what I mean is–"

"Captain!" came a panicked voice. Silver whipped her head around to see Tom racing up the ladder to see her.

"There's a ship, Captain, and I'm afraid it's one we've seen before."

Dread filling in the pit of her stomach, she turned to where Tom pointed just behind her. She cursed, turning back to Nathaniel, fear building in her chest. "They've found us."

Now she knew why no one had given chase when they left the Kri's domain. They had already alerted the Cleansers, so there was no need. She immediately began shouting orders to her crew.

Nathaniel was always near when an extra hand was needed, seeming to know what she needed before she even had to ask. After preparations were made, there was nothing else to do but wait. Silver stood by John with Nathaniel on her other side, watching as the ship grew closer and closer to them. There was nowhere else to run.

CHAPTER SIXTEEN

Peter

Peter woke to a bright light. It took a while for his tired eyes to adjust, but when they did, he thought he was dreaming. He was laying on a four-poster bed, like the kind they have in fancy dorm rooms and although the curtains were drawn around him, they seemed to be fluttering in some kind of breeze.

He groaned, feeling his body ache all over. He felt like he had been run over by a horse. But he wasn't about to let things like body aches keep him down for long.

He sat up and had to pause with his head swimming. He took some deep breaths, waiting for the dizziness to pass, so he could continue exploring. He leaned over to the curtain and drew one back, then gasped in surprise.

He was outside, sleeping on a bed, in the middle of a forest clearing. "What in the world?" he asked no one in particular as he gazed around in awe.

There was greenish-gray light that filtered down through the huge tree canopy above him. How the hell had he gotten here?

He swung his legs over the side, gritting his teeth against the ache that was threatening to take over his body and stood. Too quickly as it turned out, his vision went black, and he had to sit back down on the bed for several more breaths before he felt like he could try again, preferably without passing out.

Standing slowly, he tested his weight before walking straight in front of him. He had no idea where he was going, but he figured the most logical place to start was forwards.

He moved painfully slow through the trees, each one looking exactly like the one before, almost like a copy. He turned to look behind him and found himself no longer in a forest but in a building.

"This just keeps getting better and better," he said to himself as he began exploring. The building was small. It really was more of a small home than an actual building the more he looked at it. It had a roaring fire in the middle of the room, with the flames almost reaching the ceiling.

Peter was briefly worried that the ceiling would catch fire before realizing that it was no ceiling at all but the open sky. Then he saw he wasn't surrounded by four walls, but by trees in a similar clearing to the one he started in. However, this clearing had a large log on its side with two figures seated upon it.

His eyes must've been playing tricks on him but he could have sworn that one of the figures looked exactly like Aisling. After all, he had just seen a house thirty seconds ago, but to his disbelief, the figure turned and let out a cry, bounded towards him.

"Peter! How're you feeling?" she asked when she reached him, tracing over him with concerned eyes.

"Aisling? Where are we?"

"Oh, I'm so sorry! If I had known you were going to wake up I would have come to explain everything to you, but I guess time sort of got away from me. Here, come and sit, you must be getting tired."

His legs felt like jelly but he wasn't planning on collapsing, especially in front of Aisling, so he walked forwards on unsteady legs until he reached the tree stump. He lowered himself down onto the log before looking up at the other figure ahead of him. It was good he sat down first because when he looked at the man in front of him, he had to swallow down a shout of surprise.

The man, at least what he assumed was his gender, was the ugliest man he had ever seen. He had warts almost completely covering his face that seemed to glisten in the firelight. The part of his face that wasn't covered in warts was bumpy and uneven, like he had been sick before and it had left a mark.

His nose was long and crooked, almost as if it had been broken several times and never put back into place. After Peter took in all of this, he began to notice something odd, but he couldn't put his finger on it. This was probably because a man covered with warts was sitting in the middle of the forest and was grinning from ear to ear.

"Welcome!" His voice was strong and clear, completely clashing with his face in every way possible. This is not how Peter imagined someone like him would sound like.

"Th-thank you," answered Peter, trying and failing to sound as nonchalant as possible.

The man chuckled at him. "Not used to seeing someone different than you? Well, that is surprising considering everything you and your sister have gone through."

Peter cleared his throat, trying to get his voice under control. "I'm sorry, sir, but I'm not quite sure what you mean."

"Oh, you know," said the man gesturing with his hand. "Just the fact that you and your sister deal with all sorts of problems from people not understanding the way you look."

Peter was growing increasingly uncomfortable with the direction of this conversation. So, to change the subject he said, "I'm sorry, who are you? And how do you know about Silver?"

"I know a great many things, my boy," he answered in a booming voice. "As for who I am? I go by many names, but you may call me Eli."

How had he somehow not answered both of Peter's questions? "What happened? How did I end up here? Wherever here is."

Aisling joined in the conversation, "I'm afraid you got the disease."

Peter tried to jump away from Aisling to put space in between them. "What're you doing sitting so close to me, then?"

"Peter calm down!" she exclaimed, reaching out a hand to steady him. "Eli healed you."

"I'm going to need you to start at the beginning," said Peter, calming down but feeling as though Aisling was talking to him underwater.

She explained everything, from how he collapsed on the deck and Silver calling a white dolphin to Eli's healing power. "It was amazing to watch!" she explained. "You were so close to death, with the black spidery veins running through your body. Eli placed his hands over you and though at first nothing happened, the veins slowly began to recede."

"What, like magic?"

"Something like that," Eli finally broke in, continuing to smile. Peter noticed that his teeth were crooked, like fencing that hadn't been placed properly.

"How is that possible?"

"How is anything possible?" Eli asked him in return. "How do sea turtles survive in the sea without being able to breathe underwater? How is it a young boy can see moments in the future before they happen? Don't you see? It's all connected."

Peter didn't see, but he guessed that was part of the point. "How do you know about my gift?"

"I'm the one who gave it to you, silly boy."

"But," Peter said, trying to understand. "I've never met you before, and I've had this gift for years."

"And that makes a difference? I've always known you, Peter."

"But I haven't known you," answered Peter.

"Haven't you?"

Peter was about to answer no but found the word somehow trapped in his mouth. There was something oddly familiar about this man, he was positive he had never met him before. There was no way he would have forgotten a face like his. But there was something he couldn't quite grasp, something just out of his reach.

He looked into the man's eyes and had to swallow down another gasp. His eyes wouldn't stay one color. They morphed and changed, never staying one color for long. He was mesmerized by his eyes, and for a moment, he couldn't look away. It was his eyes. That's what was familiar. Again, Peter wasn't sure how or where he had seen them before but he had seen them somewhere.

"I thought so," Eli said smugly. "Now on to business!"

Peter felt his heart drop at that. Did this man expect something from him for the healing?

"I need you to tell me what you saw when you came into the clearing."

"Um, I saw a building."

"Interesting," Eli said, his eyes twinkling. "Describe it."

"It's hard to explain," said Peter, trying to gather his thoughts. "I walked out of the trees and turned, then I was somehow not in the trees anymore. Somehow, I was inside a building that turned into more of a small house. It had four walls, kind of yellow, and there was a huge fire in the middle of the room that looked like it was going to hit the ceiling. Then it morphed and turned into this clearing."

Eli was quiet for a few moments, looking thoughtful. "Anything else?"

"Not that I can remember," said Peter, beginning to feel frustrated. "What's all this about?"

"I think you may have an idea."

Peter thought hard but this wasn't his kind of thing. "I don't know," he said, anger leaking out of his voice. "So, why don't you tell me since it looks like you have all the answers."

The man continued to pleasantly smile at him.

"Fine, if you won't tell me, then I think I'll be going." Peter stood, then somehow found himself lying on his back in the deep leaves.

"Peter! Are you alright?" Aisling was leaning over him, concern clear on her face.

"Fine," he said through gritted teeth. He slowly got back on the log, glaring at Eli.

"Someone's got a temper there," said Eli cheerfully. "I'm afraid if you're not careful, it'll be the end of you."

"Now," Eli continued. "Since you are so determined not to think about what the room could mean, I'll tell you. Everyone who comes into the clearing has a different trial they have to face. Since you were already technically in the clearing even though you weren't conscious, doesn't mean that you got to skip the trial."

"This is in place to make sure the person coming in is of good heart. These trials aren't meant to harm you, however, if you fail there will be some kind of consequence. In this case, you didn't quite pass, which is why you just passed out briefly. The goal was to see whether or not you'd do what I asked, especially if it was something you weren't particularly skilled at which just so happens to be: interpreting metaphors."

Peter sat in silent shock as this strange man in front of him seemed to spill all of his secrets. He felt strangely exposed, like there was a bright light on him and everyone had taken a step back.

"Now in regards to the room, this represents your desires. You desire to settle down, in a house similar to this, nothing too big but something nice and cozy. It overlooks the sea because whether you like it or not, the sea is a part of you. Now the fire you saw represents what is to come. You won't be able to get to your house and settle down until you've finished your task. There is still much work for you to do."

Peter sat in silent shock for a few moments. How could this man know so much about him when they just met? Perhaps there was something at work here.

"And what task is that?" he asked, finally breaking the silence.

Eli leaned forward, the firelight causing weird shadows on his ugly face. "That's for you to decide."

Peter thought about all of the things Silver and he had been through. The Cleansers chasing them and the disease that was spreading through the world. He looked up at Eli in shock.

"Wait, you don't mean save the world? How cliche is that?"

Eli leaned back, grinning like a child. "Oh well done! I was hoping you'd say that!"

"But wait, how can one person save the world?"

"One person, can make all the difference. That's the very thing! One person though their actions may be small, just like a stone dropped in a quiet pond sends out ripples of change. But for the record, it's not just you that is tasked to save the world. Many groups have already been sent out and are fighting their own battles."

"This is a lot to take in," said Peter, his head beginning to spin.

"Why don't you go rest, and we can talk some more tomorrow? After all, your body has been through quite a lot." Eli smiled at him kindly. "Aisling, why don't you take him back to his bed?"

Aisling stood, taking Peter's arm and leading him away from the fire and into the forest. When they were out of earshot Peter asked, "Did you tell him any of those things about me?"

"No! I swear to you I didn't!" Aisling said concern in her eyes. "Do you think I would betray you like that?"

"No, I don't," Peter said, sighing. "I trust you, I'm just not sure I trust him."

"Eli has been very kind to us. When I showed up with you unconscious, begging for help, he didn't even question me. Also, he knew both our names without me having to tell him. It's strange how much he knew about both of us."

"That's what I find so strange," Peter replied, using Aisling for more support than he would like to admit. "How can someone know you that well when you've never met?"

"I don't know," she answered, leading Peter around a tree branch. "There was something super familiar about him when we first met. It was almost like somehow I knew him, even though I'm pretty sure we've never met before."

"Yes, that's it exactly! How can you feel like you know someone you've never met?"

"I'm not sure," she said as she led him into another familiar clearing. She led him over to the bed where he sat down heavily. His body was aching all over.

"All I do know is I trust him. I'm not sure why, but there is something about him that seems good, somehow. Nothing is straightforward with him, I've spent a couple of days talking with him, but somehow, I feel like we can trust him."

Peter sighed again, but he knew that he would follow Aisling's instinct. It hadn't been the first time someone smarter than him had a feeling about something. He had learned just to go with it.

"Come on, go to sleep now, I'll see you in the morning."

Peter was already nodding off, his body feeling like lead. He laid down, and before his head hit the pillow, he was asleep.

CHAPTER SEVENTEEN

Silver

They had been battling the Cleansers ship for fourteen hours straight. Silver wasn't sure how much longer her men could hold out against them. The Cleansers had been shooting at them as soon as they were in range and hadn't stopped. The missiles weren't like normal ones, which they only knew anytime one of them hit something. One hit a pile of rope and made the strangest sucking sound before disappearing. Luckily, none of her crew had gotten hit by any. But it was only a matter of time.

The men had hunkered down below decks out of range of the missiles, but that made it difficult to man the ship.

Silver was more afraid than she wanted to admit, but she wasn't sure what choice she was going to have if this continued for much longer. She was worried the next phase of the Cleansers attack wasn't going to leave her any choice. All they had to do was sink the ship or set it on fire, and they would easily be able to capture them all.

Desperate times called for desperate measures so she had made a plan, one she hoped would stop all of this. She was packing a bag when suddenly her door flew open. Her heart in her throat, she jumped fearing the worst, and then relaxed slightly when she saw it was just Nathaniel.

"What happened? Is everyone alright?" she asked, trying to cover her bag with her body to hide it from his view.

"Everyone is currently fine," he answered, coming farther into the room. "But they won't be if you abandon them."

Silver felt her mouth drop open at his words. "Abandon? How dare you?"

Nathaniel crossed his arms over his chest. "Well, isn't that what you're doing? I see a bag packed behind you. How could you, Silver? I thought you were a better captain than that."

"I– Now hold on! I'm not abandoning anyone!"

"No, you're just going to turn yourself in, therefore allowing them to win and your crew to be captainless."

"I am doing what I think is best for this crew!" said Silver, anger flaring. "And I don't need some guy who has had no experience with ships to tell me otherwise!"

"Oh really?" he sneered. "And then what would you like me to tell your crew when they've found your chamber empty?"

Silver ignored him and went back to packing. She was angry and hurt by his words. Whatever Nathaniel thought, she was going to do what she thought was best for this crew.

"Look at me!"

She felt herself being whipped around as he took her arm. "I will not allow you to treat me this way!" she shouted, pushing him away from her.

"I can't see you throwing away your crew! Can't you see? If you go to them, then you're playing into their hands! They won't be satisfied until they have everyone."

"And I suppose you're the expert, then?"

His eyes grew sad as the anger left them. "Yes, actually," he said, taking a deep breath. "In this case, I unfortunately am."

Silver felt the anger leave her like how a huge wind turned into a gentle breeze. She took a breath, too, and then said, "I'm sorry."

"Me too," he answered.

"Well, what would you have us do?"

He looked around the chambers, running a hand through his hair. "We need something that can go on deck but not be affected by their strange weapons."

"Kind of like a decoy!"

"Exactly," he snapped his fingers.

"Do you have any idea what the darts are? How they work?"

"They were just developing them when I was last involved with them."

"You mean before they left you to die?"

He smiled sadly. "Yes, something like that. The darts used to have some major malfunctions. It could transport people but never where they wanted them to go. It would shoot them off into another place somewhere way off of where they intended."

"Is it possible they fixed that problem, or do you think they're just trying to dwindle our numbers?"

"Unfortunately, it could be either of those. I thought they still had a lot of work to do, but they may have fixed all the bugs."

An idea was beginning to form in Silver's mind. "Are there any weaknesses the Cleansers have?" When he looked at her in confusion, she continued, "Like any animals?"

His face brightened at her words. "You know, they might. They never kept any animals around except for me."

"And the cat!"

"Come again?"

"There was a cat, one besides you, I mean." She explained what had happened when they explored the tunnel and the interaction with the cat they had that led them to Aisling.

"Wait! How could I have been so stupid?" she whirled and began rummaging through her trunks. "Where is it?"

After several overturned trunks, she found it and placed the orb on the table between them. "There! I'm almost positive this is how they keep finding us."

"And you said the cat led you to it?"

"Yes," she said, coming closer to get another look. "That's why we were on the island in the first place. I had a buyer but they killed him."

"What? When did this happen?"

"It was right before we met you, that was before the Sirens... You know what," she said at the shocked look on his face. "Let's move on."

"Are you always in danger?"

"Or about to be, it seems, but hey, life wouldn't be exciting without a little adventure!"

"You're a strange one, Silver," he said, shaking his head.

"You're one to talk. Anyway, what's the plan?"

"Well, they've been pretty eager to have both Aisling and the sphere back. I'm surprised they've let you keep it this long to tell you the truth. This must be why they've pulled out the big guns to try and take it from you."

"But we may be able to use that to our advantage," he said, thoughtfully. "While the Cleansers aren't exactly afraid of anything animal-wise, I can think of one, that if we're smart about it, might be just the thing to trick them until we can get away."

He grinned at her, with life finally coming back into his eyes. She smiled back, and for the first time in days, felt like she had a plan that she could work with.

After a bit more discussion, they finally had their plan ready. Silver and Nathaniel waited under the cover of the doorway leading up to the main deck. All was quiet, both sides at a standstill, waiting for the other to make the first move. Maybe they had finally run out of weapons or knew that they were wasting ammunition with her crew hidden below decks.

She took a deep breath, trying to calm her nerves. She knew if this didn't work, they would all be captured, but it was a risk she was willing to take.

Nathaniel nodded at her and promptly turned into a beetle. He scuttled off and she counted to ten slowly. When she reached ten, she felt out with her mind and found exactly what she was looking for. She felt the animals respond to her calling, and then she waited. After what felt like a century, she heard the noise of the other ship being attacked. The cannons were fired and there was an overall panic from the surprise attack.

"Now!" she shouted, and her crew jumped into action. Several crew members ran to the canons that were loaded and aimed at the enemy ship. Their cannons fired, adding to the overall confusion of the ship. She ran above deck with a few of her selected crew members, John, Sam, and Cedric, to be exact.

They charged above deck, and she began climbing to the crows' nest. She heard shouting and the overall chaos of battle. The ship rocked once, making her swing out precariously over the deck. She swung herself back on the rope ladder and continued climbing with her heart in her throat.

Once she finally reached the top, she faced the other ship. Taking out the sphere, she reached out with her mind and told the strange sea creatures she had found in the ocean to abandon the ship. She still wasn't entirely sure what she had called up from the depths. All that she knew was it was big.

Then she reached out for the next phase of the plan: find jellyfish and have them surround the enemy ship. Holding up the sphere, she pointed it at the ship and pushed the side just like Nathaniel had told her. She felt a jolt, and the sphere began vibrating, making her hands numb.

Struggling to hold onto it as she lost feeling in her hands, she somehow managed while also asking the jellyfish to zap the ship. It seemed like nothing was happening, but then she saw the black smoke beginning to recede, until finally, the last of it blew away. She cheered and heard the rest of her crew cheering as well. They had done it!

Or so she thought. Just when it looked like their ship was sinking, she heard a horrible noise. It sounded like metal grinding and squeaking together added to the groaning of machinery. She watched in horror, as the ship began to mold itself into something else. Right before her eyes, where the wooden ship once was, there was now a metal one, one where their cannonballs bounced off harmlessly.

She looked down at the sphere, realizing that she had made a huge error in judgment. What she had thought would dismantle the ship's inner workings had somehow charged it up. Thinking fast, she called off the jellyfish and taking out her knife strapped to her thigh, began hacking at the sphere. It was surprisingly weak for being such a powerful weapon, and she was able to break through the outer shell much easier than she thought she was going to be able to.

She heard her men screaming as panic began to take hold of her ship. She ignored it and kept working, completely focused on the task at hand. Without a backup plan, she was making it up as she went along. The only thing she was certain of was that the birdmen couldn't get their hands on this device. Even if she lost the ship and her crew, she would make sure they wouldn't get this.

She finally tore the thing apart, and taking the pieces, she began stacking them together. Finding a match in her belt, she lit the piece using a bit of her shirt as kindling. They caught surprisingly well, she was just getting a good flame going when she heard a metallic voice say, "We have taken over the ship. Surrender now or prepare to die."

CHAPTER EIGHTEEN

Peter

The next day Peter woke feeling well-rested and much more like his old self. This time being ready for the forest. He walked straight until he reached the clearing with the fire. Eli was sitting there, and so was Aisling, and they were deep in conversation. Peter caught the tail end of it as he got closer.

"I must find him. Do you have any idea where he went?" he heard Aisling ask, her back to him as he approached.

"He is on the same mission as you. Your paths are bound to cross, just be patient and follow your heart. It will lead you to him. Ah, and here is young Peter! Did you sleep well?"

"Yes, thank you," said Peter as he took a seat next to Aisling. He wanted to ask what they had been discussing when he walked in, but he wasn't sure how. He was about to try and figure out a way to broach the subject when Eli handed him a large leaf.

"Eat up, you need your strength for what's ahead."

He looked down and realized it was some kind of food. It looked like vegetables with some sort of grainy bread. Not typically the kind of food Peter went for, but as his stomach gave a painful clinch, he figured anything was better than nothing.

Maybe it was that he couldn't remember the last time he'd eaten, but there was something strangely perfect about this food. It was lightly seasoned with something that made it flavorful without taking away from the freshness of the vegetables. It was one of the best meals he'd ever had in his life, and he found himself licking the leaf once the contents had been consumed.

"Enjoy it?" asked Eli, smiling at him.

Peter promptly stopped licking the leaf and while clearing his throat, replied, "Yes, it was delicious. Thank you."

"Now onto the plan for today!" said Eli, clapping his hands. "First, I would like to introduce my son Joshua."

A man stepped out of the shadows. He was tall with dark hair and a dark, full beard but besides his crooked nose, didn't resemble his father in any way. He stepped fully into the light, and Peter was able to see him more clearly.

He wasn't ugly by any means, but he wasn't particularly handsome or striking. He looked just like any man you've seen but he did have one feature that resembled his father's, his eyes. They were the same swirl of colors that were constantly changing and morphing, never settling on one color in particular.

Peter somehow felt at ease in Joshua's presence, a kind of peace washed over him. It wasn't like Eli where he felt a bit on edge anytime he was around him. Joshua felt like someone he could have a meal with.

"Joshua, why don't you take Peter and show him our land?" Eli asked, thoughtfully. "I think he could use some fresh air."

Peter stood and looked at Aisling, who had been extremely quiet this whole time. She wasn't looking at him, she was staring at a spot over Eli's shoulder. She hadn't looked at him once since he came into the clearing.

"No, no, not her. Just you." Eli said with a mischievous twinkle in his eye.

Apprehension filled Peter but he did as he was told. Following Joshua, they walked out of the clearing. Peter found himself suddenly going uphill. It was difficult terrain but manageable. The trees began to disappear, and he could see patches of the blue sky.

Joshua didn't say anything, he just continued walking, so Peter followed obediently. He was in awe of the beauty that surrounded him. The trees were all different shades of brown, some reaching just to his chest, while others stretched past the point where he could see the top. There were birds singing and squirrels playing tag in the trees. A family of rabbits watched them pass, their big ears following their progress.

Peter had spent so much time at sea where everything was open that it was an odd feeling to be surrounded. Not unpleasant, just different. He knew Silver would find it stifling, but he enjoyed it. His heart gave a ping at the thought of his sister. This was the first time they had been separated in years, and he was beginning to feel her loss like a physical wound.

His breath began coming out in gasps and pants as they continued. The hill they'd been climbing had taken a sharper incline, and Peter was having trouble keeping up. Joshua never walked any faster, nor did he reach out and try to help him. But Peter felt his presence, and somehow knew that he wouldn't let anything happen to him.

They continued going up and up, with Peter growing more and more tired. Just when he thought he couldn't keep going, he would glance over at Joshua and a new strength would fill him. He would find the will to put one foot in front of the other. The trees were beginning to thin now, with more and more blue showing. A rock face began to poke through the thinned-out trees, showing the side of what looked like a rock pass.

The path had become even steeper, and Peter didn't understand how that was possible. He stepped down on a loose stone, twisting his ankle as it flew out from under him. Falling, he braced his hands in front of him to catch himself. Joshua was there in an instant, throwing out an arm and catching him. When he touched him, energy flew through him, filling his veins. He felt strengthened by his touch, the ache in his ankle suddenly vanished, almost like it was healing itself. Joshua gently pulled him back to his feet.

"Thank you," Peter said, realizing these were the first words he had spoken to him.

Joshua nodded, and they continued on their way. Peter was refreshed after Joshua's touch, so he completed the hike without feeling like he was going to die, or at the very least, pass out.

Finally, they made it to the top, and Peter caught his breath as he looked over the view. They had climbed an entire mountain, which seemed odd considering it hadn't taken them nearly as long as it should have.

The sun was just setting on the horizon, leaving streaks of orange and pink stretching across the sky. There was a stream that cut through the forest below on the western side of where they stood, creating a pathway. The trees created an almost perfectly flat surface and stretched to the horizon. There didn't seem to be an end to them.

Peter looked out over the beauty of it all in silence just taking it all in.

"You did well," came Joshua's voice pulling Peter out of his thoughts. His voice was warm and comforting, like a silky cup of hot chocolate on a cold day.

"Was this another test?" he asked, turning towards him.

"Of sorts," Joshua shrugged. "Then again, most things are some kind of test. A test of wills, a chance to prove yourself. It's all part of it. Some of it are tests we put on ourselves, while others are perhaps put on us. The important thing is how we react, and if we learn from the mistakes we've already made."

"But that's hardly fair," argued Peter. "Why does everything have to be a test? What if I don't want to be tested?"

"Well, that's the question, isn't it? Do you have a choice?"

"Probably, at least I'd like to think so."

"Interesting, and in what way can you choose?"

Peter thought about it for a long moment. "I can choose not to partake in anything, I can choose not to play the game."

"You could do that," Joshua answered thoughtfully. "But is that any way to live? What is the point of life if not to learn and grow? Sure you could stay stagnant. That is completely in your realm of choice. But then by choosing to do nothing, you've sealed your fate far worse if you, as you say, "played the game"."

"I don't think I'm enjoying this conversation," Peter answered, hearing the bitterness in his voice.

"No, most things that are good for us aren't enjoyable. When faced with the idea of change, most people fight it, wanting everything to stay the same. By doing this, they use up much more energy and time than if they'd just changed. Whether they like it or not, change is inevitable. Just like how a rose blossom grows so uncomfortable that it must burst forth out into the world. It's the same with people."

"Did you bring me up here to lecture me on change?"

Joshua chuckled. "Your bluntness is refreshing, Peter. In truth, that is part of the reason."

"And the other?" Peter prompted.

"The other is to talk about what's bothering you."

Whatever Peter had been expecting Joshua to say, this wasn't it.

"Bothering me? How did you know something was bothering me? Wait, let me guess," Peter said, holding up a hand. "You're gonna say, "you know many things" or something like that."

Joshua smiled at him. "Or something like that. Come now, I won't bite."

So, Peter told him. He spoke of his dreams to settle down, but being afraid to leave his sister. He spoke of this new burden that had been placed on him to somehow save the world when he didn't feel worthy. And he spoke of Aisling, the feelings that had been growing for her since the moment he saw her, and how those feelings were scaring him more than anything. Joshua listened in complete silence, not offering anything other than his presence.

When he had finished, he felt like a huge weight had been lifted from his shoulders. Although he hadn't come to any conclusions, he somehow felt like he could do anything. He took a deep, cleansing breath and let it out slowly, feeling the pine-scented air in his lungs.

"It would seem you have a lot of work ahead of you," said Joshua after a few moments.

"Yes, it would," answered Peter, not feeling worse by his words, just acknowledging them. "I don't know where to start."

"Usually the best place to start is what presents itself first. You'll know what to do when the time comes."

"That's a very cliche answer."

Joshua laughed a huge belly laugh. "Cliches aren't always a bad thing, typically there's quite a bit of truth to them. After all, why do you think they're so overused?"

Joshua clapped him on the shoulder and gestured back down the mountain. "Come, the way down is not always easier, but I'll catch you if you fall."

Joshua was right, the way down certainly wasn't easier, but Peter knew that having him by his side, he had nothing to fear.

They made it back to the clearing in what felt like far less time than it took to climb up. Aisling was still deep in conversation with Eli, but they stopped when Joshua and Peter entered the clearing. "Welcome back," said Eli, spreading his arms wide. "Have a nice trip?"

"I did actually," answered Peter, taking the spot next to Aisling. She glanced up at him when he sat down, and he saw something was wrong. "What is it?" he asked, his heart dropping at the sight of her distressed face.

"It's– It's Silver," she answered, her eyes wide with fear.

"Is she alright?" he asked urgently.

"I can't be sure," she said, shaking her head. "But we need to go to her. Quickly."

Peter jumped to his feet, ready to leave this instant. Eli came over with Joshua at his side. "We've packed a few necessities for you," said Eli, handing them a bag. "Inside you will find something that may come in handy." His eyes twinkled mischievously but he said nothing more on the subject.

"Wait just a moment." Out of the trees stepped a beautiful woman. She had light blond hair and was tall and slender.

"Allow me to introduce my wife, Lydia," said Joshua, holding out his hand to her. The way they looked at each other was one of pure love, the kind you read about in stories. It almost felt like they were intruding, walking in on something so pure and intimate it was almost painful to look at.

"I have a gift for each of you," she said, coming forwards. "Hold out your hand," she said, and Peter and Aisling complied. Around each of their wrists, she wrapped a kind of bracelet. It was made of what looked like different colored twine with shells sewn in. "These will come in handy, you'll know what to do when you need them the most."

"Thank you," said Peter, overcome with everything they had done for them. "For everything."

"You both are most welcome," said Eli, smiling a crooked smile. "Now off with you! There's no time to lose!"

Joshua whistled, and a great white deer with antlers that reached to the sky trotted forwards. "Ziv will take you where you need to go. Then, it's up to you."

Peter nodded, Ziv bowed, and he helped Aisling up before climbing up behind her. He wrapped his arms around her, feeling a tingle race up his arms from where he touched her. Ziv raced off into the woods, going much faster than Peter would have thought was possible. He glanced back, but the trees had already closed over the clearing.

CHAPTER NINETEEN

Silver

"And where is your captain?" came the horrible metallic voice from below. Silver grabbed a rope from next to her and made sure the small fire was still going before swinging from one rope to the next until she was directly above them.

She swung down, landing in front of the Cleanser saying, "She's right here." She made sure to land in a position where the Cleanser's back was to the crows' nest. All she needed was to distract him long enough for the parts to get beyond salvageable.

"Excellent," the Cleanser practically purred. This was the first time she had seen them in broad daylight, and they were almost more horrifying. She could see its mask more clearly, the ugly bird's beak, and the cloak completely covering the rest of its body.

She heard a grunt and looking around him, saw to her horror that the crew members who were the distraction were tied together and efficiently being gagged by another Cleanser. The rest of her crew was being hauled up from below decks and pushed into the circle to be tied with the others. She counted at least five Cleansers but still had no idea how many there were. John looked at her with such sadness in his eyes that it broke her heart.

"Now then," said the first creature addressing her. "We believe you have something that we want."

"Oh, and what might that be?" she asked, stalling for time.

"Don't play stupid with us girl!" the creature spat. "We have captured your crew and taken over your ship. There is nowhere else to run."

Out of the corner of her eye, Silver could see there was a real fire going now in the crows' nest. Hopefully, she had done enough to destroy it.

"We know what that shock you sent our way was, and now we would like our device back."

"You didn't say please," answered Silver, crossing her arms over her chest.

Lighting fast, the creature was upon her and slapped her across her face before she could even think of defending herself. She stumbled back but didn't fall, and then out of nowhere, Nathaniel came charging out from behind a pillar and tackled the creature to the ground. The other Cleansers were at their fallen brother's side in an instant before pulling Nathaniel off of him.

"Well now," said the first Cleanser, rising slowly as the other members held Nathaniel securely. "I thought we had disposed of you."

"I offer myself!" Nathaniel shouted, struggling against his captures. "My life for the rest of the crew and their captain."

"Interesting," said the Cleanser, turning to look over the crew and Silver. "It seems our little shapeshifter has grown attached. Let's see if they return his affection."

He nodded to one of his brothers, who took something out of his cloak and pressed it to Nathaniel's arm. Nathaniel let out a scream, one that chilled Silver to the bones.

Acting on instinct, she rushed forwards, not knowing what she was going to do but knowing she couldn't let them hurt him. She didn't get very far before the first Cleanser hit her again, this time in the stomach. The wind was knocked out of her, and she fell to her knees gasping. Nathaniel's screams had stopped, and she could hear him gasping for air as well.

"Ah, so this one does care for you," from this vantage point, all she could see were a pair of black pointed shoes that stopped right in front of her.

"Please," she heard Nathaniel's voice panting out the words. "Take me instead. Don't... Don't hurt her or the crew."

"Aw, Nathaniel," came the silky voice of the Cleanser. "How sweet of you to sacrifice yourself. But you forget, you have nothing to bargain with. You belong to us. Just because you survived our last attempt doesn't mean your life is yours. This time, we won't make any mistakes." Finally getting her breath back, she lifted her head in time to see the creature walk forwards and brushed a gloved hand against Nathaniel's cheek. "Take him below."

"No!" Silver yelled, getting her feet under her just before the Cleanser struck her down again.

"Now, now Captain," said the Cleanser, towering over her as she struggled to rise again. "Let's not be too hasty. You still have a crew to think about. I would hate for anything to happen to them."

Anger and helplessness coursed through her, making it hard to breathe as she watched them drag Nathaniel below. He didn't fight, he simply hung there, suspended between two Cleansers until they disappeared.

Just then, one of the Cleansers shouted and pointed to the burning crows' nest. The other Cleansers burst into action, putting out the flames in record time with strange contraptions that looked like guns and seemed to shoot smoke out of the barrels. She felt her gun and sword being ripped out of her belt, and then she was roughly pushed to her feet.

"Now little Captain," rasped the Cleanser, holding her shoulder in his iron grip to face him. "What, was so important that you caught it on fire, with the possibility of burning down your ship?"

"The device of course," she answered, in a calm voice. "Oh, I'm sorry, was that something you needed?"

She couldn't see his expression behind the mask, but she felt him vibrating with anger. He made it as if to strike her again but one of the Cleansers ran up to him. "There's no sign of her!"

Momentarily forgetting about Silver, but keeping her in his grasp, he asked, "Are you sure?"

"Positive sir," said the creature in a calculated voice. "She's not on this ship."

He excused the other Cleanser with a flick of his hand, and then turned back to Silver. "Well, it would seem we are at an impasse," he said, in a deadly calm voice. "How about we make a deal?"

"What kind of deal?" asked Silver, crossing her arms over her chest.

"It's rather simple, really," said the Cleanser, coming even closer. "You tell us where the girl is–"

"What girl?" asked Silver, trying her luck. "You can't expect me to make a deal about something I'm unsure of."

In a flash, the Cleanser rushed at her again at an impossible speed. In a matter of moments, she found herself dangling over the railing of the ship. The Cleanser had its hand around her throat and was holding her with one arm over the waves below. Her crew cried out in muffled voices because of the gags, and she heard them struggling against their bonds.

"Let me be clear," said the Cleanser, in a deadly, calm voice. "The girl you stole from me has been missed. We are ready for her to come back home to us. So here is my deal: turn over the girl to us, and we won't kill you and your crew."

She felt herself blacking out from lack of oxygen. Honestly, how did he expect her to answer him when he was cutting off her windpipe? Just as the edges of her eyes were getting fuzzy, she had a crazy idea.

Reaching out with her mind, she called all the creatures she could reach. When her vision had gone almost completely black she heard the Cleansers' cry out. The one holding her drew her back on board and dropped her roughly to the ground. She gasped, taking in big breaths into her lungs, sputtering like a fish on land for the second time that day.

When she finally had gotten enough oxygen to get her vision back, she saw that crabs and lobsters as well as other crustaceans had flooded onto the ship. Birds and other flying creatures had joined in as well and were attacking all the Cleansers that were on the main deck. The creatures that couldn't come aboard were circling the water below, making the ocean look as though it had come to a boil. Silver saw a shark fin pop out of the water before sinking back down below.

Knowing she didn't have much time, she got to her feet, tripping slightly, and rushed to where her crew was bound. She began frantically trying to untie them and had almost made it past the first set of knots when she was ripped away. She struggled fiercely, but felt the cold bite of metal handcuffs placed on her wrists. As the cool metal bit into her skin, she felt all her energy leave her and was bone-tired as if she had just run several miles.

Breathing heavy, Silver lifted her head and looked directly into the face of the first Cleanser. He looked a little rough of wear, his cloak had holes in it and one of his eye lenses had been broken. Silver tried to see into his mask, but it was pitch black.

"So," panted the Cleanser, also slightly out of breath. "It's going to be difficult, is it? Interesting that you have a gift. We knew someone aboard this ship did when we were attacked, but I never expected it could be you. This could be very useful."

Silver's heart began to pound, and her stomach clenched. They knew. They figured out she had a gift, and now there was no escape for her.

"I will give you one last chance to answer me: where is the girl?"

"I… don't… know." Silver answered in all truthfulness.

The Cleanser shook his head, his broken lens flashing before her like a gaping wound. "I tried to be fair. Know that this death is on you."

He nodded to one of the other Cleansers who brought forth one of her crew, Tom.

"NO!" Silver yelled, her adrenaline giving her new strength. She struggled to her feet, but the Cleanser came behind her and held her in place.

"No more fighting," he spoke quietly in her ear, making the hair on the back of her neck stand up. "Watch the consequences of your actions."

She watched in mute horror as the other Cleanser brought Tom to the middle of the deck. His hands were bound behind him, his mouth still gagged, and he looked up at her with pride in his scared eyes. He was proud to give his life for his crew and his captain, but Silver never wanted him to have to.

The Cleanser came behind him, forcing him down to his knees. Tears were streaming down Silver's cheeks, her eyes completely glued to Tom's face. He gave one last brave smile around his gag, breaking her heart. Then, the Cleanser behind him pulled out some kind of weapon. There was a strange sound, almost between a gunshot and a thunderclap. His eyes rolled, back and he fell forward, twitching once before laying still.

Silver's knees went out from under her, and the Cleanser that was holding her let her fall. She felt empty, like something in her had died when Tom did. He was so young. So young.

She heard the Cleansers talking among themselves but didn't hear what they said. It was like they were far away or underwater, she could hear that they were speaking words, but it was just sound with no meaning.

One of the vile things picked her up and half dragged her away. She didn't care. They could do anything to her now. There was no point in fighting. She didn't have any fight left in her anyway.

CHAPTER TWENTY

Peter

Peter and Aisling were making good time. Peter found out the hard way that time was counted differently in Eli's world. Since they were finally back in their world, time was back to a normal speed. Ziv had taken them to the ocean, where he dropped them off and after bowing to each of them, bounded back into the forest.

They looked around unsure of their next steps. "How did you get here from the ship again? Where's the boat?" asked Peter, looking around the rocky shore.

"I didn't take a boat," she answered nervously. "Silver called a dolphin, and that's how we got here."

"What? And I missed it?" Peter exclaimed.

"I'm not sure now is the best time to be worrying about that," she said, bringing him back to reality. Aisling sat down heavily, and Peter rushed to her side. "Aisling? What's wrong?"

"Your sister is in danger," she said, looking up at him with fear in her eyes. "We need to get back to her. Now."

"Well, that may be difficult," said Peter, beginning to pace. "Give me a moment."

He paced back and forth, creating a tiny trail where his feet packed down the sand and rocks. "Wait, let me see that bag!" He rushed over to the bag that Eli had given them and dumped it out on the ground.

There were several things he took in. First of all, everything was tiny. It was almost like Eli had given them a bag full of children's toys. There were a total of six items, one tiny metallic thing that looked almost like a gun, two mini cloaks, a tiny wicker picnic basket, a mini wooden paddle, and a tiny wooden boat.

"Why would Eli give us this stuff?" Asked Aisling, coming over to inspect each item.

Getting a crazy idea, Peter looked down at his bracelet. It had three shells sewn into the blue twine. Looking at the basket, and feeling his stomach rumble, he picked it up and looking at it, pressed it up to one of the shells. The shell warmed on his skin, stopping just before becoming painful. The basket began to grow and grow until he was holding a full-sized picnic basket in his hand. He looked over at Aisling, grinning at her shocked face.

"How? What?" she asked, coming over to inspect the basket.

Peter shrugged modestly, "Lydia told us we would know what to do when the time came. Maybe I just knew. Although," he said thoughtfully. "It would've been just as easy for her to tell us to use it to make the other gifts work. I wonder what would've happened if she hadn't come in time? Oh well, let's see if this is what I think it is!"

He opened the basket, and sure enough, it was filled with fresh bread that was still steaming somehow, more of the strange vegetables he had eaten earlier, and a canteen of fresh water. They both ate until they were completely satisfied, and then Aisling went over to the objects. She inspected each of them, and then looked down at her bracelet.

"Peter? How many shells do you have?"

"Three," he answered confidently before looking down at his wrist. "Strike that, only two now."

"It looks like we have just enough shells to make everything. I wonder how long the spell lasts?"

Just as she said that the basket began to shrink until it was once more toy-sized and fit in the palm of Peter's hand. "Oh," she said, clear worry stretched across her face.

"Well, we don't know if it was the timing or if it was because it served its purpose," said Peter, trying to be reasonable. "Surely everything won't only last a few minutes."

She looked at him doubtfully. "What if we get the boat and it only lasts until we're far enough away we can't swim back? Or what if the paddle shrinks? What if–"

"Hey, Aisling," said Peter, walking over to her. He wanted to reach out for her, but he hesitated when she turned to face him. "Do you honestly believe Eli would trick us like that? These were gifts, and we don't know how they work. And sure, an explanation before we left would've been nice, but we'll figure it out."

"You think so?" she asked, hope filling her eyes at his words.

"Of course I do," he said, trying to convince himself just as much as her. "Come on," he said, gathering up the rest of the gifts. "If you're worried, why don't we test it?"

"How?"

"Well, it's already getting a bit late," he said, seeing the purples and dark blues already beginning to deepen across the sky. "Why don't we use the rest of my bracelet to make the boat and paddle? We'll let it sit out overnight and then if it hasn't shrunk, we will know it's not on a timer."

"And what if it has shrunk?"

"Then we'll figure something else out," he said, smiling what he hoped was a confident smile.

She nodded, looking up at him with her emerald eyes. This was the first time they had ever been alone together. At least while he had been conscious. Now that he had a moment to think, he realized that it was something that didn't make a lot of sense.

"Aisling, why were you the one who brought me here?"

Her eyes flashed. "Oh, did you wish it was someone else then?"

"What? No! Of course not! That came out weird. I–"

"Well, it's fine. I already know you hate me, so–"

"Wait just a moment! Where did that idea come from?"

"You pretty much admitted as much before the Kri siblings took us!"

"As I recall, I said I didn't hate you!"

"Well, you didn't say you didn't! All you've done is told me what to do, where to be, and ignored me! What was I supposed to think?" she turned away from him, staring out over the ocean as the waves lapped on the shore.

Peter rubbed a hand over his face, trying to figure out how he had messed things up this badly. He walked over to where she stood to stand next to her. "Aisling, I don't hate you. For the record, I… like you a lot."

She whipped her head around, her eyes meeting his. "Then why haven't you shown it?"

He lost his breath for a moment at the intensity of her stare. He cleared his throat. "I haven't…I'm not always good at expressing myself and…"

"And?" she prompted when he didn't continue.

"And I didn't know how you'd react. I… I don't want to hurt you."

"Is that all? That's really what you're afraid of?"

"What do you mean is that all? I just bared my soul to you and here you are saying is that all? My god," he took a few steps away from her just needing to walk it off.

Then he felt a tug on his arm, as her hand pulled him back. He lit up from where her hand touched his bare skin and the feeling spread to the rest of his body.

"No, wait! I'm sorry I just thought that was silly because you know you've been hurting me."

He whirled on her. "What? How?"

"Peter, when you ignore me, that hurts me," she spoke as if speaking to a child.

"What– I didn't mean–" he felt himself rambling but couldn't seem to stop.

"Well, I know that now but I thought you didn't like me, and that hurt. Especially considering I like you, too."

"You– what now?" Peter felt like his head was spinning.

"I like you too," she repeated, smiling up at him.

Her eyes bore into his, and he felt himself getting lost in their depths. They were close, much closer than they had ever stood before. As he opened his mouth to respond, someone coughed behind them.

Heart in his throat he spun around, pulling Aisling behind him. There was a little blue man, about the size of a toddler. He had bright green clothes that seemed to be made out of leaves, and he was looking at them with amusement in his eyes.

"Well, I don't mean to interrupt," he said, taking a few steps closer.

Peter, missing his sword, tried to look intimidating. "Who're you? What's your business?"

The little blue man laughed and said, "The name's Rasful," he gave an exaggerated bow. "My business currently is to keep you safe. And given how easy it was to sneak up on you," he said with a twinkle in his eye, "I'm going to say I've got my work cut out for me!" he sat down on a tree stump, and crossing his arms across his chest, grinned at them happily.

"Who sent you?" asked Aisling, coming out a little from behind Peter.

"Can you think of no one?"

Peter stayed uptight, not trusting himself to move.

"Oh, very well, if you need me to spell it out, E-L-I sent me," he said, pulling out a small pipe and began puffing on it happily. It was somehow already lit. "Although, I don't know why I always walk in on people kissing. Must be my impeccable timing."

"We weren't– we were just–"

"Alright, alright, keep your shirt on," Rasful shrugged and began blowing perfect smoke rings.

Aisling was the first to approach him. "How are you going to keep us safe?"

"Well, for starters, I was going to explain how the bracelets work. However," he said, eyeing Peter's wrist. "I can see you've already figured it out, at least in part. I would advise not activating something until you need it," he said, his face growing serious.

"Why not?" asked Peter, a bit more harshly than he needed to.

"Oh ho! Looks like I made someone unhappy with being interrupted," he sang. "You've got quite a hold on him don't you," he winked at Aisling. "Because, hot-headed Peter, once you've activated something, you can't activate it again."

"Oh no," said Aisling, eyeing the basket.

"Yes it is unfortunate, but at least it was only the basket! You could've messed up everything if you had started with the boat."

"Now wait just a minute!" Peter exclaimed, striding forwards. "How were we supposed to know any of this!"

"Well, that's what I'm for," said Rasful, puffing out his chest. "Come on, Peter, why don't you use some of that frustrated energy and gather wood for a fire? Make yourself useful."

Peter stood there, shaking with rage until he felt Aisling's hand on his arm. He looked down at her and she said, "It's alright, I'll go with you."

"Wait a moment," came Rasful's sing-song voice. "I would actually like a word with the lady. So go on! Hop to it!"

Aisling looked at him helplessly. Peter clenched his jaw and marched into the forest. He grumbled the whole time about tiny blue creatures that messed everything up. He gathered several pieces of wood in record time and hurried back to the campsite.

"Welcome back," Rasful said cheerfully as Peter came out of the trees. He briefly thought about chunking one of the logs at Rasful's face but thought better of it. Aisling was sitting too close to him and with the way his luck was going, he would accidentally hit her instead.

He began building a fire, moving dirt around so that it would be in a little hole. Stacking the wood just so, he reached in his belt for his flint when he remembered he didn't put on his belt before they left.

Cursing, he began searching around for stones that he could use when he felt a hand on his arm. He looked up, and Aisling made a scoot-over motion, before placing both hands in front of her. He did as she bade and watched in fascination as two green electrical bolts came out of her hands instantly lighting the wood. A few moments later, a happy fire was blazing in front of them.

"Amazing," he said, facing her again. She smiled up at him and for a moment, they were close enough to be almost touching. Remembering Rasful, Peter turned to see him grinning mysteriously at them from his perch on the stump.

Peter stood facing Rasful and said, "Anything else?"

"No," he answered cheerfully. "You may relax now. Trust me, you'll need your strength for tomorrow."

He bristled at Rasful's condescending tone but sat down with his side to the fire enjoying its warmth. Aisling reclined next to him, closer than she ever had before. "Are you cold?" he asked, worried that her linen shirt might not be enough against the cool night air.

"Not to worry!" said Rasful, jumping up and startling them both at his sudden movement. "I brought supplies!" he reached behind the stump and pulled out an impossible number of blankets and sleeping rolls. There was no way that all of those things would be able to fit behind the small stump.

He handed them out, then he spread himself out on the smallest mat directly in between them. "I can't have you two love birds keeping each other up all night. We need you to get your rest cause we have a busy day tomorrow."

"Wait, aren't you supposed to keep us safe?" asked Peter, his annoyance at this little man coming out in his voice.

"I am! Whether that be safe from enemies, or each other," he said, giving him a suggestive look.

"We don't need a chaperone!"

"That's for me to decide," said Rasful, leaning his short arm over to pat him on the cheek.

Peter swatted his hand away and rolled himself upon his mat, angry at the way the little man was so belittling.

"Don't worry, Aisling," he heard Rasful say behind him. "Peter will be fine in the morning. He just needs to rest."

Everyone quieted down at those words and seemed to fall asleep. Peter didn't feel like he could, with anger boiling away in his stomach. When he had finally begun to doze off, he felt a hand roughly shake him.

Rasful stood next to him, "Come," he led the way slightly into the woods. Peter looked over at Aisling's still form for a moment, before begrudgingly following.

Rasful led him only a few feet in before turning to face him. "Well?" asked Peter, not even trying to hide the annoyance in his voice.

"I needed to talk to you. Alone," said Rasful, his usual mischievous face looking somber.

"I'm listening," despite his best efforts, he was curious as to what Rasful had to say.

"Your dreams are valid."

Peter felt goosebumps rise on his arms at Rasful's words. "What do you mean by that?"

"Just because you don't dream of the same things as your sister, doesn't mean that they aren't important. You've protected her and been her support for the majority of your life. It's alright to let her go. It's alright if your dreams are different from hers."

Peter was quiet. Rasful's words had struck something within him. He had always been there for Silver and placed his dreams aside so she could live hers. He didn't want her on the ship by herself. He didn't trust anyone else to take care of her the way he did, nor did he think anyone could ever know her the way he did. They were twins. Weren't twins always supposed to stick together?

"Just something I needed to tell you," he said, shrugging nonchalantly.

"But Silver needs me."

"Does she?" Rasful asked. Peter opened his mouth to answer, yes of course she did, but no words came out. The answer would've been yes if he had been asked that question before Aisling came into the picture, before… Nathaniel. Maybe he and Silver were better off separated, living their own lives and following their dreams?

"Think about it," said Rasful, as he began to lead the way back to the camp. "You are allowed to make your own decisions. And if those decisions involve someone else," Peter could just make out Aisling's sleeping form. Her red hair flowed behind her, twinkling in the moonlight. "Then that's alright too."

They came back into camp quietly. Peter laid on his back staring at the stars, more awake than ever.

CHAPTER TWENTY-ONE

Silver

Silver was thrown into a dark room somewhere below decks. She landed heavily on her side, her hands still cuffed behind her giving her no way to break her fall. But she didn't feel pain. She didn't feel anything. Only numbness. She laid there doing nothing, not trying to get in a more comfortable position. It didn't matter. Nothing mattered.

"Hello?" came a voice from the back of the room. "Is someone there?"

Something about that voice was familiar, even if it was raspy. Silver lifted her head, unable to see anything from her position, she wiggled to her feet. It wasn't dignified, but she didn't care at this point. She, unfortunately, or fortunately, had spent way too much time in handcuffs from various times she had been arrested. Knowing how to make it in one swift movement, she lowered her arms behind her and smoothly jumped through her arms, now putting her cuffed hands in front of her so she'd have more control.

Creeping forwards, she darted in between crates, sticking to the shadows and hardly making a sound. Her curiosity had gotten the best of her in the worst of times, so it wasn't surprising that she was moving towards someone who may or may not hurt her.

She peeked around the last crate and saw a figure standing straight up. Leaning over to get a better view, she saw why the voice she heard was so familiar. It was Nathaniel.

Crying out, she rushed to him, glad that he was at least alive. "Silver? Is that you?"

Silver stopped short at his voice. Could he not see her? She reached up to his face, afraid of what she might find. Her fingers brushed something she couldn't quite identify.

"Nathaniel? Are you–"

"No, I can see!" he said, anticipating her question. "They just blindfolded me. Can you..?"

She pulled, and what must've been some kind of cloth, came away easily.

"Ah, thank you! Although, I suppose it doesn't make that much of a difference. Why is it so dark here?"

"Well, the sun's probably gone down by now," she answered, beginning to lower her hands. "Wait a moment. Let me see if I can find a light."

She began going through the crates, knowing they must have a box of candles somewhere. Finally, she found it, and after a bit more digging was able to find a small box of matches as well. She lit a candle and carefully brought it back to where she had first seen Nathaniel. When the light fell on him, she gasped and almost dropped it.

He was covered in bruises and he had bloody, swollen lips. His eyes were almost completely sealed shut by how swollen they were. He was shirtless, meaning she had a full view of the bruises that covered most of his chest and arms. "I must look pretty bad then," he said, attempting a grin that broke open his bottom lip, causing it to bleed again.

Silver saw that his arms were tied in and were hanging above his head tied up in some kind of rope.

"What's that sound?" she asked, ignoring his last statement. There was a tapping sound like a faucet dripping. Coming in closer for further inspection, she saw that his right arm was heavily bleeding. Not enough to kill him, at least not immediately.

She untucked her shirt and began ripping the bottom half of it. "What are you doing?" Nathaniel asked, trying to see her better through his squinting eyes.

She ignored him and continued ripping until she had several long strips of fabric. Crawling over some of the other crates, she was able to find a bottle of rum, not exactly medicine but the alcohol would clean out his wounds. She also found a letter opener and a hairpin of all things. She brought her goodies back over to him.

"Silver?"

She grabbed the rum first and uncorking it, tipped it back into his slightly open mouth. He sputtered slightly, as the alcohol hit his injured lip but he drank a good amount. "Delicious," he croaked out. "If not particularly refreshing."

"It's all we have down here," she answered, turning so she could pour some of it onto the stripes of cloth. "But it wasn't to refresh you."

"What was it for then?"

"Unfortunately, I'm going to need to leave you tied up a bit longer."

"What–" he began to ask, then his body went taut as she pressed the alcohol-soaked cloth onto his skin. He muffled a cry in pain, trying to be quiet, but she continued cleaning the wounds until she was satisfied.

"You could've given me a warning," he said, panting slightly when she had finished.

She shrugged at him, and took a swig of the rum herself before wrapping his now clean wounds in the rest of her shirt. In hindsight, she could've given him a warning but she hadn't thought about it. She felt his breath on her face as she moved around him, trying her best to stop the bleeding. They hadn't been this close in a long time, and she felt her heart pounding in response to it.

When she had finished, she turned again, going back to her supplies.

"You know," he said in a lazy voice. "I seem to always find myself tied up around you."

"Physically or emotionally?" she asked, walking back over to him.

He laughed, which turned into a cough. She grabbed the rum bottle again and gave him another sip. Then standing directly in front of him, she reached above him to begin sawing at the rope holding his hands. She stood on tiptoe, bringing them face to face. They were quite close again, this time she could've sworn she heard him catch his breath, but it could've just been the fact he was in pain. He was quiet for a moment, letting her work.

"Thank you," he said softly, his breath warm across her face.

She nodded, almost losing her nerve for a moment, and then continued. "This might take a while."

"Well, how would you like to pass the time?"

"No idea," she answered, continuing.

"Hmm, how about a question for a question?"

"Like when we first met?"

"Exactly," he said smiling. "You have to answer completely honestly."

"Fine, but I get to go first."

"Of course, I wouldn't have it any other way."

She thought for a moment, then asked before she could overthink it, "Why can't you always control yourself?"

He was quiet for a moment before answering, "The Cleansers developed me. I'm one of their failed experiments. My father was a wolf and my mother was a human. Trust me," he said, seeming to read her thoughts. "I try not to think about it too much. My mother isn't around anymore and left me in the hands of the Cleansers."

"They… they've done many things to me. One of their experiments was trying to turn me into a weapon. They would say certain words, trying to use them as a brainwashing code. For a while, it almost worked. They almost broke me. But they didn't account for one thing."

"What was that?"

His eyes grew hard, seeming less puffy than before. "My ability to fight back. I have learned to hide everything about myself. My form, my thoughts but most importantly: my emotions. This was the one thing that was mine. Something they couldn't touch. However, sometimes I lose it. I don't know what's the mask and what's me. Am I confident and unbothered or am I something else?"

His eyes flicked over to her, and she realized she had stopped cutting, completely wrapped up in his story. "My turn, and I get two questions since I answered two from you."

"Oh very well. Go ahead." She continued her sawing.

"What happened when they took me down here? There is something weird. You've been off since you got here."

She sighed, not wanting to get into it. It was still too fresh, too new. But he had answered her question truthfully and fully. So she told him. She told him about Tom, about what the Cleansers had done. And when she started talking, it was almost like she couldn't stop. The words continued to tumble out of her mouth as she kept her eyes firmly above his head on the rope.

"I don't know if I can protect everyone. I have fought so hard to get to this point, to prove to them that I'm worthy to be their captain. But then something like this happens and I realize how powerless I am. In everything."

Finally, she stopped the flow of words. She couldn't look at him. Couldn't believe she had said all that. It was almost like she had been waiting for him to ask. Tears fell down her cheeks, embarrassing her but she couldn't stop them.

"It's not your fault."

"I don't know if I believe you." She bit her lip, trying to prevent the sob that tried to bubble out.

"Silver, look at me."

Nothing was forcing her to do it. It wasn't like he could force her head up to look at him. Yet for some reason, she found her eyes meeting his blue ones.

"Part of being a leader is knowing when to take the blame. The Cleansers are monsters. You couldn't have done anything different to save him."

She nodded, hearing the truth in his words, even if she didn't completely believe him yet.

"Now hurry up," he said gruffly. "It's driving me crazy. I can't wipe away your tears."

"You want to wipe away my tears?"

"Yes," he said as if this was obvious. "But it's not your turn. Why do you feel like you need to prove yourself?" he asked quietly, making her heart drop. This was the true heart of the matter, wasn't it? The real thing she had been feeling and striving to achieve.

"Because–" she broke off, her thoughts tumbling over themselves. "Because don't all captains need to prove that they're meant to be in charge?"

He was already shaking his head before answering, "None that I've ever met before."

"But you grew up in a lab."

"Not all the time. I was sent on missions sometimes, and I ran away more times than I can remember. But we aren't talking about me right now."

"I–" she felt herself floundering slightly. Why was this so difficult to answer? "I guess I just felt like I didn't deserve it. It's always been my dream to sail. I love the ocean. I love being out on the water with the sun beating down and fighting the waves. Everything that comes with it, even the hard work."

"I never thought I would be given a ship. I never expected to be made a captain. I was just thankful that they let a woman on board. Some ships can be superstitious and that has become more of an issue as time has gone on. But not from my crew. They're all–" her voice broke. Taking a deep breath she continued, "They are good people. All of them. I just don't know if I can lead them the way they need to be led. Everything I've done is to prove that I'm meant to be here. Meant to lead them."

"But can't you see that's the very thing," he said, with an eagerness like she was getting somewhere. "The fact that you're thinking that way, the fact that you're worrying about whether or not you should be captain, is the very reason that you should be."

"What does that matter?"

"Well, any other captain I've ever sailed with hasn't cared. They were all horrible and didn't care if they deserved to be captain; they didn't even question it. The only thing they cared about was making more money or gorging themselves on whatever they pleased. The fact that you care makes all the difference in the world! It has nothing to do with deserving anything. Silver, Tom was happy to die for you."

"But I didn't want him to die. I don't want him to be happy about it."

"I'm not saying that you did or you should want that. What I'm saying is his willingness and happiness to sacrifice himself shows so much more about you. He loved you, Silver. Your entire crew does. They would all gladly lay down their lives if it meant keeping you safe and that sacrifice will not be in vain. You love them, and they love you. This is what it means to be a captain."

Something suddenly clicked into place for Silver at his words. It wasn't that she didn't deserve it or had to prove herself. She had their approval the whole time. More than that, she had their love, and she loved them just as much. Maybe that's what it meant to be a friend, to be willing to lay down your own life for them. She took a deep breath and let it out slowly. "Thank you," she said, feeling the weight of the world she had been carrying ease up.

"You're welcome," he said, smiling. His eye suddenly seemed less puffy, and his lip wasn't bleeding anymore.

"Do you have magic healing or something?" she asked, scanning the rest of his body with her eyes.

"I can heal faster than most," he admitted sheepishly. "The blindfold was to prevent that. But thanks to you, I am healing nicely."

"So, you didn't even need the bandages? Or the alcohol?"

"Well… no," he said smiling. "But I did appreciate the effort. Ouch!" she had elbowed him in his bruised ribs.

"I don't feel bad about hurting you now."

"Oh, that's not fair! If you had told me what you were doing then I could've told you not to."

The rope suddenly snapped in two, the knife finally cutting through it. "There," she said, about to lower her hands.

Before she could move, he grabbed her hands in his own and gently pried the knife out of her fingers. "What did you use, a spoon?" he asked as he dropped it over to the side of them.

"It was a letter opener," she admitted, her heart pounding at their closeness.

He lowered both of his arms to encircle her waist while saying, "That explains why it took so long then."

"It was all I could find," she rested her hands on his bare chest, feeling his skin against her palms.

"Well, then I suppose I should thank you, not only for releasing me but also for your excellent healing skills."

She snorted at that in a very awkward way. He looked down at her surprised, so embarrassed she tried to duck under his arms. "Where do you think you're going?" he asked, tightening his grip, and pulling her in closer. "I didn't mean to embarrass you. I've just never heard you laugh before. It's beautiful, and I'd love to make you do it again."

Her hands were pressed tightly against his chest, the metal of her handcuffs biting into her wrists. "Now about that thank you," she said, changing the subject. "What did you have in mind?"

"Well, I don't have much I can offer you," he said slowly, his eyes flickering down to her lips. "But I do have something in mind if that's alright with you."

He leaned in closer, the last word whispered across her lips. Then he waited for centimeters away, their warm breath intermingling. "May I?" he asked, eyes locked on hers. She realized that he was waiting for her to answer. He could've just kissed her without even considering if she wanted to or not. This was a different side of him that she had never seen before.

"Yes, you may," she said a little breathlessly. His mouth went up in a small smile before he leaned in and closed the distance between them.

His lips were warm and soft and as they pressed gently against her own, she felt herself melt into them. She had some experience with men before, usually hot and rough and to the point. This time was so different. There was nothing rushed about it, nothing frantic. It was slow and steady, like the beating of Nathaniel's heart under her palms. His lips explored hers almost lazily, softly. Through all of her time knowing Nathaniel, she had no idea he could be so gentle so tender.

He pulled back, his lips finding other places to explore, her cheeks, her eyelids. When they finally came back to her mouth, she was hungry for them. She deepened the kiss, wanting to know a different side of him. His body reacted almost instantly. Turning her expertly around, he pressed her back against the wall of the ship, pushing his own body against hers, his arms no longer around her waist but in her hair, cupping her cheek.

The kiss was more of what she was used to, yet it was somehow still so different. There were teeth and tongue, yet there wasn't anything violent about it, there was hunger, but it still wasn't frantic. Whatever it was, she liked it and wanted to go deeper, to know more. Her hands slid down from his chest and made their way to his pants.

She felt him freeze, and faster than she would've thought possible, pulled back and brought his hands to her own, stopping her. "Silver," he said, panting slightly. "I think that's enough."

She felt as if she had been slapped. She tried to wiggle out from his grasp but he held her firmly in place. "Well, if you're done then let me go," she said, frustration and anger leaking out of her voice like venom.

"Let me rephrase," he said, his iron grip preventing her from moving. "That's enough for now."

"Why?" she asked, hating how pitiful she sounded.

"Well, let me think. One," he said, counting off on her fingers. "The Cleansers could be back at any moment. I would prefer not to be indisposed when they do. Two," he held up another of her fingers.

"We need to be making up a plan. And three, I don't want you to regret anything about us."

"I won't regret it," she said, firmly.

"We don't know that right now," he said smiling. He kissed each of her three fingers before wrapping her hands in his own. "There's no rush. I'm not going anywhere. Unless you tell me to. Plus the setting isn't right."

"What do you mean?"

His all too familiar grin was back, "There's no romance, Darling. Although it would be so simple to do this now, I'd prefer to wait for the right moment."

"But what if we don't get another chance?"

"Come on," he said, leaning in and kissing her forehead. "Don't think that way. We'll get through this, and when we do, I want to make this special. Let me plan this. I want it to mean something. I don't want to be just another man on the list. When I take you," she felt her, chills all down her body as he leaned in and whispered this last part in her ear. "I want you to see stars."

He leaned back and smiled at her, making her knees grow weak. She could see the hunger in his eyes. She knew he wanted this just as much as she did. He kissed her again softly, and she knew he was right. Now wasn't the right time.

"How long?" she asked when he pulled back.

He laughed, and pressing his forehead to her own, said, "Not long. I don't know how much longer I can wait. But right now, let's focus on surviving the next few days."

She nodded, then pressed her lips to his again feeling like she would never grow tired of kissing him. First, they needed to survive the night, then maybe they could test that theory. She was the first to pull back this time and stepped away. He released her and stepped back as well, looking at her.

"Right," she said, all business. "First let's try to get these handcuffs off."

He nodded, amusement at her business-like tone all over his face. She went back to her pile and pulled out the hairpin. "Any idea how to pick a lock?"

In no time at all, her hands were freed. Silver could feel her strength flow back into her. She felt tired but not drained as she had before. Nathaniel seemed to be feeling the same way. He stretched similarly to how he did in cat form, and Silver took the opportunity to admire his strong muscled figure. Catching her, he grinned and then faster than she could blink had her in his arms and somehow pulled her down on his lap. For a few more minutes, there was no talking as they explored each other.

"This is ridiculous," said Silver, coming up for air. "We're acting like teenagers."

"You started it," he mumbled against her neck.

She wiggled out from his arms and sat, panting a few inches away. "I can't think when you're kissing me! Alright, what do we do? We need to come up with a plan."

He leaned back lazily on one elbow. "Off the top of my head, I can think of a few things. However, it's your crew I'm not sure about. I know we could get away, but them."

"Well, I'm not leaving without them, so we'll have to think of something." She didn't remember standing but found herself pacing, trying to get her brain to work. There had to be something. She felt Nathaniel's eyes on her, not offering anything helpful, just watching her pace back and forth.

"I've got it!" She said, snapping her fingers. "What if we put my handcuffs back on when they come. It almost seems like they forgot about you. Wait–" she broke off and stopped walking. "Why did they put me in here with you?"

Nathaniel shrugged. "I think they planned on me being dead by the time you got here. That blindfold wasn't as strong as they thought it was."

"That's horrible," she said, shivering slightly at the idea of being locked in here with Nathaniel's body.

"Are you cold?" he asked, coming up to her and wrapping his arms around her.

"You're the one who's probably cold," she said, but she leaned into his arms nonetheless. "I'll see if I can find you a shirt."

"Hurry back," he said, leaning down to kiss her neck again.

"Nathaniel," she said, feeling her eyes lose focus slightly. "You need to let me go so I can do that."

He chuckled and did as she asked. She shook herself slightly and began going through the crates. "What's the rest of your plan?"

"Wcll," shc said, not finding anything useful and moving on to the next one. "You can turn into something small, something they wouldn't expect. I can tell them it was awful and your body disappeared when you died. Then you can begin freeing the crew. I assume they're going to come back for me so they can try to get more information. Aha!" she said, producing a black, silk shirt.

"Where did you get this?" Nathaniel asked when she handed it to him, a look of shock on his face at the quality.

She shrugged. "Merchants. We get all sorts of stuff that needs to be shipped off to other locations. I don't ask questions, I just deliver what I'm told. Or not. Sometimes we keep it."

"You know, the more you talk, the less I think you're pirates and the more I think you may be smugglers."

"Just put on the shirt, Nathaniel."

"Yes, Captain," he said, admiring the shirt for a moment longer before doing as he was told.

"After you set the crew free," she said, continuing her plan. "I'll call on animals, and we'll ambush them."

"This sounds like a wonderful plan," he said, coming over to her slowly, and wrapping his arms around her. "Only one thing: how will you call on animals if you have these handcuffs on?"

"Oh right, I didn't think about that," she said, frowning.

"You're so cute when you're thinking," he said, leaning down and kissing her again. "I feel like I could eat you up."

She pushed him away. "Stop, I can't think," she began pacing again. "What to do, what to do?" Picking up the handcuffs, she turned them in her hands looking for a switch or something that made them work. Eventually, she found it, a small, almost microscopic knot in the metal. Taking her hairpin from before, she jammed it into the knot before completely scraping it off. Putting the handcuffs back on, she waited for the draining feeling to come but it didn't.

"I think I fixed it!" she said, as Nathaniel expertly picked the lock again.

"Well done," he said, not releasing her hands after placing the handcuffs to the side. "I think your plan could work. We'll just need to get it right the first time, there'll be no room for error."

"I don't think we have another option," she said, softly.

"Perhaps not," he said, bringing her trapped hands to his lips. "We'll do it. When I've finished untying everyone, I'll whisper in your ear. That'll be the signal. Then with the rest of the crew, we'll rush them. Hopefully, the surprise we have on them will be enough."

"It'll have to be," she said, chewing on her bottom lip in worry.

Nathaniel leaned down to nibble her lip as well. "We'll do it. It will work. Now," he said, looking up into her eyes. "Why don't we try and get some sleep? We'll need all the rest we can get."

She nodded, and together they searched for blankets. After finding some, they got rid of the evidence of the crates being looked through as well as the candles that were used.

They spread out the blankets, Silver beginning to make her own pallet before Nathaniel took her blankets over to his. "Come on," he said. "I need your warmth."

"Oh, is that all?" she asked, but climbed in dutifully after him.

It was cool below deck, and the blankets were thin, so she was grateful for his warmth. He wrapped his arms around her, pulling her in close. "Good night, Silver."

"Good night," she said, turning her face up to his. Knowing what she wanted, he kissed her. He pulled back far too soon, and tucking her head to his chest, he held her close.

CHAPTER TWENTY-TWO

Peter

The next morning, Peter woke to the sound of rustling. He opened his eyes to see Rasful's blue face grinning down at him. "Good morning!" he said cheerfully.

Peter shoved him away and got out of his bed roll. Aisling was already up, rolling up her mat, and putting it away. Peter did the same, keeping one eye on Rasful.

"I can take care of those for you," Rasful said. With a snap of his fingers, the mats disappeared.

"How… never mind," said Peter rubbing his eyes. It was too early for these kinds of games, and after not enough sleep and anticipation for the day ahead, he didn't have the brainpower.

"Well, let's get to rescuing!" Rasful said, clapping his hands together.

"Rescuing?" Peter was having a very hard time keeping up with the little bouncing man. "Who're we rescuing?"

"Oh, didn't I tell you? The Cleansers have your sister and the crew captive," he said in with same annoying cheerfulness.

Peter felt his stomach drop like a stone. "What?" he asked, only now feeling wide awake.

"Yes, the Cleansers came and took over the Silver Shadow about two days ago."

"And when were you planning on telling us this?" Peter asked in a dangerous voice. He felt his temper rising, the corner of his vision going red.

"It must've slipped my mind," he smiled, mischievously.

"Then why did we spend last night sleeping? We could've rescued them by now!"

"Come now, we all needed the rest. Can't rescue people if we're falling asleep where we stand." He grew serious. "They're alright currently. There was nothing we could have done for them last night. But now, it's time to get moving. Are you ready?"

Peter nodded, still fuming.

"Excellent. Now Aisling, my dear, if you'd press your bracelet to the boat, and Peter use yours for the paddle."

They did as he was told, and in no time at all they had a boat and paddle big enough for all three of them. Peter dragged the boat to the water with Rasful not helping at all, of course.

"Why is there only one paddle?" asked Peter after a lot of pulling and pushing, successfully getting the boat afloat.

"I'll show you." Rasful helped Aisling into the boat and waited for Peter to get in before walking over to the back. He placed the paddle in what looked like a small holder. At first, nothing happened, but when Rasful jumped into the boat, the paddle began vibrating, almost like it was caught on something. Then before Peter was prepared for it, the boat took off over the ocean, almost skipping over the waves. Peter was thrown to the floor, grumbling his thanks to Aisling who rushed over to help him.

"Don't quite have your sea legs, do you?" asked Rasful, laughing. Peter glared at him and then stared out over the water. They were traveling at an impossible speed. No ship or creature as far as Peter knew could go this quickly.

In a quarter of the time it usually took, they had made it far enough out to sea that Peter could no longer see the shore. The wind whipped his face, making it hard to keep his eyes open. Even at the speed they were traveling, he kept wanting the ship to go faster. All he could see were visions of Silver being hurt by the Cleansers.

He startled at the feeling of something touching him. Looking over, he saw that Aisling had slipped her hand into his. He gave her a smile and a reassuring squeeze. She squeezed his hand back, giving him the strength to stop his spiraling thoughts. If Rasful noticed their hand holding, he didn't say anything about it.

After about an hour, the boat began to slow. Worried that it was shrinking, Peter glanced over at Rasful. The blue man didn't seem at all bothered by this new development, so Peter decided that it wasn't anything to worry about. Although, maybe Rasful was a better swimmer than he looked.

Just as the boat slowed down to an almost crawl, Peter saw it. A huge metal ship, about three times the size of the Silver Shadow. It puffed out this continuous stream of black smoke, which just so happened to be what they were heading into.

The boat somehow knew to use the smoke as a cover, and it stealthily crept up to the other ship. Peter was tense, waiting at any moment for the alarm to sound and them to be spotted, but nothing happened. They just continued moving forwards until their tiny boat gently tapped the side of the metal one.

Rasful had taken out the cloaks and handed one to each of them. Gesturing for them to use their bracelets, he turned and began removing a part of the metal that Peter wouldn't have believed could be separated from the rest of the ship.

Peter swung his cloak around himself and helped Aisling to do the same.

"Now," Rasful whispered. "The rest is up to you. The cloaks will protect you from anyone seeing you, but you have to be fully covered."

"Is my sister on this ship?"

"No," said Rasful. "But this is where you can save her."

"What–"

"I think I understand," said Aisling, interrupting Peter.

"Good girl," said Rasful, smiling. "Now go."

He helped Aisling on the enemy ship and left Peter to climb up himself.

"Will we see you again?" asked Aisling once Peter climbed into the side of the ship.

"Oh aye," he said with a little bow. "Trust me I'm never that far away. Take care of each other."

Peter blinked and in Rasful's place was just air and a tiny boat that looked like it was a toy.

He and Aisling looked at each other before taking the piece of metal and gently propping it up to look like there wasn't a hole. They turned and found themselves in what seemed to be a small metal tunnel. Peter could stand up but just barely. The top of his head brushing the roof.

"Are you alright?" he asked, turning to her. He realized this must be hard for her to be back so close to the creatures who had hurt her.

"Yes," she whispered, turning her face up to look at him. He saw fear in her eyes. "As long as I'm with you."

"Trust me," he said, brushing her damp hair out of her eyes. "I'm not going anywhere."

Their eyes locked again, and Peter had to physically take a step back to get some distance from her. "Now do you have any idea where we are?"

"Unfortunately yes," she said, glancing around. "We're in the center of the ship. Rasful brought us as close as he could to the engine rooms."

"What's in the engine rooms? You know, besides the engine?"

She smiled at him, making his heart quicken. He would do anything for that smile. "We need to destroy it," she said, pulling out the last item that Eli had given them.

"The whole engine room?"

"More like the whole ship," she tucked the strange gun-like item back into the bag. "This is a… well some sort of explosive. It only works with a spark."

"That's convenient."

"Terribly," she gave him a small smile. "Come on. I know where we need to go."

"How do you know where to go?" Peter followed her down the strange metal hallway.

"Ah, now I get to be the one with all the answers," she said, smugly. "I came aboard this ship quite a bit. The Cleanser's life force is attached to it. They worked halfway on the island and halfway on the ship. If they needed to recharge then they would come here. When I was younger, they would take me aboard and then leave me to my own devices. I'm not entirely sure why," she said, thoughtfully. "Maybe they just figured I couldn't run away, so they didn't need to watch me. I'm sure if they knew what I was up to now they probably would've kept a closer eye on me."

"How many of them are there?"

"Ten, I think," she walked forwards, and the tunnel made a sharp turn to the right. "It's a little bit difficult to tell them apart. Wait, I hear something."

Pulling up their hood, they both crouched down and waited. Peter's heart pounded against his ribs. If they got caught now, it would be disastrous. At first, Peter couldn't hear anything above the sound of his heart. And then he heard it, a tip tap. It almost sounded like claws scratching against the metal of the tunnel.

Sitting perfectly still, Peter strained his eyes in the near darkness, until he saw something moving. It was small and hard to see with how dark everything was. It wasn't until it was almost right next to them that Peter finally was able to make out what it was, a black cat. The same one from the cave where they rescued Aisling.

They both held their breath, praying that Rasful had been honest with them and the cloaks would hide them. It passed so close to them that Peter thought the cat's tail may brush his leg. As it passed, Peter noticed that the cat had a red blinking light in the corner of both eyes.

They waited until they were sure it was gone. Aisling was the first to stand, "We need to hurry."

Peter stood and silently followed her. They walked on, stopping briefly to take off their shoes and tie them to their belts. "It'll help us move quietly," Aisling explained when she suggested it.

Finally, they made it out of the metal tunnel and into a wide-open space. Peter felt anxious after the small space of the tunnel, now he felt overexposed. She led him to the center of the room.

There was a huge pillar that was completely covered in wires. It reached the ceiling which, was several feet above Peter's head. The rest of the walls surrounding it had weird red blinking lights with exposed wires running up and down the walls. Aisling snuck into the room, Peter following in her footsteps.

"Why are there no guards?" Peter whispered, just as they heard something.

Crouching down in the corner of the room, they made sure to cover themselves with their cloaks. There was the sound of metal on metal getting closer. The cloaks worked for the cat, so they could only hope it would also work on the Cleansers. They waited. And waited. Peter's anxiety was getting to the point he almost just wished they would find them, just so he wouldn't have to be so stressed.

The creature finally rounded the corner and walked into the room. He checked on something on the pillar of wires. Peter held his breath, trying to quiet any noise that he was making. Then the creature turned to look directly at their hiding place. Peter and Aisling sat stock-still as if they had turned to stone. After several long heartbeats, the creature turned and walked back out of the room.

They waited for a couple more beats before Aisling nodded at him. He let out his breath slowly. "You just had to ask where the guards were?"

Peter's eyes shot over to her, but she was smiling. "Come on," she whispered, leading him to the center of the room. "Another will be back soon. We don't have much time."

"Any idea how this thing works?" he asked, coming up behind her.

"No idea," she answered inspecting it. "But I also don't think anything exploding here would be good for it."

She pressed the last shell on her bracelet to the tiny toy. Before Peter's eyes, the gun-like thing grew until it was a little bigger than Aisling's hand. Looking at it closer, he was able to see that it wasn't a gun but some sort of bomb.

"Where did Eli get this?" he whispered.

"I'm not sure," she answered. "But we don't have time to worry about that now." She snapped her fingers, which sounded like a gunshot in the quiet room, then pressed the spark to the device. It lit up and began blinking rapidly. She placed it in the middle of the wires and stepped back.

"What happens now?" she asked, looking at him.

"Now we run!" he grabbed her hand and dragged her back down the metal tunnel they had come from.

"Where are we going?" asked Aisling, as they ran.

"Back out from where we came!"

"But we don't have a boat! It shrank, remember?"

Peter let out a string of curses as they ran. "Any idea how much time we have before that thing goes off?"

"Absolutely no idea."

More cursing on Peter's end. "Aisling, how are you at swimming?"

"Fine, I guess."

"Well," he said as they rounded the corner. "We're about to put that to the test."

Aisling stopped dead in her tracks. Peter, having no idea what was going on, looked in front of them and saw the black cat staring right at them.

CHAPTER TWENTY-THREE

Silver

Silver woke to Nathaniel pressing a finger to her lips. Opening her eyes, she saw the gray light of morning shining in through the cracks in the wood. "They'll probably be here soon," he whispered. "We need to get ready."

She nodded, heart-pounding and stomach tying itself in knots. They shoved the blankets into a crate, and Nathaniel helped her back into her handcuffs. "I don't know if this is going to work," she whispered, voicing her fears. Now that this was happening, all of her confidence from the night before had vanished.

"Don't think like that," he said, pressing tiny kisses on the inside of her palm.

"But what if this doesn't work?"

"It will work," he said, tucking her short hair behind her ear. He rested his hand on her cheek, forcing her face up to meet his eyes. "It will." He leaned in and pressed his lips against hers. She kissed him back with all the fear and hope that this plan was a good one.

He pulled back and held her face in both his hands. "Are you ready?"

She let out a long breath, trying to answer him honestly. "Ready."

They decided she should be sleeping on the floor when the Cleansers came in. Nathaniel was going to change into a bug and try to fly out the door as soon as they opened it. She watched his body shrink until he disappeared. She laid down and shut her eyes, trying to make her breathing slow and steady.

The door flew open and two Cleansers walked in. She sat up, not having to pretend to be surprised as they came towards her. "Well," said the now familiar voice of the leader. "How was…" it drifted off as its masked face turned towards the place where Nathaniel had been tied up. They had done their job well. It looked exactly as it had the night before, just without Nathaniel in it.

"Where is he?" the Cleanser asked, turning to Silver.

"He disappeared," said Silver, trying to keep a tremble in her voice. This was the tricky part. She had to act like she was distraught but also like she was hiding the fact she was. "He was bleeding all over. I…" she made her voice break. "I tried to bandage his wounds but it was too late. When he died," she took a breath like she was steading herself. "His body turned to ash." She looked over at the scene that they had set up. Luckily the matches were cheap, so there were enough of them to make it look like he had turned to ash.

The Cleanser walked over to inspect. She heard the Cleansers discussing this in hushed tones as she tried to make herself seem upset, which wasn't too difficult given the circumstances. They seemed to be having a quiet argument, but after a few tense moments, they came back over to her.

"We have decided to trust your story, for now," it leaned in towards her until its ugly black beak was almost touching her nose. "But if we find out you're lying, we'll kill you on the spot." It nodded to the other Cleanser, who hauled Silver up to her feet and pushed her outside to the main deck.

The rest of her crew was here, sitting in almost the same place they had been the night before. Silver wondered if the Cleansers had even moved them. She noticed a few new bruises on several of the members, which made her blood boil.

"Now then," said the main Cleanser, rubbing its hands together. "Have you had time to think about where the girl is?"

"I have," answered Silver in a voice that she hoped sounded defeated.

"Well?"

She knew she just had to keep them talking to give Nathaniel a chance to cut the ropes. "I– I'll tell you."

"Wise choice," said the Cleanser in what sounded like a triumphant voice. "It's as easy as that, isn't it? Come now, tell us where she is."

"She left the ship."

"I'm well aware of that," the Cleanser said, an edge beginning to grow in its voice. "Where did she go?"

"She left five days ago," Silver's heart dropped, realizing how much time had passed since she last saw them. She hoped nothing had happened to them. "On a small boat in the middle of the night."

"That would explain why the crew knew nothing about it," it said, referring to one of the other Cleansers next to them. The other Cleanser seemed to be taking some notes.

That would be why the crew all had fresh bruises, thought Silver as she looked at all of them. Her eyes rested briefly on John's, who met her gaze with a steady stare. She knew him well enough to know what he was thinking; he was telling her not to say anything else.

She tried to give him a sign with her eyes to show that she knew what she was doing. His body twitched ever so slightly, in what she hoped was surprise at his bounds being suddenly chewed off. He gave her the slightest head nod, showing he understood. Nathaniel must be at work. Just a little longer.

"Yes, she left, without telling any of us where she was going. My crew knew nothing about this."

"But you did?"

"Yes," she said, acting like she didn't want to say anything. "We had become friends while she was aboard."

"And now you'll betray that friendship? Why?" it asked, seeming genuinely curious. She realized it was looking at her the way a scientist would, dissecting her decisions so that it can learn from them.

"You threatened my crew," she answered simply. "No friendship is worth my crew dying for."

"Interesting," it said, nodding to the other Cleanser who hastily began scribbling things down. "Well, I'm glad you've decided to come clean on this. I would hate for any more of your crew to die because of your unwillingness to speak."

"So would I," she said, in all honesty. Its curiosity was making stalling surprisingly easy for her. She only hoped it would last a little longer.

"Well, then let's get down to it," it said, practically rubbing its hands together. "Where is she?"

"She went to an island," she began making up on the spot.

"An island," the Cleanser said, cocking its head to the side, the way an animal does when they're trying to understand something.

"Yes, as I said, she went to an island."

"Why?"

"She wanted to see the world and where she grew up. It wasn't a deserted island, but one with people. I guess she wanted to start there."

Instantly, she knew she had said something wrong. The Cleanser looked at the other one, who slowly lowered its pen. "She rowed to an island." The creature took a step towards her. "Would you say that is something that would be difficult?"

Silver shrugged trying to look nonchalant. "That's all we had to give her. Maybe she was planning on getting a lift from another boat."

"You know," it said, continuing his slow pace towards her. "I realized something last night. Wasn't there another one of you?"

"What do you mean?" She took a step back, trying to put distance between them. Not that it mattered. She knew they could move fast.

"I remember, there was a boy just like you," it said, snapping its fingers in mock realization. "That's right! He looked just like you, except for the eyes. Now, what an odd thing for him not to be here as well."

"I've found something!" Silver jumped at the other Cleanser's voice. She had forgotten anyone else was there. She looked up and felt her heart drop like a stone to her feet. The Cleanser was holding up a struggling white rat.

The speaker turned back to her. "Thought you were so clever, didn't you?" it purred like the way an engine does before revving up. It turned back to the other Cleansers. "Kill them all."

CHAPTER TWENTY-FOUR

Peter

Not blinking, the cat stared at Aisling and Peter. At first, Peter thought that maybe the cat hadn't seen them until he felt something beginning to choke him. Ripping at his throat, he realized the magic cloak's power was fading, and it was shrinking back to its original size.

In horror, he looked over at Aisling who had fallen to her knees, clawing at her throat. He rushed over and ripped the now tiny cloak out from around her neck. She gasped big lungfuls of air as she rubbed her throat.

"That would've been nice to know how long they lasted," he said, as he helped her to her feet. She nodded but kept her eyes on the cat.

"Can we just sneak past it?" he asked.

"It's worth a try, but he may have already alerted them."

They began walking forwards, and the cat moved to further block their path. Peter was just contemplating giving the cat a good strong kick, when suddenly they heard footsteps racing towards them. With inhuman speed, there were two Cleansers directly behind the cat.

"I see we have visitors," one of them said. "And one of them looks strangely familiar."

Peter felt Aisling freeze next to him. Her fear was almost a living thing in the room with them.

"Hello, don't mind us, just passing through," said Peter, angling his body so he covered Aisling standing between her and the creatures. He was missing his sword and was silently cursing Rasful for not giving him some kind of weapon. "So, if you'll excuse us, we'll be leaving now."

Both Cleansers laughed a strange, scrapping laugh that made hairs on the back of his neck stand up. "There is no escape," said one of them, as they began to advance forwards.

This was bad. Peter began backing up, keeping Aisling behind him. Having no idea what else he could do, he cleared his mind. He felt the fear, anger, and panic slip away. That's when he felt it. Time began moving in slow motion. It was like he was looking at the scene as an outsider, as opposed to something that was happening to him. He saw himself lunge and pick up the cat that was currently licking itself, throwing it at the two Cleansers. Then he saw himself and Aisling run past them.

Time sped back up, and he knew what to do. He picked up the cat that felt strangely metallic in his hands, then he threw it at the two Cleansers as hard as he could. The cat hit them with the sound of metal hitting metal. All three of them went down, and then Peter grabbed Aisling's hand, and they spirited down the hall as fast as they could.

Peter knew that wouldn't hold them for long, in fact, he was already hearing them get back up. But he knew if he and Aisling made it to the place where they came in, they might have a chance. Time slowed again, this time showing the Cleansers grabbing Aisling. Peter saw himself throw his tied-up boot at the creature, hitting it in the face and tripping up the other Cleanser.

Time sped up again, and as he turned around, he grabbed his boot and slammed it into the Cleanser's face. This did indeed slow them again, which gave them enough time to make it to the panel.

Peter ripped off the panel, ready to use it as a weapon as he yelled, "Go!"

Aisling obediently jumped out of the ship and landed with a splash. Peter turned to face his oppressors.

"Do you think you've won?" asked the one on the right as they moved closer to him. "After all, you've got nowhere to go."

"I believe we do have somewhere else we can go. Have a nice life," he said before jumping out of the ship himself. As he jumped, there was a massive explosion. The bomb must've worked, Peter thought right before the shock wave hit him. He felt himself being thrown back and hit the water hard. His last thought was of Aisling, and he hoped she really could swim well. Then the water closed over him.

CHAPTER TWENTY-FIVE

Silver

Silver was thrown on her back by the force of the explosion. Before she could even begin to sort out what had happened, she was hauled back up to her feet. This time by a familiar, welcomed face. John held her gaze, and she nodded her gratitude. "It's their ship," he told her, loosening her handcuffs. "Somehow it just exploded." She turned her head and saw that indeed there were little bits of floating metal that were on fire. "Go! We'll take care of the crew."

Turning, she ran full force at the Cleanser who held Nathaniel. It had already dropped him and was on its hands and knees. Nathaniel was nowhere in sight. Slipping her hands out of her handcuffs, she began to use them as a weapon.

"What–" the Cleanser asked, looking over the railing to his ship. Silver walked up to him and hit the Cleanser across the mask, pushing its head to one side with the force of the blow. She heard a scuffle behind her, but didn't turn to see what was happening. Her focus was solely on the Cleanser in front of her. It was moving slower than usual. She couldn't see anything but red as she hit the Cleanser over and over again. Finally, it went down, and she stepped on its chest.

"Silver!"

She turned and saw John had taken care of the rest of the Cleansers. They were no longer moving, whether from the ship blowing up, or the beating her crew gave them, or maybe a mix of the two. Nathaniel was running up to her and pointed over the side of the ship. Aisling's head was bobbing in the water, and she was carrying Peter. Silver kicked the Cleanser in the face one more time for good measure, and then began giving orders.

A rope was lowered, and her battered crew hoisted them up on deck. She rushed over and felt Peter for a pulse. He had one, but just barely. Cedric came and took over, pumping his heart and having Aisling breathe into his mouth for air. At first, it didn't seem to be working. Then with one last kiss from Aisling, he sputtered. Turning on his side, he coughed up enough seawater to fill a fish tank.

"Was I dreaming or was Aisling just kissing me?" he croaked out. Silver rolled her eyes but laughed, throwing her arms around him.

She leaned back and hit him in the arm. "Ouch! Hey, I almost died!"

"Exactly," she said with tears in her eyes. "That was for almost dying." She turned to Aisling, "Thank you," she threw her arms around her in a hug as well. Aisling hugged her back.

"I hate to break this up, but I could use a little help over here!"

Nathaniel was single-handedly trying to tie all the Cleansers together, who were all trying to sneak away. They were all very slow, so they didn't pose a threat but one did get close to the edge of the ship.

Silver rushed to help with the other crew members, and in no time, they had all the creatures tied together in a circle. "What should we do with them?" Biff asked. His right eye was almost completely swollen shut. It made her want to hit the Cleanser again for doing this.

"Well, we need some information out of them," she said. She started thinking about all the horrible things these creatures had done. How they had hurt Aisling, Nathaniel, and her crew. How this one, sitting in front of her, had killed Tom. "And I think I know how to get it."

She took a step forwards, but was stopped by a hand on her shoulder. She turned to see John standing behind her. He leaned down and said very softly. "Think carefully about this. Once you go down this path, there's no way back."

He let go and stood back, allowing her to make the final decision. She debated for a moment before nodding and stepping forwards.

The Cleansers were slumped against one another and seemed to be growing weaker and weaker by the moment. The leader's breath was coming out in whistled gasps, like steam being let out of a pipe. She bent down in front of it until she was at eye level.

"It's over," she said to them, over the sound of its gasping.

"Not quite," it huffed out. "Our mistress is not finished yet."

"Your mistress?" she asked, taken aback. "What do you mean?"

"Our great mistress," the creature seemed to be talking without even realizing she was there. "If only we had served you better. The spread of the disease wasn't enough. We should have done more."

"Are you saying she was the one who started this terrible disease?" she asked, horror gripping her.

"No, I've already said too much," the creatures gasped. "This conversation is done."

She grabbed the beak of its mask, forcing its goggled eyes to meet hers. "No I don't think it is," she said. "You're going to tell me what I need to know."

"Or what?" it spat. "You'll kill me? My time is already almost up. We die with the ship. I have nothing more to say to you."

While she was this close to them, she saw something that made her pause. A small, red blinking light that she was sure wasn't there before. "Goodbye, Silver one." the creature said, just as the blinking red light intensified.

"Everyone move!" she yelled, before launching herself away from the creature.

All three of the creature's bodies blew up, marking the second explosion of the day. Luckily the crew had already been on the other side of the deck, so they were out of harm's way. Silver wasn't so lucky. She did feel the heat of the blast burn her skin as she landed heavily on the deck.

Ears ringing, she felt herself being hauled up yet again by strong arms. Looking up, she saw Nathaniel's face. As he came into focus, she saw his mouth was moving but no words were coming out. Just as her eyes fully focused, she was able to hear what he was saying.

"Are you alright? You're burned! Cedric!" She felt lots of bodies pressing around her, and the last thing she saw was Nathaniel's worried face. Then she blacked out.

Silver woke to feel like her arms were on fire. She cried out and tried to sit up. "Shh," said a familiar voice. "It's alright." Nathaniel was there and held out a glass. She drank from it greedily, and then he gently pushed her back down to a lying position.

She looked around, realizing that she was in her chambers laying on her bed. Her arms were hurting as she looked down and saw they were covered in bandages.

"What happened?" she managed to croak out. Her voice sounded strange, like it hadn't been used for a long time.

"Well, the blast from those creatures burned your arms."

"I can feel that," she said, growing impatient. "What about the crew? Is everyone alright?"

"Yes, everyone else was out of the way when the blast hit."

"And the ship? A blast like that must've done some damage."

"Lucky for us, the blast only damaged the main deck. The rest of the ship is fine. It was a pretty easy fix, all things considered."

"That's a relief," she said, settling back into her pillow. "It must not have been that bad if you already fixed it in a few hours."

"About that," her eyes flew to him and narrowed. "Silver, you've been unconscious for two days."

"What!" She sat up again and tried to get out of bed.

"Easy, easy," he said, pushing her back down. "Silver, you need to rest, you're going to hurt yourself."

"That doesn't matter! How could I have been out for so long? I need to take care of the crew and–"

"Silver," he said, placing a hand on her cheek. This stopped her instantly, and she looked into his icy blue eyes. "We've got it handled. Please rest, or am I going to have to make you?"

She felt her heart flutter at that. "What did you have in mind?" she asked, her heart beginning to pound.

He grinned the all too familiar grin. "Not what you're thinking," he chuckled before stepping back and turning himself into a cat.

"You can't be serious," she said looking at him, a strange disappointment began to settle on her. "How can a cat possibly stop me?"

She tried to get out of bed again, but he jumped up and sat directly on her chest. "Nathaniel," she sat looking at him. "This isn't funny."

He ignored her and stretched in a very catlike way before laying down on her chest.

"Your move," he said, yawning and closing his eyes.

"All I have to do is stand up and you'll go flying off," she said, trying to wiggle out from under him.

"Is that what you're going to do?" he asked, cracking one eye open at her.

She sighed and settled back down.

"Fine, you win. But it's only because I'm too tired to fight you right now."

"Of course it is," she heard him say before closing her own eyes and promptly falling asleep.

CHAPTER TWENTY-SIX

Peter

Peter sat around the table, looking at all the faces in front of him. They were in Silver's chambers having another meeting. It felt like a lifetime ago since they had their first meeting with the four of them. It felt good to be around them all without all the fighting there was before. Well mostly.

"Nathaniel, you can't sit in my chair."

"Why ever not?"

Silver was looking irritated, and Peter didn't blame her. Nathaniel had been taking her things all night, from drinking out of her cup to taking her last bite of dessert. When she had gotten up to let Sam in with the tea, Nathaniel had hopped over into her seat. Sitting in her chair was the last straw.

"You have your chair, Nathaniel," she growled.

"But I like yours better," he grinned. "Besides, what's the fun of sitting in my chair when now we can do this."

Before she could stop him, he leaped up, grabbed her by the waist, and promptly pulled her into his lap. Peter spit out his drink, and Silver sat there for a moment in complete shock.

"Nathaniel, let go," Silver tried to stand up, but his arms snaked around her, keeping her seated.

"Well then, let's continue this meeting," he said, grinning as he rested his chin on her shoulder.

Their argument continued, and Aisling started laughing. Peter felt a slight ache in his chest. He was happy for Silver, although Peter was surprised to admit it, Nathaniel had more than proven himself as someone who cared for her. He was happy they had each other and how comfortable they were around one another. The only thing was he had hoped for the same with him and Aisling. She hadn't spoken to him since they had returned from their trip. He had hoped for a moment alone, but when he tried to talk to her, she was somehow always busy or with someone else.

"Alright," Silver said, having untangled herself from Nathaniel and was now sitting in the chair next to him. "Since you already know what happened to us," they explained while they were all eating. "We need to hear what happened to the both of you."

Peter nodded, and between him and Aisling, they told the whole thing, from going to Eli's forest to the bomb exploding on the ship. Once they were done, Silver said, "So, wait, some ugly man in the forest–"

"You forget it was a magical forest," added Nathaniel helpfully.

"Told you that we were all going to save the world?" she finished, ignoring Nathaniel's interruption.

"Yes," answered Aisling. "And I'm afraid there is more. There's something Eli told me and… well, I'm leaving the ship."

There was a shocked silence at her declaration. "What? Aisling, why?" asked Peter, heart pounding.

"I need to find someone. It… turns out I have a family who's alive. I have a brother who's out there. He had already passed through Eli's forest ahead of us. I feel like he's the key; he can tell me about my family and where I can come from."

"What's his name?" asked Silver curiously.

"Robert."

"I don't know anyone by that name," she said, frowning. "I was hoping to give you something helpful to go off of."

"That's alright," Aisling said, smiling. "I appreciate your help, but I think I know where to start."

"We'll give you whatever you need for your journey."

Peter felt his world slowly crashing down around him. How could she be leaving? He stood from his chair, hitting the floor in his haste, stopping the conversation.

"How could you not tell me you had a brother?" he burst out.

Her eyes narrowed as she looked up at him. "With everything going on, there didn't seem to be time," she said in a deadly, calm voice.

"But we've had all this time back on the ship! You couldn't find a few moments to, I don't know, share this monumental discovery?"

She stood up, facing him head-on. "I just found out! I needed time to process this! Also, I didn't know how to tell you! How do you bring that up in a normal conversation? 'Here's the rope you need. By the way, I have a brother.'"

"You could have at least told me you were leaving!"

"I didn't know how you'd react. I didn't want to upset you."

"So, you wait to spring the news on me right now? Before you leave?"

"What do you want from me, Peter?" she asked with exasperation clear on her face.

"I want to go with you, damn it! I would have said let's go!"

"You would?"

All the anger went out of him with a whoosh. Her emerald green eyes stared up at him with something that looked like hope.

"Aisling," he said, gathering his courage. "I would go anywhere with you. Just say the words, and I would leave everything."

"But this is your home, and you'd be leaving your only family. I can't ask you to give all that up."

Hesitating for only a moment, he took her hand in his. When their hands touched, he felt a shock go through him. Whether that be from her powers or by just being near her, he didn't know or care.

Clearing his throat, he continued, "You don't have to ask me. I want to. Unless you don't want me to come?"

"No, of course, I do!"

"You do?"

"She does! Just get on with it!" Nathaniel interrupted again, and was again, ignored.

"I mean as long as it's alright with Silver," said Aisling, looking over at her.

Silver was quiet for a moment, looking between the two of them. Peter recognized that look, it was the one she wore whenever there was a problem among the crew. "Yes, of course it is," she answered, after a tense minute. "I always knew Peter would be destined for bigger and better things than this ship." She smiled at him. "When do you two leave?"

Peter looked to Aisling who answered, "Well, I'd like to leave in a few days."

"Perfect," said Silver, smiling. "Now will you both sit down, please? I have some other news to share."

They both sat back down, with hands still interlocked under the table. A kind of joy he didn't know he could feel filled him up from the inside out. He tried to focus, and all three listened intently as Silver explained what the Cleanser had said right before exploding.

"So, they were the ones behind the disease?" asked Peter, incredulous.

"It would seem so, they didn't mention anything about a cure, but they were the ones who created it and spread it. Did either of you know about this?" she asked, addressing Nathaniel and Aisling.

"I had heard something about it," said Aisling, slowly. "But I was in and out of consciousness so much it was difficult to tell what was a dream and what happened."

Silver shrugged, "That's alright, I just thought I would ask. Nathaniel?"

"Hmm?" he asked, looking as innocent as a cat can. All wide-eyed, as if they didn't do what you just saw them do.

"Did you know about this?"

"I might have heard an inkling or two."

"And you didn't think this was information worth sharing?"

It was his turn to shrug. "I didn't think it was relevant."

Silver pinched the bridge of her nose. "No more withholding information. We'll need to have a sit down so you can explain everything."

"Aye, aye Captain!" he said, giving a little salute. He was almost believable, but then he ruined his act by adding a wink.

Rolling her eyes, she continued. "The Cleanser also said they were working for someone. He referred to her as his mistress."

Aisling was shaking her head before Silver even finished. "Never heard of them working for anyone."

Six eyes turned to Nathaniel. "What?" he asked.

Silver made a go-on sort of gesture, which was met with a long, drawn-out sigh. "Oh very well. Yes, I knew about the Mistress. No, I don't know where she's located before you ask. But there was talk of her controlling the population with a disease. The whole point was for her to create the thing people most feared, then she was planning on swooping in magically with the cure."

This statement was met with shocked silence. "Well, that sounds like a whole lot of work," Peter said, breaking the silence.

"No, it makes perfect sense," said Silver. Peter could see the gears turning in her head. "Think about it: she could bargain anything for this! Kings and Queens would probably give up anything to get the cure, money, riches, even their kingdoms. She could become the supreme ruler of the world in a matter of days."

"But this disease has been going on for years from what you've told me," Aisling said logically. "How much longer is she going to wait?"

All six eyes turned to Nathaniel again. "Ah, this I do not know," he said with an apologetic smile. "I wasn't invited to the inner circle's meetings."

"Any idea where we can get more information?"

"Well, since you two destroyed their life force, very commendable by the way, well done, all of the Cleansers are dead. All the evidence was destroyed probably in a very similar way to how they blew themselves up onboard. But I do happen to know where a few of their labs were."

"If you can lead me there then we may be able to glean some more information. Also, we could rescue whoever else they had been experimenting on. Now that no one is there, they–"

"I wouldn't say no one," Nathaniel interrupted. "Just because the Cleansers are gone doesn't mean that they don't have others who worked for them. If you want to rescue them all, you'll need someone on the inside."

"Well, it's a good thing I have you then."

"Wait, I never agreed–"

"So, it's settled," said Silver, ignoring Nathaniel entirely. "You two will go and look for Aisling's brother. We will go and rescue the rest of the experimentees."

"What are you planning on doing with all of the people you rescue?" asked Aisling.

"Well, someone is going to need to fight this mysterious mistress. What better way to build an army than from the people who have the most against her?"

That night once everyone had gone to bed, Peter came above deck to find Silver standing at the railing. He came up next to her, and they stayed in comfortable silence for a few moments.

"I know what you're thinking," Silver said after a moment. "You want to know why I let you go so easily."

"Well, you were always so hard on me not fulfilling my duty as first mate," he said a little sheepishly. "Why now?"

She sighed and continued looking out over the sea, not meeting his eyes. Her hands seemed to be gently stroking the railing of the ship, almost in a way someone would stroke a pet.

Finally, she said, "I always knew this was my dream. When we were kids we talked about our dreams, do you remember?"

"Yes," he said, smiling at the memory. "You said you wanted to be a pirate, and I asked if girls could be pirates."

"Do you remember what you said?" when he didn't respond, she continued, "You wanted to be a knight. Save damsels, ride horses, win battles of epic proportions."

She turned to him, "Peter, it's your turn. I know why you've stayed this long. It's because you were worried about hurting my feelings which I get but–"

"I'm gonna stop you right there," he said, holding up a hand. "The reason I stayed is that you're my sister, Sil. We're all that's left of our family, we've only ever had each other. I stayed because I love... the ocean."

"I love you too," she said, bumping his shoulder with her own. "I'll say it even if you won't."

They laughed together, soaking in the last few moments of normalcy. "Everything is going to change now," Silver said, leaning against the railing again.

"Everything already has," said Peter, joining her. "But that's not necessarily a bad thing."

"I suppose not."

"After all, the last time we were separated, the only things that happened were I almost died, I survived two explosions, and people took over the ship. Nothing we couldn't handle."

"Right," she said laughing. "That's all."

"Besides, if anything goes super south, our twense will kick in."

"That will never be a thing, Peter."

"You don't know that. I, for one, am planning on spreading it anywhere Aisling and I go. Just wait, you'll be hearing it from strangers in a matter of months."

"Sure, Peter."

She rested her head on his shoulder, and they looked out over the ocean together.

A few days later Aisling and Peter were gathering the rest of the supplies they needed for their trip. They were below in the storage area and Aisling had already talked him out of bringing five swords, ten bottles of rum and a shirt she said was ridiculous.

"Come on! The shirt doesn't weigh hardly anything!"

"Peter, where are you planning on wearing a shirt like that? We're going to be traveling the whole time, it's way too dressy!"

"But think about it: what if we're invited to a fancy ball or something? Then if I have this shirt. What?" he asked at the look on her face. "It could happen!"

"Fine, bring the stupid shirt," she said shaking her head. "But nothing else! And don't blame me if you never get to wear it!"

They bickered back and forth a little longer with Peter trying to sneak a couple more things into their supplies. Aisling found most of them. They sat back and admired their work.

"I'm tired," said Peter sitting down.

"Yes, it's exhausting putting things we don't need in the supplies."

"And hiding them too," he said, before taking her hand and pulling her down next to him.

This was the first time they'd been alone since the whole Rasful incident. Peter kept a tight grip on her hand, rubbing little circles with his thumb on the back of her hand. "I thought you were upset with me," he said softly.

"Fine, you can bring something else," she sighed.

"No, not about that, but I will hold you to that," he said, grinning. "I thought you were upset after the last time we were alone."

"Oh," she said, tucking her hair behind her ear. "No, I wasn't. Mostly… I don't know. I just didn't know what to say or how to react. Things have been strange between us from the beginning, and I'm just not sure where to go from here."

"I never meant to make you feel anything negative. I was just trying to protect you. But now I can see that maybe I was just trying to protect myself. After all, I don't doubt your ability to handle yourself. I just feel bad for causing you any pain."

"Thank you, that means a lot for you to say that," she smiled up at him, and his heart quickened. This girl was doing things to him that he didn't even know were possible. She was so strong, yet gentle. He would do just about anything to make her smile.

"Thank you for trusting me to come with you. I can't promise we'll find him, but I'll do whatever is in my power to help you."

She nodded, continuing to smile. He felt drawn into her emerald eyes, and for a moment, he thought about closing the small amount of distance between them and kissing her. But now wasn't the time. He didn't want to mess up this fragile thing they had just started. Perhaps there would be time later.

"Well, these bags won't pack themselves," he stood, breaking the spell and pulling her to her feet.

"Especially at your speed," she teased, squeezing his hand.

"Hey, one human can only be good at so many things. I've got to save some talent for the rest of the population."

"I'm already regretting asking you to come with me," she said, with an exaggerated sigh.

Her comment made a laugh burst out of him. He was just happy to go wherever she went. Anywhere she led him, he would gladly follow.

CHAPTER TWENTY-SEVEN

Silver

When Peter and Aisling came out from below deck, the whole crew shouted in celebration. Silver walked up to them, laughing at the surprised and slightly afraid look on both of their faces. "What's all this?" asked Peter as she handed him and Aisling drinks.

"A going away party," she said smiling. "It was the crew's idea to celebrate your last day as the first mate. Also, I think they were slightly afraid that you'd sneak off before saying goodbye."

Peter looked around with tears filling his eyes. Before he could get too sappy, the crew surrounded him and the party began.

There was dancing and music with the crew showing off for each other. Cedric was a surprisingly good flute player, and Gwane took over the drums. There was also amazing food that Sam had made, who was offering it around like a proud mother hen. The rum poured like water, which wasn't too different from normal. After all, they were on a ship.

They hadn't had many parties aboard the Silver Shadow, but Silver was wondering if that was something that should change. She watched Biff do some fancy footwork, while Gwane started playing off beat on the drums, trying to mess up Biff's dance. Everyone was laughing at their performance and gave a huge applause when they were done. Her crew worked hard and deserved to let loose every once in a while. Maybe she could make this more of a regular thing.

Everyone wanted to dance with Aisling, who gladly obliged whoever asked. They kept her dancing most of the night, until Peter stepped in, waving them off. Silver was standing off to the side, smiling and enjoying all the chaos that happens during the best kinds of parties.

Suddenly, she felt her arm almost yanked out of the socket. About to tell off whoever was pulling her, she turned to see Nathaniel's grinning face smiling down at her, as he promptly dragged her to the dance floor.

"Nathaniel! I don't want to dance!"

He ignored her and pulled her to the center of the dance circle. She looked up at him in panic, but he just continued to smile and smoothly turned her around until she was facing him. "Just follow my lead," he whispered, and then the dance began.

He was an excellent dancer, much to Silver's surprise. He led her through a series of complicated steps like it was the most natural thing in the world. Dancing was never her strongest subject in school, yet dancing with Nathaniel was different. He made it fun and took all the pressure off of it. Silver found herself enjoying it and felt herself relaxing.

When the music came to a close, the crew cheered and whooped, applauding their performance. Embarrassed, Silver tried to go back to the sidelines but was stopped by one of her crew, and then another, until she had danced with all of them. While she was being twirled and spun, she would occasionally catch a glimpse of Nathaniel standing off to the side laughing.

Once everyone had danced with her twice, she did start telling them no and made her way over to him. "I'm going to kill you," she said cheerfully as she sat down to rest her aching feet.

"Come on," he said laughing and bumping her shoulder. "You know you had to have enjoyed yourself a little."

She was just about to retaliate when John came up to her. "May I steal you for a moment?" he asked in his quiet way. Nathaniel bowed out of the way and went to go dance with Aisling, much to Peter's chagrin.

"Is everything alright?" she asked, worry clear in her voice as he sat down.

"Yes, everything is fine, better than fine in fact," he said, smiling at her. "I wanted to check on how you were doing."

"Oh," she said softly, looking over to Peter who was trying to break Aisling and Nathaniel apart. He was unsuccessful. In the fact, Nathaniel, Biff and Gwane kept twirling Aisling away from him.

"I'm alright," she answered after a moment. "I'm certainly going to miss him, but this is what he wants. I can't expect him to stay with me all the time. Besides, it's not goodbye forever." They sat in silence for a few moments before she said, "John, can I ask you something? I mean, besides the question I just asked."

At his nod, she said, "Do you think I'm doing the right thing?"

He was quiet for a moment thinking it over. "Yes," he said finally. "I think this is what's best for Peter and you. Aisling complements Peter in a way that makes them both better people. I believe the same can be said for you and the man who seems to always be hanging around you."

"Do you think we can make it work?" she asked quietly, the fear bubbling out before she could stop it.

"That's entirely up to you," he said, shrugging. "Relationships will only give you back what you put in them. It's easy to let them fall by the wayside, but as long as you are both working hard to love each other, then I think anyone can make it work."

"Thank you, John," she said smiling. "For everything."

"Anytime," he said standing.

"Oh, and John?" he turned to face her. "Any interest in being my first mate?"

He looked at her thoughtfully for a moment before saying, "Are you sure I'm the right choice?"

"Of course! I wouldn't want it any other way!"

"Hmm," he said, his face unreadable. "Why don't you think about it and ask me again in a few days."

"Alright," she said, confused by his answer.

He smiled, giving her a slight bow before heading back to the party. After that, she was asked again to dance. She felt bad for saying no before, so she did. She really would kill Nathaniel. The rest of the party was a blur as she danced, letting go and enjoying herself.

Silver waved with the rest of the crew as the small rowboat became a speck in the distance. She had wanted to drop them off at a port, but Peter insisted that he didn't want her and the whole crew giving a tearful goodbye in a town they'd never been to before. So they got as close as he would allow and then sent them on their way.

She stayed far longer than everyone else, staring off into the horizon, even when she couldn't see the boat anymore. Arms encircled her waist, and she jumped, turning to see Nathaniel had snuck up behind her.

"You know, we need to work on your perception skills," he said as he tucked her head under his chin.

"It's incredibly unlikely that someone as quiet will be sneaking up on me," she said while she leaned up against him.

"So," he said after a few minutes of standing. "I heard you had a position open."

"Oh?" she asked, only half listening.

"Yes, I heard the position of first mate is available, and I was wondering what I needed to do to apply for the job."

"What?" she asked, wiggling out of his arms. "You want to be my first mate?"

"Is that a problem?"

"No, it's just… well."

"What Silver, do you not want me as the first mate? Do you think I'd be a bad fit?"

"It's not that."

"Then what?"

"I–" she broke off, trying to figure out what it was. "I already asked John," she said, thinking quickly.

"And? Did he accept?"

"No, he didn't... wait a moment," she looked at him suspiciously. "Did he set you up to this?"

"Well, if he didn't want it," he said, ignoring her question. "Then doesn't that mean the position is open?" He took a step towards her.

"Yes," she said, trying to keep up with him.

"Then what's stopping you from picking me?" he smiled down at her, his body just inches away from hers.

"Nothing I can think of," she said, sighing. "Fine, you can have the position. But there are going to be some rules in place."

"Aw, that's not fun," he said, pretending to pout.

"The rules are for my sanity. Do you want the position or not?"

"I do. Very well, lay them on me."

"First, there'll be no kissing or grabbing me in front of the crew. I need to keep some kind of leadership over them, and I can't do that if you're kissing me all the time."

"No promises."

"Then no position."

"Fine, done," he said, giving in. "Anything else?"

"Yes actually," she said, beginning to enjoy herself. "If I tell you to do something as your Captain, I need you to do it. This could be anything," she warned.

"Done," he answered with a grin she wasn't entirely sure she liked. "Anything else?"

"No undermining my position, especially in front of the crew. They need to know I'm their leader and not get confused with conflicting orders."

"I wouldn't dream of undermining you," he said, moving closer.

"That somehow doesn't comfort me," she said, taking a step back. He continued moving forwards, so she kept backing up. "Now, I need the freedom to make more rules as I think of them. I can't think of any more right now, but I know they'll come to me."

"I'm sure they will," he said, continuing his advance.

"And," she said, trying to keep control over the situation. "I–" her back hit something solid. She turned to see that it was the wall just below the deck. He stepped forwards until there was no space between them.

"I'll do whatever you ask me to," he said, leaning down towards her.

"Then there's something else I need," she said boldly. Then, she reached up and pulled his head down to hers. Sealing their promise with a kiss.

The crew wasn't completely sure what Nathaniel had done to become the first mate but, they were happy for him. He was someone everyone respected and genuinely liked. The fact that they all enjoyed how he got under the Captain's skin might also have something to do with it. Occasionally, they would see a white cat riding on her shoulder but they learned not to question it. This is how the crew had learned to approach most things being a part of Captain Silver's crew. After all, there was never a dull moment aboard the Silver Shadow.

The End

ACKNOWLEDGMENTS

I can't believe I get to write one of these again! It has been an amazing journey and I'm just so excited that this book has made it out into the world.

I wrote this book during the beginning of the pandemic. There was so much uncertainty and fear, so I wrote this book as an escape. There are portions of this book that are a nod to what was happening at the time. Things are maybe a little better now. There will always be uncertainties in life, but I hope that this book can give you a small bit of escapism from the world just like it did for me.

As per usual, this book would not be what it is, without some truly amazing people.

First of all, Robin. What you did to help me with this book is beyond words! Thank you for your willingness to be completely honest with me about what wasn't working, but then looking me dead in the eyes and saying, "But you are a good writer. I'm just trying to help you be better." I will never forget all of those conversations in between sorting carts and in passing. This would have been a very different book if not for you and so I can't thank you enough. I owe you at least 1,000 boba teas!

To my incredible editor and friend Laura. Thank you for taking a chance on my story and being so kind and thorough! When I saw you had left hundreds of comments leading up to chapter seven, I knew my story was in good hands! The amount of work and care you put into editing my book is truly amazing. I am so grateful for you and your friendship.

Thank you to my cover designer Vlkncharlie and Daniel at global_design for formatting this book! You both always do incredible work, which helps bring my story to life! Thank you both again for your amazing work!

To my amazing co-workers at the FP Library. Thank you for always asking how my writing is going and asking me when the next book is coming out. I feel weird bringing it up myself so I am always excited when people seem interested.

Thank you to all the librarians everywhere. You all do amazing work for the community, and for authors as well. Libraries attract a certain kind of people who are willing to put in long hours, and are really caring for people. Also, libraries are just awesome!

Thank you to my family for your excitement and support. A special thank you to Courtney who promoted my books on all of her socials and probably got me half of my sales. Thank you all so much!

In this same vein, thank you to Jen who sent out a companywide email at the library promoting my first book. It was such a kind and thoughtful thing for you to do and also probably got me the rest of my sales. Thank you so much!

Thank you to my wonderful partner in crime Jase. I wouldn't be able to write if you didn't help me take out the dog and order us food while I was in the middle of a writing session. Thank you for letting me gush about my books even if it sounds like the ravings of a mad woman! Every love story I write has inspiration from you, so thank you for loving me the way you do.

And lastly, thank you dear reader for making it this far. My intention with these books is to give you just a moment to not have to think about the world around you. While I would absolutely still write if no one read it, the fact that people have and enjoy it is crazy to me! With that said, I look forward to seeing you in the next one. Onward!

Jessica Harden has been writing for the last 14 years. She loves all things fantasy and secretly hopes to be a mermaid someday. She doesn't understand people who don't want to live in a fantasy world and looks for magic every day. She lives with her very old dog and husband in Texas. This is her second novel.

You can follow Jessica Harden on:

Instagram: @jjbear226

Twitter: @jjbear226

YouTube: Jess Go Write

www.ingramcontent.com/pod-product-compliance
Ingram Content Group UK Ltd.
Pitfield, Milton Keynes, MK11 3LW, UK
UKHW041636190726
13854UKWH00006B/2521

9 798218 123284